The Netanyahus

The Netanyahus

An Account of a Minor and
Ultimately Even Negligible Episode
in the History of a Very Famous Family

JOSHUA COHEN

 New York Review Books New York

This is a New York Review Book

published by The New York Review of Books

435 Hudson Street, New York, NY 10014

www.nyrb.com

This is a novel.

Library of Congress Cataloging-in-Publication Data
Names: Cohen, Joshua, 1980– author.
Title: The Netanyahus / an account of a minor and ultimately even
    negligible episode in the history of a very famous family by Joshua
    Cohen.
Description: New York : New York Review Books, 2021.
Identifiers: LCCN 2021004715 (print) | LCCN 2021004716 (ebook) |
    ISBN 9781681376073 (paperback) | ISBN 9781681376080 (ebook)
Subjects: LCSH: Jewish fiction. | College stories.
Classification: LCC PS3553.042434 N48 2021 (print) | LCC PS3553.
    042434 (ebook) | DDC 813/.54—dc23
LC record available at https://lccn.loc.gov/2021004715
LC ebook record available at https://lccn.loc.gov/2021004716

ISBN 978-1-68137-607-3
Available as an electronic book; ISBN 978-1-68137-608-0

Printed in the United States of America on acid-free paper.

1 2 3 4 5 6 7 8 9 10

To the memory of Harold Bloom

"Eliminate the Diaspora or the Diaspora will eliminate you."

— ZE'EV JABOTINSKY, Tisha B'Av, 1938

1.

MY NAME IS RUBEN BLUM and I'm an, yes, *an* historian. Soon enough, though, I guess I'll be *historical*. By which I mean I'll die and become history myself, in a rare type of transformation traditionally reserved for the purer scholars. Lawyers die and don't become the law, doctors die and don't turn into medicine, but biology and chemistry professors pass away and decompose into biology and chemistry, they mineralize into geology, they disperse into their science, just as surely as mathematicians become statistics. The same process holds true for us historians—in my experience, we're the only ones in the humanities for whom this holds true—the only ones who become what we study; we age, we yellow, we go wrinkled and brittle along with our materials until our lives subside into the past, to become the very substance of time. Or maybe that's just the Jew in me talking... Goys believe in the Word becoming Flesh, but Jews believe in the Flesh becoming Word, a more natural, rational incarnation...

By way of further introduction, I will now quote a remark made to me by the who-shall-remain-nameless then-president of the American Historical Association, when I met him at a symposium back in my student days just after the Second World War: "Ah," he said, limply pressing my hand, "Blum, did you say? A Jewish historian?"

Though the man surely intended this remark to wound me, it

merely succeeded in bringing delight, and even now I find I can smile at the description. I appreciate its accidental imprecision, and the way the double entendre can function as a type of psychological test: "'A Jewish historian'—when you hear that, what do you think? What image springs to mind?" The point is, the epithet as applied is both correct and incorrect. I *am* a Jewish historian, but I am *not* an historian of the Jews—or I've never been one, professionally.

Instead, I'm an American historian—or I was. After half a century in the professorate, I was recently retired from my post as the Andrew William Mellon Memorial Professor of American Economic History at Corbin University in Corbindale, New York, in the occasionally rural, occasionally wild heart of Chautauqua County, just inland from Lake Erie among the apple orchards and apiaries and dairies—or, as dismissive, geographically-illiterate New York City–folk insist on calling it, "Upstate." (I myself was once one of these city-folk and though that old wisdom is false that teachers learn more from their students than vice-versa, I did manage to pick this up, early on: never call Corbindale "Upstate.") Though my initial focus was on the economics of the pre-American, British Colonial period, my reputation, such as it is, was made in the field of what's now referred to as taxation studies, and, especially, from my research into the history of tax policy's influence on politics and political revolutions. To be sure, I never much enjoyed the field, but it was open to me. Rather, the field didn't exist until I discovered it, and, like a bumbling Columbus, I only discovered it because it was there. By the time I got into academia, America was already crowded, even American Economic History was already crowded, and I've always had a decent head for numbers. Taking on the history of taxes got me out of the ghetto of Colonial catallactics and eventually even out of America itself, into the European city-states, feudal tax-farming, Church tithes, Antiquity's development of customs duties and trade-tariffs . . . all the way back to the Rosetta Stone and even the Bible, both of which—most people forget—are substantially just tax-documents . . .

What else is salient? I wish I knew. But do we ever know? I used to open certain of my classes by paraphrasing Twain, who himself was paraphrasing Franklin, who for his part was presumably plagiarizing Britons untold: ". . . nothing can be said to be certain in this world, except death and taxes and the due dates of your papers . . ."

I'd like to think my profession has made me more attuned than most to the selective use of facts and the way that each age and ideological movement manages to cobble together its own tailor-made chronicles to suit its aims and flatter its self-conceptions—from Washington's "I cannot tell a lie" after he took a hatchet to his father's cherry tree to the pruriently cherry-picked film-and-TV accounts of the Kennedy assassination, which give the sense of the mafia, the CIA, the KGB, and Marilyn Monroe all meeting up for a planning powwow in some screened-off back-booth at The 21 Club. My own version of this choose-your-own history is my academic bio, which can be found online. Forgive an old man his overexplaining: go to Corbin.edu, click Faculty, click History Department, then click on my name, and you'll find what's basically a reproduction of my CV, rife with only the highlights: the nine Corbin Distinguished Teacher prizes (1968, 1969, 1989, 1990, 1992, 1995, 1999, 2000, 2001), the American Historical Association Historian of the Year award (1993), the honorary degrees from LSE and the National University of Singapore, and a fairly up-to-date publication list and bibliography. My books still in print include *A General History of*

Taxation; Taxation Without Representation: A History of America in Ten Taxes; Import Quotas, Export Subsidies: A Journey through Non-Tariff Barriers to Trade; Embargo: A History; Blood Money: The Taxation of Slavery, and *George Sewall Boutwell: Abolitionist, Suffragist, and Father of the IRS.*

Don't get me wrong: I'm proud of these achievements, or I was trained to say and even to think I was proud of them, mostly because each notch on my ever-expanding accomplishment-belt was supposed to bring me farther from my origins—as Ruvn Yudl Blum, b. 1922 in the Central Bronx to Jewish immigrants from Kiev, who raised me up to the middle class. They made sure I had a good education, by sending me to good schools, and by berating me in shameless Yiddish when I turned out to be an intellectual.

The day after the attack on Pearl Harbor, I was married to my high-school sweetheart and drafted into the US Army, which assigned me as a finance clerk, due to my half-completion of a bookkeeping course (attended at my family's insistence), poor posture (mild scoliosis, 12-degree curve), and prodigious skills as a typist (76 WPM). I passed the war without leaving the country, spending most of my stint typing up precious elegant little thesicles on advanced pretentiousness by Eliot ("The smoky candle end of time / Declines. On the Rialto once"), and Pound ("Usura slayeth the child in the womb / It stayeth the young man's courting"), posting them to precious elegant little poetry journals and getting rejected; processing paychecks and disbursing travel expenses between Fort Benning and Fort Sill.

Following the war, I enrolled in CUNY, where my incipient bent for the humanities, and for literature in particular, was straightened out by various pressures (parental, practical) in column-style, so as to better arrange a career in sums. The compromise was this: my preference for literature became history, everyone else's preference for accounting became economics, and America stayed America. I stayed on at CUNY through my terminal degree and, after a despondent wallow in adjuncting sheol, I became the first Jew ever hired by Corbin College (in those days Corbin University was still a College), and I don't mean the first tenure-track Jewish faculty member in the Corbin College History Department, I mean the first Jew in the whole entire school—faculty and, as far as I could tell, student-body included.

The excellent now-forgotten critic Van Wyck Brooks coined the phrase "a usable past" to mean a past that every "modern," dissociated, deracinated American intellectual must create for himself— herself—themselves, in order to find meaning in the present and direction for the future. I'd be reminded of that phrase every time I drove on the Van Wyck Expressway, crawling from a city airport to my parents' and alternately frustrated and glad about being late; or, to put it another way, I hated the traffic, but was happy for the postponement. Ahead of me was just nagging, begged favors, and interminable reenactments of internecine neighborhood conflicts: can you believe what Mrs. Haber said? (no, the other Mrs. Haber!), can you believe what happened to Gartner? (no, the Gartner already with the dead wife, the heart condition, the polio child, and the carbuncle!); the under-counting, over-charging sins of the unregenerate butcher, baker, and grocer, the tenacious charity-collection of the rabbis—the full weight of what I thought of as "a useless past," the Jewish past, which I'd escaped for pagan academe and the hills and dales of my peaceful sub-Niagaran woodland.

In sum, for almost all of my life—until fairly recently, actually, when a spate of foot-leg-and-hip injuries forced me to trade mobility for mortality—I found no strength in my origins and took every opportunity to ignore them, when I couldn't deny them.

I came into the world with a skin that wasn't quite white, but as I grew up, it thickened; in a Depression-era Jewish neighborhood that bordered the Irish and Italian, it had to. The streets off the Grand Concourse were filled with mindless abuse, but unlike some of my peers, I wasn't a fighter. Instead, I was raised to react to provocations in the style of Jesus Christ, whom I was regularly accused of having crucified. Teased, taunted, I'd turn the other cheek, hoping for the best, expecting the worst, and understanding throughout that though life was beset by troubles, no relief or revenge and surely no dignity would ever be had by complaining. As the only Jewish family residing in our minor hamlet on the wrong side of the Catskills in the postwar milieu, the Blums (myself, Edith my wife, Judith my daughter) faced regular slights. To be sure, these slights weren't city-violent, but were almost always more passive than aggressive and what helped us endure them wasn't any internal fortitude so much as the thought that we weren't Mrs. Johnson (our once-a-week cleaning-lady) or any of the College's cafeteria workers or maintenance workers or groundskeepers—we weren't black or, as we said then, "Colored" or "Negro." (Edith and I were of the age that said "Colored," while Judy's generation said "Negro.") It was never lost on at least me and Edith that the stupid quips about cheapness by the Maytag repairman who fixed our appliances were uniquely soft and ineffective weapons in the annals of anti-Semitism —so much so that to regard them as harmful felt impertinent, disrespectful of the ancestors. After all, the Greeks strangled Jewish newborns with their own umbilical cords; the Romans flayed the flesh of sages using hot iron brushes and combs; the Inquisition used the strappado and rack; the Nazis used gas and fire. Compared to those historical harms, what damage could be caused by a joke like "How many Jews can you fit in a car?" or even an under-the-halitotic-breath "yid" or "kike"? What did it matter that when I'd brought our truculent Pontiac into the Corbindale Garage, the old rosaceated mechanic pulled a greasy hand out of his jumpsuit to take my cash up front and pet my head: "When's the last time you got your horns checked?" More regularly, what Edith and I had to deal with as the first Jews in Corbindale was a constant sort of low-level condescension: the sense that we should feel lucky to be there at all; that we'd been admitted, we'd been given a pass. We were talked-down-to, deigned-to, patronized, studied. Our presence was a nuisance to some and a curiosity to all. The opposition came mostly in the earlier days, when the Corbindale Golf-and-Racquet Club would constantly claim to have lost our membership forms (and by the time they started soliciting our membership, we'd lost interest), the constant spring-break stream of fellow faculty members who, mistaking my scholarship for practical knowledge, would beg me to help them "do" their taxes, and the constant winter-break parties where Edith and I were treated like drooling deficients who didn't know Rudolph from Blitzen or Donner or what to do with our lips under the mistletoe. It's true that for the first Corbin History Department Christmas party we ever went to (the year before the events I'm about to recount), I was asked by my Department Chair, the now-departed Dr. George Lloyd Morse, to take over his customary role as Santa Claus by donning the costume and distributing gifts: "It was my wife's brainwave, an inspirational bingo," he explained, "because you have a real beard like her father had . . . they

7

were common in his day but rarer and rarer now, which is a shame, because a real beard's so much more dignified and effective than a fake one . . . I knew I was smart to hire a man with whiskers and if it pleaseth the wife . . . not to mention that with you doing the jolly old St. Nick honors, it'll free up the people who actually celebrate the holiday to enjoy themselves." I recall going around the room dragging my pillowcase-sack filled with tiny letter-openers, essentially tiny daggers engraved with the school seal (trussed crow bearing olive branch) and motto (*Petite, et dabitur vobis*), which kept slicing stigmata into me as I handed them out to the assemblage, and then coming home that night and, still in costume—the suit and hat that were due back with the Theater Arts coaches in the morning so the English Department could use them for its own party—washing my gashes and the talcum that whited my beard and shaving my face clean . . . (Before I continue I think it bears remarking that when I began teaching at Corbin, the school had only just gone co-ed and the sum total of students of color was zero. By the time I retired, however, the school had both an African Students' Union and an African-American Students' Union, a Hispanic Queer Alliance, and a Transsexual Safe Space Task Force. The pep rally cheers that had once travestied indigenous chants—"The Iroquois Whoop," "The Allegany Banzai"—have been canceled; and the statue of the College's founder—the Tammany-connected developer and one-time caudillo of the New York State Canal Board, Mather Corbin—which used to reign in the Quad without contextualizing qualms, now sports an interactive plaque at its base that calls the man's slaving and profiteering from immigrant peonage "incompatible with the University's values" and "problematic." All of these changes are certainly remarkable, and yet the fact remains that the youth today is more sensitive than ever. I admit I don't know how to understand this phenomenon and have sought to approach it "economically," asking the question of whether an increase in sensitivity has brought about a decrease in discrimination, or whether a decrease in discrimination has brought about an increase in sensitivity to when, where, and how it occurs. Or, I should say, to when, where, and how it's perceived to occur by a student-body whose laudable penchant for acceptance has been nurtured into a culture of grievance that I find anathema. So many of my former students— especially those from my last stretch of teaching—were so tolerant of others' psychosocial fragilities and resentments as to become intolerable themselves, junior Torquemadas, sophomoric Savonarolas, finding fault with nearly every remark, finding bigotry and prejudice everywhere. I don't want to rehash the campus wars, those bloody battles over equal rights that began, as so many of the most important American civil-libertarian battles began, with Jews on the front lines. And I certainly don't want to be understood as saying that every single student nowadays has too light of a trigger, or takes things too personally, or takes good intentions in bad faith, or that misogyny and racism and homophobia and so on have all been totally eliminated from campus life. I'm merely asserting that for my generation, a Jew would be lucky to pass as white, the color hated most openly was Red, the plural pronoun was not a preference, and for every minority the fashion as well as the most reliable protection was to assimilate, not to differentiate.)

Of all the limp-swung slings and rubber gag-arrows that Edith and I suffered at Corbin, perhaps the only truly wounding one came—unexpectedly, unintentionally—from another request made of me by this Department Chair, Dr. Morse, when he summoned me to his office toward the start of the winter term 1959, the first term of my second year of full-time employment at Corbin. I was on my way to my American History seminar (a core curriculum requirement even now, which in those days still opened with the Pilgrims and these days opens with African chattelship and a raised palm in greeting to the native Seneca) and stopped by my faculty mailbox. In that era before email, and before I became a bit less neurotic about my status and future, I was in the habit of checking my mailbox multiple times daily, always looping back to that wall of wooden cubbyholes before and after every class and bathroom trip and errand, no matter how far-flung. What if someone wanted me? What if I missed something urgent (the messages that were stamped at top, URGENT)? Usually, of course, my box was empty, or at most was graced with slim slips of memoranda mundana: *seeking faculty advisor for Mock United Nations, interested parties please contact* ... But this time, there was a folded note, typewritten on Dr. Morse's Department stationery: "Rube," it read, in his characteristic mélange of the casual and turgid, "If you'd be so obliging as to slot me in today, I'd very much enjoy the favor of your audience. Might I suggest my office directly after your day's last class?" Yes, you might. Yes, you have. Yes, sir. The tone was no suggestion, but a summons. Even now, I can close my eyes and hear Dr. Morse booming out the text to Ms. (Linda) Gringling, who at the time was his secretary, and later, his second and ultimate wife. Incidentally, you could always tell a Ms. Gringling production—one of the missives she typed from his dictation and signed with Dr. Morse's name—because of the neatness and propriety of her *M*'s. George's own *M* was a capacious manse that roofed the *o* and *r* and often the *s* and *e* as well. It was a signature that communicated, in effect, "you're mine,

you dwell at my pleasure, I contain you," while Ms. Gringling's forg-
eries tended to have more respect for boundaries.

I must've read that brief note a dozen times that day, trying to
read into it, to read between its lines, like a Talmudist or Bible her-
meneut or lovestruck adolescent: what's in his heart? More like,
what does he want? What have I done? What catastrophe awaits
me? My Jewish anxieties are surely hackneyed by now—they
might've been hackneyed even then—but that doesn't discount their
reality. They were real once. And at one time or another they were
interesting. I don't want to fall into the trap of dismissing these
anxieties, these inherited neuroses, when what's actually to blame
for their present banality is how they've been represented in books,
in film, in TV—in "media"; when what's actually to blame is the
lack of creativity on the part of those who've channeled them over
the past half-century. As a city boy who also happened to be the
newest faculty member of the History Department just beginning
the second of two probationary years preliminary to a verdict on
tenure, I was the bloated, hypertensive, and above all apprehensive
and even dread-fueled embodiment of the under-coordinated, over-
intellectualizing, self-deprecating male Jewish stereotype that
Woody Allen, for instance, and so many Jewish-American literary
writers found outlandish financial and sexual success lampooning
(Roth in the generation younger than mine, Bellow and Malamud
in the generation older). In ways I still find occasionally painful to
recall, I was of the cohort that taught America the words *schlemiel*,
shlimazl, nebbish, and *klutz*; a potbellied kettle of black-humored
guilts and cathexes, hirsute, sudorous, sebaceous, complicated by
complexes, and constantly afraid of slipping up, constantly afraid
of saying the wrong thing, or of wearing the wrong tie, or of wearing

a tie-bar instead of a tie-clip, or of wearing cuff links when mere buttons would do, or of wearing madras when corduroy was once again in-season, or, above all, of confusing something basic: the order in which the states were admitted to the union ... Delaware, Pennsylvania, New Jersey ... As I followed my seminar students out into the crush of school-color scarlet, I repeated the rosary, counting each like a soothing bead: Georgia, Massachusetts, Connecticut? Or Georgia, Connecticut, Massachusetts?

Ms. Gringling ushered me into Dr. Morse's office and lingered in the doorway for a moment to take his drink order, his order for the both of us: "Gimlets, Linda. I think the mood is gimlets." Again, let's register the change: once upon a time, it was the job of nice, honest, competent-enough middle-aged women like Linda Gringling to take dictation and schedule meetings and fix mixed drinks for professional historians, though sometimes Dr. Morse wanted a sloe gin fizz or a gin and tonic and sometimes, in the gimlet mood, which functioned as something like his subjunctive, lemons had to be substituted for limes. Ms. Gringling squeezed the citrus herself, with the result that some of Dr. Morse's correspondence—including the note I now placed on his desk—was faintly citrus-scented.

As if I was handing in some sort of permissions-slip back in my own student days, or back in the army, I slipped a corner of the note under the cannonball on his desk, that fierce pocked spheroid that resembled the shrunken cranial trophy of some leaden tribe of head-hunters. Those were the only items atop his desk, this cannonball-pa-perweight and now my chit of paper. Dr. Morse sat tilted in his chair, tilted back into his lax immensity—"All day I was telling myself, no drinking till Rube shows up ... no drinking till Rube shows up ..."

"My apologies, Dr. Morse."

"Rube, I almost didn't make it."

"I came directly from class, as quickly as I could."

"But you're still not sitting…and you're still not calling me George…"

Though I was never much of a drinker, this cocktail hour reassured me. No one got fired at Corbin over cocktail hour.

With a flourish, Dr. Morse took the lid off his cannonball: stored inside the scooped-out brainpan of the thing was his smoking paraphernalia. The underside of the scalp, inverted, became an ashtray, and when the drinks came, we both lit up. I'd smoked cigarettes in my youth and cigars in the service, but Corbin had brought me to pipes. Though Dr. Morse tended to alternate between a calabash by day and a churchwarden by night, pretty much everyone else in the Department went with billiards, both straight and curved, while Dr. Hillard dangled a desiccated corncob. My pipe was a billiard, not as straight as some, not as curved as others. In retrospect, it was all just a vain experiment in blending: drinking the Ms. Gringling–served gin and smoking the sweet-spicy burley that burnt my throat and stung my eyes and clouded the head that joined them, while the body wore suits whose plaid was as wide as the mullions of the window in brilliant orange-yellows like the autumn outside.

Dr. Morse was a breezy, barely passable historian of the so-called imperial century of the British Empire (ca. 1815–1914) and, officially speaking, our relations were those of a capital to a colony: diplomatic and vigorously cordial. It definitely helped that I knew my place, I knew why I'd been hired. Dr. Morse was the monarchical boss and I his Loyalist-Semite liaison and spy among my fellow Americanists in Corbin History. With my Jewish initiative, my Jewish drive to impress, I was to be his eyes and ears in this incomprehensible hemisphere, helping to keep my New World colleagues in latitudinal line; demonstrating just enough industriousness to keep them productive and just enough scrupulosity to keep them honest. It's notable that today, decades after Dr. Morse's reign, Corbin still excels at American Studies of all hyphenate-stripes, but lags leagues behind when it comes to the study of what Dr. Morse, but not only him, used to call "The Continent." Of course, students now take this as a sign of the Department's liberality—its willingness to evolve—but the truth is far more damning. The truth is, Dr. Morse never developed a deep Europeanist bench because he couldn't stand the competition. Europe was his (maps of it by Ptolemy and Rand McNally took up the entire wall of his office, opposite the window); the invaded, occupied, annexed, and partitioned outposts of every European empire belonged to him, and to a few approved crony-mediocrities who knew, just as well as he did, that they weren't scholastically equipped to defend themselves from challenges. This was the aspect of Dr. Morse I found the most perplexing: the man knew his limitations but wasn't ashamed of them. He didn't care. He wore his averageness lightly, almost proudly, like a transparent scholar's gown, underneath which he was nakedly an administrator. His WASP complacency was astounding, at least to a fusser like me, a child of the Garment District. Nowadays, they'd call his condition something like privilege, I guess. The complete calmness, the complete comfortability, the totally untroubled capacity to relax inside of one's own blanched-dry dermal girdle that comes from being swaddled in money, bonds, and stock certificates from birth, a patrimony honed at Groton, Yale, and Harvard. I don't want to come off like I'm putting him down, though, because Dr. Morse in all his ease, his simplicity and ease, taught me an important lesson. What he taught me was that all the gumption and smart-assery that had been an asset to me in my youth and certainly in my student days was actually a liability to me as a teacher. Now that I was quite literally at the head of the class, I could finally stop acting like a show-off kid. To be clear, I should continue to research, write, and publish like a greenhorn dervish on fire, but I shouldn't ever sweat or display even a smidgen of ambition to anyone. I was a Corbin Man now, or I had to pretend to be one. I'd made it, or at least I had to learn how to fake having made it by breathing deeper. This, I thought, was what Dr. Morse was trying to communicate by plying me with drinks, but then: the guy also just liked his boozing. He drank his gimlet and puffed on his calabash and in his genial vastness was even closer to being a Santa Claus than I was, a jolly old St. Nick gone glabrous, his bald head resembling the pumpkin left outside Fredonia Hall to ripen past its season; some odd crooked warty pumpkin flushed with red broken veins and purple capillary-dapplings, frozen-over in a white skin of rime.

I now come to the portion of this account where the real dialogue starts—the first real stretch of person-to-person dialogue that isn't some negligible *hi, snookums* ... or *how goes it* ... or *help yourself to a lousy chair* ... and before it starts, I'd like to announce a policy. Quotation marks, or "quotes," or, as various students of mine have called them over the years, "rabbit ears," "raised eyebrows," or "the little tiny raindrops that tell you who's talking," are holy to historians. In academic writing, quotation is the guarantee, the two-spanged, or four-spanged, seal that certifies facticity and says, "These words have been written or spoken by someone before me, scout's honor." And because a sole scout's honor is never enough, each quotation is traditionally accorded a citation that says, "For all of my doubters, here's the author (last name first), the book title (in italics), and the page number because you're lazy, now get thee to a library and check me up." A lifetime of being guided by these dictates has made me wary to forsake them, even if no record exists to contradict me and I myself am the only source. In what's to follow I'll endeavor to express only what was expressed to me, as verbatim as my memory is able, and with the reminder that unlike most writers who violate the sanctity of quotation—that unlike the religious, who have the chutzpah to put words into the mouth of God—I'm only recalling events at which I was present, and the time elapsed between those events and the current moment has been considerably shorter than, say, the span between the Creation of the universe and the Exodus from Egypt, and shorter even than the span between the ministry of Christ and the composition of the canonical Gospels.

Our conversation opened with this: the College Library and high-school drama. And if I had to produce my own verifying note, I'd put an asterisk next to both topics and write: "Cf. every conversation with Dr. Morse I've ever had, all of which opened with my wife and the College Library and my daughter and high-school drama." Ibid. Ibid. Ibid. Ibid. Someone in Dr. Morse's childhood must've told him that the polite thing to do to get by in the world (in his world) was to memorize one fact and one fact only about each of your colleague's family members, so that when you met that colleague, or met their family members, you could, by mentioning this fact, appear solicitous and engaged.

He asked, "And how is your Edith getting on in our great but disorganized collection?" and instead of answering him, "not-so-good," or "they're still just using her part-time," or "they're still just using her for shelving," or "actually, she thinks she's being punished by her supervisors, who've called her proposals to increase the library's hours and extend borrowing privileges beyond the college to the general public, 'controversial' and 'the height of arrogance'"—instead of answering anything like that, I said, "She's OK."

Dr. Morse then went on to Judy, who the previous year, as the mysterious new arrival at Corbindale High, had gained some local notice by landing the leads in productions of Gilbert & Sullivan and Shakespeare, so that he sometimes called her Juliet, as in, "And how's fair Juliet faring these days? She was superb in *The Mikado*."

"Thank you," I said. "She's fine."

"What is she now, a junior?"

"A senior. Top of her class. With any luck, she'll be graduated as valedictorian."

"What a success! To matriculate in the middle of high school and garner top honors—everyone must loathe her!"

"She's managed to make a few friends."

"And of course she'll be applying here? Now that we're taking women, we might as well take the best."

"Of course she'll apply."

Dr. Morse grinned.

"You're a terrible liar, Rube, you know that?"

As I was fretting about how to reply, he said, "I hope you know that's why I like you."

Next on the conversational checklist was class-talk. Again, this was the classical order, Loc. cit. Antiquity was Bronze Age followed by Iron Age, Dr. Morse had family-chat and school-chat, always in sequence, always in proportion. Though I thought it was ridiculous at the time, I can now appreciate my Department Head's habit of never inquiring about the material I was teaching or the level of my students or really about anything except the physical rooms: he wanted to know what rooms my classes had been assigned to and how they were heated, whether there was a draft and if so from where, whether the lighting was adequate, whether the blackboard was regularly cleaned and the erasers clapped and the sill resupplied with chalk—whether my surroundings were "congenial." That was his word, his criterion. "Because," he explained, "it's important that our surroundings be congenial." A year in, I'd already learned to answer these questions with faint cavils or gripes of inconvenience, even if I had none. By telling him that the radiators were leaking and pipes were clanging in, say, Fredonia Hall, Room 203, I was enabling him to file a maintenance request, which made him feel effective. Rather, he'd jot down the room number and problem ("203: radiator, leaking; pipes, clanging...would you say Loud? or Very Loud?") and, when Ms. Gringling would come in to refresh our drinks, she'd leave with our old glasses and the request, which she'd file in his name.

After the first sip of his second gin, Dr. Morse settled down to business: "Money... maybe it's your favorite subject, but it's certainly not mine... And every department in this school is clamoring for more... for more money, more hires, higher salaries, better supplies... English, Classics, German, French: this is the situation everywhere or everywhere but History and yet it's in History's nature to partake of every suffering. Philosophy suffers, so suffers History. Psychology, invariably. Russian suffers and History does too, a cosmic Russian suffering. But the worst of it's in the sciences with their laboratory needs. The sciences aren't just expensive, they're greedy. They run their departments as if another war's on. You'd think they weren't just electrocuting pigs in there, but cooking up a bomb. Their time and effort would be better spent setting up a mint and developing novel methods of counterfeiting currency. Because money's what's required and the purse is empty and the pocket's got a hole. The regents and deans have been beancounting and you can imagine how that's gone. I don't need to tell you that economies are best left to the economists. Instead of fundraising, instead of going after donors or endowments, they're going through the departmental budgets one by one, line by item, in the hopes of finding unused funds that might be redirected."

Dr. Morse's ice-cubes clinked, as if in applause, while mine shivered against the glass in my shaking hand. "So it's not a matter of making cuts?"

He frowned. "Please don't worry, Rube. You have no reason to worry... And anyway, haven't you been cut already?"

The fright must've shown in my face, because he said, "Take it easy, please, take it easy. I was merely trying to lighten the occasion by making reference to circumcision."

I coughed a laugh and he went on, graver: "You have my word, Rube, you won't be trimmed or snipped again. It's History, we're being pillaged."

"Why us?"

"Because History is the exception. It always is. History is rich. Our treasury is the envy of Mathematics, it makes even Geology and Physics jealous. This is because we don't waste here. But the administration and the president had the temerity to disagree: they told me it's because we don't hire. Can you imagine that? Can you imagine becoming impatient with someone who practices thrift, to name just one of our myriad virtues?"

"No, I can't," was what I said, but what I was thinking was: I was his last hire, the only hire the Department had made since Hiroshima and Nagasaki.

"Anyway," he continued, a trifle absentmindedly, "that's what they've done: they scolded me for failing to be profligate. They told me I had to make another hire or risk having our hoarded funds appropriated and reallocated elsewhere. To a department that could put it to use. To a department that, to be frank, would fritter it away. Between us, I hold this demand to be a species of extortion. It's most certainly a threat, but so be it. This is how the academy now conducts its business, which it increasingly regards as just that, business."

"That appears to be the trend."

He puffed and swiveled wallward, to talk to his maps. "And though I do rather like the fraternal intimacy of our Department, the choice is clear: I would much prefer bringing on another scholar than conceding a defeat and passing our hardwon spoils onto Driggert in Agriculture or, God forbid, Pumpler in Physical Education."

"So we're hiring?"

"We are. We're putting a sign on the door that says, HELP WANTED—INQUIRE WITHIN."

"Any requirements in particular?" Even as I imagined the new sign already hanging from the doorknob—NO COLORED, IRISH, OR EUROPEANISTS NEED APPLY—my head was full of preferences, and what the Department lacked: Near East, Far East, Byzantium, anti-Whig, demography, historiography, a Hindiphile, a Hindiphone, a female.

"No requirements. Constraints. They're constraining our autonomy. They're telling me that because of our wealth, our Department has to hire someone who can also teach some classes in another Department—in Departments that failed to save as well as we have. And because they failed, they're to be rewarded."

"That doesn't seem fair."

"Because it isn't. Fair is too clear and honest a principle for these people. The terminology they employ is cross-listing, cross-discipline. Streamlining, efficiencies. This is the future, I presume: poly-functional, attached to multiple commands. I wouldn't be surprised if a few years from now they'll have you teaching a preparatory class for the CPA exam. They could certainly use all the help they can get; their audits have left a mess," and he lowered his head as if to indicate the mess, but his desk was empty.

"So where do I come in?"

He snapped back to attention, to his drink. "Powerless as we are to oppose this encroachment, we're going to have a few candidates up to campus over the course of the term, to sit for interviews, guest-teach some classes, and present some public lectures." He leaned forward. "This is where you come in, Rube."

"Me?"

"I've brought you here to beg a favor."

"Anything."

Dr. Morse grimaced and swished his drink in amendment of his statement: "Actually, it's not so much a favor as a jumping of the line. As you're surely aware, it's the responsibility of everyone in the Department to serve on a hiring committee, to which faculty members are assigned on a rotating basis. As our newest faculty member, your turn wouldn't come up for a while, maybe two, maybe three hires down the road, but we think this is a special exception, and if you'll agree, we'll certainly make sure you won't have to do double duty. You'd be taking your turn now as opposed to later. Doing your duty a bit earlier."

"So we're hiring another Americanist?"

"Since we've only just hired you, unfortunately not. It seems we'll have to go scholar-shopping in the nooks and crannies of European History."

"European History?"

"I'm trying to think of this requirement thrust upon us as something of a relief, a little respite for me and the others from Europe's burden."

"But then why put me on the hiring committee? Europe isn't my field."

He puffed a bit, as if mulling his next remark by first sending it up in smoke. "Committee membership is a requirement. All faculty members must serve a term. The specialty of the candidate under review is irrelevant. And everyone else already has their committee assignments for next term, with many of us shouldering full loads. For example, myself and Dr. Hillard won't just be joining you on Hiring, we'll also be serving together on Tenure.... on your tenure committee..."

"I understand. Forgive me. I'm happy to be of service."

Dr. Morse waved that away, dispersing the fug. "Apparently one of the candidates is particularly promising. A Europeanist whose specialty is the Medieval Era."

"The Medieval Era?"

"As far as I can tell. Iberia, I think? Fifteenth century, was it? Anyway, we'd like to have your opinion."

"Mine?"

"Your opinion in particular."

This was puzzling. He'd like to have my opinion of what? The Medieval Era? Which was the same as the Middle Ages? Which was the same as the Dark Ages? I wasn't qualified. When it came to that era, I was less its expert than its citizen, its denizen, its illiterate peasant in the middling dark. I mean, I knew when the 15th century was, between the 14th and the 16th, but that was like saying I knew where the Sugar Pops were in the A&P, in the cereal aisle below the Cocoa Puffs and Cocoa Krispies. As for Iberia, I didn't even know what that meant: Portugal and Spain, sure, but Castile and Aragon and what now? And what about the Muslims? Were all Moors Arabs? Were all Berbers Moors? Ferdinand and Isabella I was liable to confuse for George Burns and Gracie Allen. The closest I came to Iberia was stumbling a rhumba or faking the cha-cha-cha. And then what was that bit of juvenile doggerel, dancing in my head? Was it from some CUNY revue or Hebrew school before that?

> In fourteen hundred and ninety-two, Columbus sailed the
>   ocean blue
> And the Inquisition expelled the Jews,
> And all the Indians who didn't have shoes
> Said, "Nu—who you calling Indian?"

I certainly didn't recite that to Dr. Morse. I merely said, "Medieval Iberia is out of my expertise. I confess the whole milieu remains rather an enigma."

He sighed and tamped his pipe. "The man's field, Rube, is Medieval Iberia and," he hesitated, "the history of the Jews."

Sitting in smoke, he gulped his drink to the bottom.

"So I'm asking," he picked up again, after smacking his lips, "if I can rely on you to sort of welcome him here and chaperone him around, sort of make him feel comfortable, because it's important to feel comfortable."

"Congenial."

"Indeed. And then please give us your opinion."

"Of what?"

"We feel like you're in a unique position to judge, given that you fit in so well at Corbin and this man is one of your own."

"One of my own?"

"I'm glad you understand my reasoning."

We sat in silence. I hadn't planned on touching my refill drink, but now I sipped.

"I will be candid. This man, this candidate, is being pushed on us. By Huggles of all people. Huggles at the Seminary. He needs someone to teach some Bible classes. We're always getting applications, even when there isn't an opening, and Huggles went through them all and, apparently, only a Europeanist with a Hebraic background is suitable." Dr. Morse banged the table with his pipe. "If Huggles wants a Bible teacher so badly, let him hire a nun. Let him pay your wife to do it. Does your wife know the Bible well enough?"

I shook my head, as Dr. Morse shooed tobacco from the pleats of his pants and reclined, his belly stretching the grass-green cardigan; patches of parboiled shirt showed through the gaps between the braided leather buttons. I stared at those buttons, those gaps, losing myself in the off-white patches to thoughts of tenure.

"Forgive me, Rube. It seems we're the only liberal arts school in America that refuses to countenance the separation of church and state. Huggles had the temerity to put this candidate's name in front of the administration, which in turn put it in front of me—he went over my head and left me no choice but to issue the man an invitation. I don't fault the man in the least, mind you. He doesn't know the machinations behind the scenes. He's merely a scholar in search of employment. And a talented scholar at that. At least I'm told."

My glass, though half-drained, felt heavy in my hand.

But Dr. Morse was smiling. "Rube, no one here is expected to be an expert in everything. Not even you. Your fellow members of the hiring committee will help evaluate the work. Drs. Galbraith, Kimmel, and Hillard are the members I've proposed. In addition, of course, to myself as Chair."

"So I'm the only Americanist?"

"That would appear to be the case, Rube. A unique figure in many ways." He craned toward the cannonball lid and tapped out his pipe. "If you have specific thoughts about this man's scholarship, I'd be keen to have them, though I'm just as keen on having your thoughts about the man himself. His character. His fitness and aptitude."

"For?"

"I want to know whether he'd fit in here. Whether he'd integrate well into the Corbin community."

"I'm flattered you'd think I'm qualified." I finished my drink. "At least for that."

Dr. Morse chuckled and let a last ember fall into the cannonball's upended scalp, where it smoldered. "I'm sure you remember that feeling, Rube—coming up here for the very first time as an outsider, having to get up in front of everyone and present your material. It's hell on a man's nerves. If nothing else, I'm sure you'll be a steadying influence."

And that was it, pretty much. The rest of our conversation was logistics, followed by Dr. Morse attempting to pronounce the candidate's name and me failing to understand him—I was getting Bento Nehru, Benzedrine Nakamoto, Benzene Natty Yahoo . . . I was imagining the Last of the Mohicans tarred and feathered and set ablaze...

Finally, Dr. Morse just ransacked his drawers and handed me some sloppily clipped sheafs of carbon copies faded and typescripts smeared, their cover pages curling like scrolls around the name: Ben-Zion Netanyahu...

Which meant nothing to me, or to anyone...not even the surname, which was still a generation from its infamy. At the time, and especially in America, it was unknown. Or beyond unknown: it was foreign, esoteric. An alien name, eons old but also from the future; a name equally from the Bible and the funny papers.

The heir of King Hoshea. The sidekick of Flash Gordon.

At my bris, I was called *Ruvn ben Alter*—Ruvn the son of Alter. If I'd had a son, he would've been *ben Ruvn*—the son of Ruvn. *Ben-Zion* was the son of Zion—my bar-mitzvah Hebrew was adequate to that, and that was the extent of it.

I was going to meet the son of Zion.

2.

IN THE BRONX, not far from the manicured jungles of Pelham Park, there's a midblock boxy edifice of scruffy whitewashed brick from whose portico juts a marquee of burned-out bulbs and jagged lettering that sometimes proclaims THANK YOU LORD GOD and sometimes offers a cryptic reference like ACTS 1:7 or ECCLESIASTES 1:9, but always states its name to reassure the skeptical: THE CHURCH OF THE ASSUMPTION. Though I'd already left the borough before this marquee appeared, at some point over the years of my visits back, the novelty of it got lodged in my mind—I used to park my car in front of it, thinking who would steal a car from outside of a church—and the church's strange appellation gradually became a kind of private joke or personal pun for whenever anyone presumed upon my Jewishness, or presumed to prevail upon me by appealing to my Jewishness. Whenever some Hasids from the Corbin Hillel would accost me with requests to don a yarmulke and donate money to their cause, or whenever some young student of poli-sci would corner me with a request to affix my name to a petition "in favor of peace in the Middle East," I'd always think, Aha, another member of the Church of the Assumption. Dr. Morse was a member of that church in good-standing, but then so too are all of us, goys and Jews alike, members in good-standing and even with good intentions. In my childhood, this scrofulated one-armed man

27

used to stand outside the Tremont Avenue El stop jingling begged pennies in a paper cup in his single hand. Years and years later, I ran into him again on a Manhattan bus and he was carrying shopping bags from Macy's, carrying them in two arms, with two hands... Who isn't a member of The Church of the Assumption? My father used to tell this story about working on some Garment District line with some benign deficient Pole who wanted to propose to his girl and so bought a diamond ring. He brought it into work one day to show it to the Jews he worked with and ask their opinion, as if cutters of cloth were synonymous with cutters of precious stones, as if Jews and Jewish expertise everywhere were interchangeable. With utter sincerity he wanted all of his Jewish coworkers to examine the diamond and give their assessments, "because you people are the experts in these things... tell me, Yankel, Yitz, did I get taken?... I bought it off one of you people, but not one of you I know, not one of you I trust... you'd tell me if I got taken, wouldn't you?" and of course all the Jews on the line dropped their shears and examined it, held it up to the light, polished it on their aprons, and cooed over it like it was a clear-eyed newborn and told him it was magnificent and at the price he'd paid for it, a deal, while the Pole just beamed: worshipping at the altar of the Church of the Assumption. And then there was that story about my mother's brother, Uncle Sruly, an ersatz grocer who'd spent most of the latter 1940s and early '50s borrowing money from my parents, and from who knows how many other families from around the Grand Concourse, to open up a store whose business and location kept changing every time you asked (a produce-stand on Webster, a shoe-shop on Park, a flower-shop down in Spanish Harlem, a civil-service bookstore somewhere beyond the edge of the known Semitoverse in the Village), until eventually Sruly stopped answering questions and vanished and even then, my mother still believed in him, she still trusted him—he'll make good, he'll turn up. Even after the Collee gang came looking for him, even after the Manzonetto boys came, and even after Sruly's almost unrecognizable—almost but not quite unrecognizable—corpse was found nearby a construction site for the Kosciuszko Bridge on the banks of Newtown Creek: he'll make good, he'll turn up... Same church, different assumptions.

When I was a kid, the Church of the Assumption, the physical on-the-ground structure, was actually a synagogue whose name was Young Israel. This was where I went to Hebrew School and where my parents prayed. I don't recall exactly when the congregation dissolved and the building was put on the market and purchased by Catholic Caribbeans and reconsecrated with a marquee, though it must've been sometime before the death of my father, who didn't call it a synagogue but a shul. I had to say kaddish for him somewhere else.

Growing up, my weekday mornings began at another midblock pile of dignified brick—PS 114, where the gaggle of old maids and young widows who taught there would yell in loud panicked voices about how America was a country where all men were equal, and where, probably, all women were equal too; a country where we could say what we wanted; where we could be what we wanted; where we could worship whatever god we pleased, and where we could even worship no god, because the law's equal protection covered atheists too; and even agnostics, if they were citizens, were free to choose their future.

Then, once that indoctrination was concluded with the tolling of bells, I dragged myself a few blocks over to the dusty bunkerish basement of Young Israel, where—in an atmosphere of mildewed books stacked on shelves that would collapse at the most unexpected, slapsticky of moments—a quorum of wizened rabbis who'd survived the Pale of Settlement pogroms would set about contradicting those verities, demolishing those verities, ridiculing them, laying them to waste. Totally careless about the fact that here in America they were free to demolish, free to ridicule, free to lay waste, they then hauled those verities out to the yard and buried them deep in the Bronxian earth, sprinkling salt overtop them—sprinkling cement overtop them—so that nothing from them would ever flower.

Today, I imagine, that basement is packed with ecstatic Haitians who bang drums at mass and shriek Creole to popes, but back then, the nonsense had a different accent, and the delirious tongues were Hebrew and Aramaic.

My childhood days were so divided between the secular and the religious and sometimes the religious arguments against the secular were so systematic and precise that I had the crazy suspicion that the rabbis had somehow been in class with me; that they'd somehow stowed away in my school-satchel and hung there on the classroom hook throughout the next day, absorbing what Ms. Ianello said about the Bill of Rights or what Ms. Murphy said about Phylogeny, Heredity, and the Fossil Record, just so they knew exactly what to contradict and rail against as the sky sheened gabardine-dark toward twilight.

It was the differences in history that got to me the most. The history in my regular schooling was all about progress, a world that brightened with the Enlightenment and steadily improved; a world that would continue to improve illimitably, so long as every country kept trying to be more like America and America kept trying to be more like itself. The past was merely the process by which the present was attained, and the present merely the most current stage of the American superlative, to be overtaken by tomorrow's liberation and capital's spread, until the ultimate transfiguration of world history into world democracy. This meliorist account knew no bounds. Like the country itself, it could only grow; it could never end; it was open, expansive, exhilarating. By contrast, my Hebrew school history was closed: it was no history; there was no past, no present, no future. Rather, there was time, as round and perfect as the earth, which from the moment it emerged from God's spoken light had been marked by a constant repetition, not of seasons, or harvests, or astral phenomena and the holidays they governed, but of oppression, violence, and death; between the recurrences of which was a perpetual waiting for a tarrying messiah, whom my public-schoolmates were convinced had already come—the messiah had already come and we, I, had failed to notice ... maybe because we, though not I, were too busy being slaughtered ... To the gaunt shuffly rabbis who were force-feeding me these recapitulative chronicles of Jewish suffering and loss amid the pallets of stale matzoh and tarnished samovar parts, American history was synonymous with goyishe history. America wasn't the new Jerusalem that my public-schooling implied. Rather, it was the newest incarnation of Rome, Athens, Babylon, Egypt—*Mitzraim*. It was Diaspora—*galut*. And its villains—Pharaoh, Nebuchadnezzar, Antiochus, Hadrian, Titus, Haman, Khmelnytsky, Hitler, Stalin, et al.—weren't individual men perpetrating individual evil of their own accord, so much as they were all just avatars of Amalek, Israel's original enemy from the deserts. American Jews were just waiting for an Amalek of their own.

Father Coughlin, perhaps. Or Fritz Julius Kuhn from the Bund. Henry Ford. The brownshirts or the stain-sheeted Klan. A bit later, it might be Lindbergh. But the particular name and face and embodiment didn't matter. All that mattered, the rabbis said, was that hate would again find its vessel and we'd be kicked out of America too, kicked out or murdered, as was our fate in Iberia, Russia, and Germany. Just wait, the rabbis promised, it's coming. Our history (the rabbis used the plural pronoun even more than Dr. Morse) was more like a chronology of trauma, as received and determinative as the commandments from Mount Sinai: the course could not be altered; the force could not be resisted; carnage was the Jewish destiny and those of us who didn't survive could at least be sure that those who did would interpret our deaths as foreordained and sacrificial.

This round of education/counter-education was enough to drive any kid nuts, especially a kid as serious as I was, predisposed to credulousness and literality. Like most smart precocious children of my generation, I grew up reading any book put into my hands and was raised to respect the wisdom of my elders. I memorized and repeated without discernment, treating everything I read or was told as the truth, as if it weren't the product of fallible mortals but of some overarching infallible intelligence—either of a collective intelligence like the American people or the Jewish people, or of a singular superhuman intelligence like the president or God, the trigrammaton of FDR or the tetragrammaton of YHVH. And so my childhood was tugged between conflicting exceptionalisms, between the American condition of being able to choose and the Jewish condition of being chosen...

I don't know that I ever resolved this conflict, I think I just matured, through deciding on my own course of reading as much as through the changes of my hormones. After my bar-mitzvah, I left Hebrew School, abolishing the seven days of creation and replacing them with the explanation of billions of years, single-celled to multi-celled, and evolution—the doctrine that everyone who adopts it as a substitute for religion always winds up treating as a metaphor for puberty, the evolution from childhood to adolescence.

It was only after I left the Army, though—and returned to the woman I'd married and our baby girl I'd never met—that it became clear: I wasn't what I was doomed to be; no one was going to murder me in this country. No one was going to drag me and my family off to a camp or shove us together into an oven. The only uniform my country would ever make me wear was decorated with medals and ribbons. The diminutive Catholic ladies at PS 114 had been right, my old civics teacher at Stuyvesant who'd lost his chin at Verdun had been right, and even my dour, disabused, Trotskyite professors at CUNY were proving right too, despite themselves—they were right and the rabbis were wrong: America was the most exceptional exception. I myself was waking proof of its dream, my accumulating higher degrees evidence of its higher beneficence, and if there were still some considerable flaws in its laws or policies or propaganda, then my vocation—the vocation of history—would issue the corrective.

That was how I felt, in that busy flourishing period between the war I tried to forget and the counterculture I didn't anticipate. Ike, the Supreme Allied Commander, was president. The interstates were being paved. The urinals were being desegregated. Alaska and Hawaii had just been admitted to the union. We ordered new flags and globes and tossed out our old ones like so many soiled rags and punctured basketballs. We had fifty stars now, in staggered rows.

And though the Soviets sprawled all over Europe, a new country was founded whose borders could barely contain its labeling and the name Israel spilled out from its green shading across the blue and lucid Mediterranean. No matter the problem, whether it be overpopulation, or the nuclear threat, Asian containment, or the creep of consumerism into intellectual life leading to an atomizing relativism, our own ingenuity would save us. Technology would save us. Within a few years, we'd be colonizing the moon. A few years after that, we'd launch our own moon and colonize other planets and open diners there, chrome-and-neon drive-thrus, fly-thrus, because cars would fly. Robots would be our servants.

At the exact time I'm describing—between my meeting with Dr. Morse at the beginning of the fall term, September 1959, and the arrival of Dr. Netanyahu at the beginning of the spring term, January 1960—if you'd stopped me on the street and asked me how I was, if you'd asked me how the family was, I would've answered: wonderful; I would've boasted about Edith's attempts at instituting classification reforms at the library; I would've bragged about Judy's grades and standardized test scores, her prospects for college admission; I might have mentioned the delight I was taking in my tax research, and even in my students. Autumn in Corbindale was the most beautiful season. As the leaves blushed their russet colors, I'd steer my students from (September) Plymouth and English America, through (October) the Revolution and Constitution, into (November) Federalism, before finally marching them (December) straight to the gate of Fort Sumter. Am. History 101. After my classes, I'd scurry over the root-split sidewalks of Hamilton, right on Wolcott, left on Dexter, right on Gallatin, to Evergreen, and our handsome, gabled house, as the dark came earlier and cooler. I'd open the door into the smell of roasting chicken. Edith would be tossing a salad or shaking up a dressing. The table would be set. Judy would be upstairs practicing her flute or figure-drawing her profile with the help of a mirror. I'd change into a robe and pile up some sticks for a fire. After supper, we'd gather by the hearth to assemble a jigsaw puzzle, pausing only to tear up old editions of *The Corbindale Gazette* ("It's Apple-Picking Season"), and thick back-issues of *The New Yorker* ("Khrushchev and Nixon Meet in a Kitchen") to stoke the cozy flames.

Of course, no historian could be satisfied with this account—no sane non-historian, no sane person, should be either. It's too wishful.

The truth was this: my wife was bored and my daughter was angry. We'd sit around the hearth, where sometimes there wasn't any warmth, because I was actually terrible at making fires and sometimes I'd use up entire boxes of matches just trying to spark the tinder. In the rare instance that I'd get the logs to catch, I'd inevitably forget to open the flue and the den would be choked with smoke. The fire had the same problem as the family: a lack of oxygen. I recall sitting by the side of cold ashes and a 500-piece puzzle of a $500 bill, trying to fit some together into the collar of that great protectionist William McKinley, aware but unable to communicate my awareness that the true puzzle to work on was us. Edith wanted a proper degree and a job that had her reading books, not just cataloging them; Judy wanted to get out of the house and be free of her nose, which she thought was too long, too big, too bumpy. Our house—like so many in our neighborhood, a Dutch Colonial, or, as it should perhaps more accurately be called, a Dutch Colonial Revival, because it dated from just after the Civil War when people were feeling nostalgic—was old and drafty and crumbling. I'd initially been in love with its clapboarded and shuttered austerity, but after a year of coming and going I'd become suspicious of its double-identity. Look at a Dutch Colonial from the front, it looks like a house. Look at a Dutch Colonial from the side, it looks like a barn. This bothered me. It made me uncertain as to whether we were humans or animals. And though there was so much to do to prepare the house for the winter—because last winter had left its lessons, especially on the shingling—I tended to procrastinate and withdraw after supper to my study upstairs. My study was at the end of the hall: a cherry-lined chamber, all my books shelved in my own order, which Edith couldn't touch. I kept the door shut, but if I stayed still, if I stilled my breathing, I could hear her getting ready for bed. A bit later, I could hear Judy getting into bed. There would be a puddle of light under the draft of the door and then, with a click, it would dry up and vanish and, for a while at least, the only indication that I wasn't alone in the house would be a certain stress, a certain tension, in the woodgrain, and the occasional creak of Edith rolling over, Judy's whinny-snoring. It was during those hours that I'd put aside my taxes and turn to the Jews. That's what I'd say—I'd get up from my desk and stretch and say, "Time for the Jews," though sometimes I wouldn't say it, I'd just think it, and, forsaking the research curriculum I'd set myself for the term (the commodity bubbles of the plantation economy), I'd head over to my cozy leather baseball-mitt recliner in the corner, switch on the floor lamp, and bury myself in Dr. Netanyahu, his journal articles, his journal reviews, his PhD thesis on the conversos, the Marranos, the Iberian Inquisition (Spanish and Portuguese).

The lamp had a banker's greenglass shade whose emerald glow meant jealousy, envy, even shame to me. I confess I felt ashamed about it, this secret study of mine, this sudden hidden lucubration, my unexpected resurgence of interest in subjects Jewish. These were the subjects I'd been forced to study at Young Israel, if not on pain of death then on pain of parental disapproval, and it felt strange, it felt illicit, to be delving into those very same tragedies now, and with more attention being paid than ever before, for the sake of my employer.

As I turned the pages (the English-language pages, whose frequent references to the Hebrew-language work of "Ben Zion," "Benzion," and "B. Netanyahu" indicated that the bulk of his scholarship was out of my grasp); as I applied myself to his introductions that read like conclusions and tried to stay reading through to his conclusions that read like prayers, I found myself simultaneously attuned to every sound in the house, from the shift and settle of the foundations up through the vibrance of the refrigerator and the ticking of the clock, to the chestnuts that clattered on the roof and the squirreled-and-chipmunked gutters; so alert and yet so spooked by the adventitious rustle, it was as if I were afraid of being caught... but caught by whom? My wife and daughter? The informer moon? An Inquisition tribunal from the College Seminary escorted by an armed posse of desperadoes deputized by the offices of the Corbindale Sheriff? And caught doing what? Caught doing my job? I kept telling myself that what I was doing was required of me; it was a committee responsibility, a Department prereq; I was just following orders! Let them bind me to a pole and set me ablaze with what should've burned in the hearth, my last words would be: In the Name of Dr. Morse!

But as I paged deeper, I was scandalized myself: It was difficult for me to feel that I wasn't blaspheming, just by reading.

What was Dr. Netanyahu's work about? I was frustrated, initially, because I couldn't formulate it clearly...though he couldn't formulate it either...But if by chance some of the creepy priests who featured in his texts were to come to life and demand a summary and threaten to slice off one finger with dull iron scissors for every word I used, this is what I'd tell them: *Everything you know about the Inquisition is wrong.*

That's eight words, so I'd keep my thumbs.

In Dr. Netanyahu's telling, the Inquisition must be understood as the Inquisitions, plural, which had to be divided between those launched by the Popes and the Catholic Church itself and those launched by the monarchies with the Church's collusion. The first of these politicized institutions were in Iberia: Spain followed by Portugal. The true purpose of these Inquisitions wasn't doctrinal; they weren't supposed to investigate heresies or convert the Jews or ensure that the Jews who converted remained faithful Catholics— not at all. Instead, their true purpose—never publicly stated, but privately acknowledged—was to invalidate new conversions and turn as many new Christians back into Jews as possible.

This was startling, to say the least, and constituted a major revision not just of the Jewish past, but of Christian history, which to Dr. Netanyahu was history in general.

The Inquisition, in his words, was a "crucial moment" or "critical juncture," a "peripety" or "climacteric" for Medieval Catholicism. For centuries—essentially, throughout the Crusades—the Church's primary goal had been to make more Catholics; this was a point on which both Jews and Catholics had immemorially agreed; for centuries this was probably their only point of agreement, and it was also a premise that Dr. Netanyahu accepted. However, he claimed, sometime toward the close of the fifteenth century—on the eve of Columbus's departure, actually—that goal was suddenly changed, and the Church became interested in culling its flock and returning its youngest lambs back to their ancestry.

Dr. Netanyahu, as far as I could tell, had dedicated his entire career to proving this claim, and to explaining why the change happened. And while I couldn't hope to evaluate the evidence myself— the arcana he quoted in Spanish and Portuguese and even Latin and Ladino without translation—it was the explanation that really got to me. It bothered me. Because it wasn't really an explanation. It was more like—I want to say a dogma.

Why did the Church restore to Judaism the very converts it had just spent the better part of the Crusades trying to obtain, according to Dr. Netanyahu? Because the converts were bad Catholics? No, not all of them. Or because they were too good at being Catholic? No, not all of them either. Rather, the reason was because: as long as the Catholics still required a people to hate, the Jews had to remain a people doomed to suffer.

I'm being only slightly flippant—and I'm not being flippant in the least when I say that though I've never been an expert on the split-hair psychoanalytic differences among sublimation, condensation, and displacement, or between projection and introjection, or the profuse blood-lines of transference, I can't help but propose that Dr. Netanyahu's reasoning was produced by some tainted strain from that unhappy family of defenses. If Freud can surmise that the libido, or sexual energy, can only be made societally acceptable by its transformation into something else, such as into energy for business or literature, numismatics, philatelics, or Korean taekwondo, it can't be such a stretch to suggest that Dr. Netanyahu was trying to satisfy his religious appetites through scholarship. His way of going about this was, in a sense, just a nomenclatural confusion; an un- or semi-conscious substitution of a more palatable vocabulary for one that felt too dangerous; so that what he called "history" was actually "theology," and what he called "facts" were actually "beliefs"; "the Jew" to him wasn't just a Medieval who subscribed to geocentrism and thought the earth was flat, but a Platonic ideal or archetype, a Hegelian absolute, an identity more or less constant and unchanging through the ages.

Like the Medievals he was purporting to study, Dr. Netanyahu took certain constancies for granted, and so had to reconcile the fixed and enduring "Jew" with the irreversible progress of time; with causality, contingency, *in esse* and *in fiere*, *impetus*, *conatus*, and the issues of what constitutes a thing and what, or who, can make things start or stop or happen. History treats time as a chain of happenings that we humans set into motion by our own free will; its first lesson is that a first cause does not exist because, as my teachers put it back in public-school, we learn history in order to learn how to change it. Theology, however, treats time as a chain of changes that are visited down upon us by the will of God, Who makes things occur for reasons of His own—Who brings about alterations and modifications in the fabric of existence not haphazardly, but according to a mystical scheme or pattern that can't be humanly interpreted as anything but miraculous, or as punishments we've earned in retribution for our sins. This, at least, was what I was taught by the rabbis, who were quite capable of insisting that the 1490s and 1940s were identical, if only because no differencing detail could make them explicable. And if I'd been troubled by this account in my childhood, I was utterly stunned to find it repeated by an ostensible colleague, a man who called himself an historian but denied the discipline. It was bewildering to realize: Dr. Netanyahu was a believer, and if there was any distinction at all between what he believed and what the rabbis did, it was that Dr. Netanyahu preferred to attribute the power of change not to a deity acting in accordance with an inscrutable design but to the world's vast stock of gentiles who acted out of hatred, constantly judging the Jews and oppressing them, and effecting change through their oppressions: converting them, unconverting them, massacring and expelling. This was how Dr. Netanyahu was able to pass off a theology as history, by divesting the divine of its responsibility for change and assigning it instead to mortals; letting that discretionary power devolve upon the monarchy, the Cortes and the Curia, dukes, barons, bishops, cardinals, and successive generations of Jew-butchering mobs who'd come down from their pedestaled clouds when least expected to wield their absolute authority over Jewish life, passing laws about where the Jews could live (in ghettos), when they couldn't go outside (after dark), what hats they had to wear (conical, pointy), and what occupations they could practice (money-lending), in addition to perpetrating on the Jews occasional autos-da-fé, blood-libel riots, and death-camps. And so it might be more accurate to say that though Dr. Netanyahu was certainly a believer, he didn't believe in an all-powerful God so much as he believed in the all-powerful goys, who were obviously more accountable and identifiable to academia than God was. Because unlike God, these kings, queens, ecclesiastics, and Jew-butchers who ruled the Jewish world had names and dates and places of residence and nationalities; they could be quoted with citation, marked by crosses and stars. But take away that supposedly secular garb, strip the texts I was reading of their robing notes and

41

endless garment-bolts of bibliography, and they weren't historical at all; at best, they comprised a theologized anti-history, or an anti-historicized theology with a psychoanalytic tinge—neither and both? Or just another credo for the Church of the Assumption?

Every once in a while in the course of my reading, I'd find a typo, a grammatical slip, or just an inelegant syntactical formulation—an ungainly aping of British English, "perchance"—and I'd correct it. I'd actually pick up a pencil or pen—and later, a red marker I brought home from my office at school for this very purpose—and make a mark, bringing tenses into agreement, turning "there"s to "their"s, crossing out "indeed"s and "therefore"s, and striking redundancies, tautologies, and every use of "pivotal."

It felt as if by doing so, I was holding my own history in check; I was blocking out the past, those lost old hoarse-cricket voices of the basement rabbis from long long ago, who with the infelicity and stiffness of another foreigner's thesaurusized English were murmuring again—warning me against complacency...warning me against America...

This wasn't the usual preparation of an academic evaluator, but closer to a self-evaluation, and the first time in my life I'd ever looked back and compared who I'd been with who I'd become. I was a tenure-track historian and an active participant in secular American life sneaking around in the attic-mind of an obscure Israeli academic like I was one of the antique Jews he wrote about, a convert forcibly returned to the faith I'd left and too consumed by internal turmoil to notice the hour, until—jolted by the chatter of amatory birds —I'd turn and tug aside the curtain and outside the window was morning.

3.

To whom it may concern [*went the letter that arrived in mid-September, which Ms. Gringling photostatted and left in my faculty mailbox*]:

I would like to take this opportunity to recommend Dr. Benzion Netanyahu for the position of Professor of History at Corbin College.

I cannot endorse his candidacy heartily enough.

As President of Dropsie College for Hebrew and Cognate Learning, I have had the distinct honor and pleasure of knowing Dr. Netanyahu (and his lovely wife, Tzila) for well over a decade (off and on).

You cannot imagine the joy we all experienced here at Dropsie at the appearance of so bold and brilliant a man. After all, it's not every day that a true genius, who also happens to be a major statesman and political hero, appears in the halls of a small—we prefer to say "selective"—rabbinical seminary in the heart of Philadelphia.

It truly was a miracle.

That said, it must be admitted that this is one of the many privileges of American academia: even our tiniest institutions can sometimes find the resources with which to attract the greatest of foreigners, though, alas, we can never seem to keep them ...

"Ben," as I call him (we are personal friends), came to us here at
Dropsie already with a formidable reputation, as one of the pre-
eminent Israeli (then Palestinian) scholars and Hebraists of his
generation, a profound expounder of Zionism, and an invaluable
translator into both Hebrew and English of some of that movement's
most important foundational texts, by Herzl, Nordau, and Zangwill,
in addition to later works by Ze'ev Jabotinsky, his mentor, and
Nathan Mileikowsky, his exceptional father of blessed memory.

As the war ravaged our brethren in Europe, Ben dedicated himself
to Jewish life here, leading classes for America's future rabbinate
(and a few prospective clergymen of other faiths and diverse denom-
inations) in Hebrew language, Hebrew literature, and Jewish history,
while completing his dissertation on the crypto-Jewry of Inquisition
Era Iberia under the supervision of yours truly. I freely admit the
absurdity of this arrangement, which was never more than a formality. Dropsie policy requires all doctoral students to work with a
faculty advisor, and I was grateful to be picked, because I was the
one who benefitted.

He was the one advising *me*.

Over the course of the dissertation process, I recall marveling at
so many of Ben's surpassing qualities, but none so much as his fortitude, his endurance—his ability to continue researching and producing chapters in draft even while meeting the heavy demands of
the classroom and absorbing the grim forecasts from overseas. Just
one of those tasks would've been enough for me—but not for Ben,
who also managed throughout this tumultuous stretch to maintain
a full slate of political responsibilities related to his position as Jabotinsky's chief representative in the United States. Under the auspices
of the NZO, the New Zionist Organization (formerly the ZO, the

Zionist Organization), Ben traveled the length and breadth of the land, lobbying politicians in statehouses and Congress, meeting with business leaders, cultural figures, and private citizens alike, in community-centers and places of worship, educating the American public about Israeli independence. And all without missing a single appointment at Dropsie! Not a single advisory session! Not a single class!

He'd come in for a session—on time!—and casually say, "I just returned from Washington. Bess Truman sends her regards." And then he'd get down to explaining to me some intricate intrigue from the court of João II or Alfonso V.

In brief, here is a man who worked tirelessly to build not just a career, but a state—the Jewish State! I simply have no idea when he slept!

Upon the declaration of Israeli independence in 1948, Ben began making arrangements to leave the comforts and safety of "Philly" for the perils of Jerusalem.

We here at Dropsie were sad to lose him, but the choice was an imperative: his country needed him, his people needed him, it was "perfectly understandable."

For the better part of the next decade, Ben and I kept in regular touch (in Hebrew, but mostly in English). He kept me apprised of his whirlwind activities—pedagogical and political both—and I followed them with an almost proprietary interest, particularly his efforts at expanding the scholarly horizons of his young country through academic publishing. It felt like each week, I'd get something new from him: some new monograph or pressing request. It was galling: the June issue of a journal he edited would arrive in Philadelphia only in December! If it arrived at all! Despite this,

I was all too pleased to subscribe to any venture he founded, be it a series of reference texts, or a leaflet of polemics . . .

Though I enjoyed getting the news, and the fruits, of these accomplishments, I was also sensitive to the frustrations: to the mentions Ben would make—in nearly every communication he had with me—of his growing impatience with the scant resources of his nation's struggling university, and his fondness for America's superior research facilities, reliable periodical access, and decent postal service. Ultimately, he let slip that if the conditions were appropriate, he'd be amenable to returning; what he was after, specifically, was some form of stipend or grant to at least partially support him while he turned his dissertation into a book.

It took some time, and some considerable cajoling on my part, but thanks to a few generous donors from the greater Philadelphia area (owners of a prominent wig-making company and three local Jewish men in the automotive business collectively known as "The Pep Boys"), I was able to offer Ben a one-year fellowship, which he accepted.

Ben—along with his lovely wife, Tzila, and their family that now numbered three handsome and intelligent sons—made the arduous journey to the Keystone State and resumed his scholarship and lecturing with all his usual energy and diligence.

Or with more than his usual—because the Ben who'd returned to us was intent on making the most of his fellowship sojourn, relentlessly pushing himself, and pushing others to match him. His zeal touched everyone and elevated every issue. For example, when he banned the use of English-language texts in his seminars, the students who didn't drop out went on to develop a remarkable Hebrew proficiency. And when some on the faculty were trying to make the wearing of skullcaps mandatory on campus, Ben mediated a compromise whereby only the Christians and those who'd already enrolled to study abroad in Israel were exempted. These incidents were Zionism in action—they were the very definition of "pragmatic Zionism"; the ideology that enabled Ben to spend the week teaching Hebrew with his head uncovered, even while serving as the most valuable early reader of my sermons; his erudition—which far outstripped that of any rabbi on the faculty—saving me time and again from making the most embarrassing mistakes of fact, grammar, and judgment. I'll always remember our strolls together home from Dropsie; Ben delivering his charitable critiques of my next Sabbath's homiletic, as we approached my house, where Tzila was showing my wife Carolina how to prepare hummus with tahini, falafel balls, and pashtida (I'm pleased to report that Carolina has since kept some of these dishes in her repertoire), and the three Netanyahu boys were out in the driveway with our own boy, Ronnie, who was coaching them for the B'nai Brith Soapbox Derby (they came in a commendable fifth, having never raced before).

The year flew by, and with Passover behind us, Ben approached me, seeking renewal. He wanted to stay, his family wanted to stay, but his fellowship was set to expire. And after his fellowship, the family's visas. It was the visas that got to me the most.

Even now, I'm humiliated by how confidently I responded: something could be done. Some agreement or accommodation could be reached, I was sure of it.

But when toward the end of the term, I went to the donors, I learned otherwise: I learned that the wig-making business has been sluggish of late, and—with so much competition from Mexico, with so many factories moving down to Mexico—they weren't going to be able to extend their commitment...I learned that "The Pep Boys" were in the process of expanding their franchising and so were regrettably unwilling to prolong their support...

I went to my board, which rebuffed me; I lunched with rich widows and went away hungry; I went toward the lights but was turned from the door.

It was a tragedy. Without outside funding, Dropsie couldn't afford him.

It was a tragedy I couldn't prevent, and yet I also can't prevent feeling responsible.

Once again, I was reminded of the limitations involved in running a practical vocational institute devoted to the training of the pulpit clergy. As I've often had the chance to lament with my priest and minister colleagues at our interfaith exchanges: it's an unfortunate but persistent truth that most people of every religion merely require the clergy to marry and bury them, and only a righteous few are ever ready to put up the cash to support the clergy's education in anything beyond the rudiments of chaplaincy...But I digress...

Ben now finds himself in a situation even more precarious than the one he'd left—stranded in America with no job and a half-finished book; not to mention a family of five, and the costs of relocating them back to Israel would effectively wipe out his savings.

And so his last option, to keep life and limb together and provide for his brood, is to put himself out on the market...

I've presented Ben's career in the detail I have, only out of an understanding that by American standards, his curriculum vitae might appear unorthodox—to have what we call "gaps." I would like to assure you, however, that the unorthodox is quite common in the Israeli context—in the general Jewish context. For instance, there are numerous professors throughout the States who fled the Nazi genocide, having been deprived of their positions at German universities by the Nuremberg edicts. I might cite, in this regard, such luminaries and American patriots as Dr. Albert Einstein and Dr. Hannah Arendt. Do we hold against these folks a "gap" in their CVs between 1933 and 1945? Do we decide against them because their employment histories have "holes"? Of course not! That would be lunacy! And while the lacunae in Ben's career are of a different nature, they're not unrelated. Because while he himself didn't suffer the European ordeal, he certainly did have to contend with less-than-ideal Palestinian conditions, from typewriter shortages and typewriter-ribbon rationing to Arab arsonists and biblioclasts who kept trying to torch the university archives. In other words, history came also to him. History kept him from becoming a practicing historian and yet far from being dismayed by this turn of events, Ben stepped up to the plate and confronted the present head-on. While younger men fought literal battles in their own backyards, Ben's war transcended borders to become a crusade waged even in the ignominy of the popular press, to gain recognition for his state and shape public opinion. I believe no measure of the man can be made without taking these political factors into account. To my mind, Ben is a true hero of the Jewish people! A warrior-historian in the olden mold, his work providing, in the words of the prophet, *or l'goyim*, "a light unto the nations" (Isaiah 42:6)!

In conclusion, I consider it a blot on Dropsie's record, as well as on my own personal record, that Ben must make his career elsewhere now. And I am convinced that it will represent an irreparable loss for American Jewry, and so an irreparable loss for America Herself, should he be forced to return to the Jewish State a pauper.

America, after all, is said to be the land of opportunity.

I can only hope that Corbin College confirms this reputation by appointing Dr. Netanyahu to a position appropriate to his stature.

Sincerely yours,

Rabbi Dr. Chaim "Hank" Edelman, President

Dropsie College for Hebrew and Cognate Learning

4.

A DECADE: the lifespan of a salamander; the time it took for the
Flavians to put up the Colosseum and for Odysseus to make it back
to Ithaca; the statutory period during which the IRS can collect on
unpaid tax, after which a jubilee is decreed and the debt is canceled...Just about a decade prior to the autumn I'm recalling, the
State of Israel was founded. In that minuscule country halfway across
the globe, displaced and refugee Jews were busy reinventing themselves into a single people, united by the hatreds and subjugations
of contrary regimes, in a mass-process of solidarity aroused by gross
antagonism. Simultaneously, a kindred mass-process was occurring
here in America, where Jews were busy being deinvented, or unin-
vented, or assimilated, by democracy and market-forces, intermar-
riage and miscegenation. Regardless of where they were and the
specific nature and direction of the process, however, it remains an
incontrovertible fact that nearly all of the world's Jews were involved
at midcentury in becoming something else; and that at this point
of transformation, the old internal differences between them—of
former citizenship and class, to say nothing of language and degree
of religious observance—became for a brief moment more palpable
than ever, giving one last death-rattle gasp.

In retrospect, the disparities between Pale of Settlement Jews and
German Jews, for example, or between Litvak Jews and Hasidic

Jews, can seem ridiculously minor; they can seem egoistic, egotistic, petty and vain, matters of custom, cuisine, or even just wardrobe, but that doesn't mean they didn't exist and substantially define people's lives: "*der Narzissmus der kleinen Differenzen*" is Freud's famous phrase, which you don't need more than *kleinen* German to puzzle out, or more than *kleinen* pride to be disturbed by.

I bring all this up to introduce my parents, and Edith's parents, not necessarily in that order—with them, you always had to be sensitive to the order.

Love is generally a one-to-one affair and mortal, but hatreds tend toward immortal typologies, with each change of identity becoming translated into more relevant terms, so that the Old World distinctions between my Ukrainian/Russian Jewish parents and Edith's Rhenish Jewish parents became, in the New World, secularized rivalries between the Bronx and Manhattan, the Grand Concourse and Upper Broadway; mass-transit v. Cadillacs; no days off v. Lorelei vacations and half the year in Florida.

To this day, the transmogrification of ancient feuds remains the primary process by which immigrants nativize: to renew a conflict is to acculturate.

Marxists might explain the Blum/Steinmetz antipathy in class-struggle terms, the tension between workers and owners: the Blums (my father a garment-cutter, my mother a garment-presser) made the garments and the Steinmetzes provided the cloth; Edith's cousins were into textiles, her parents into trimmings. Capitalists, meanwhile—capitalists such as both sets of our parents actually were—might explain the antipathy culturally: my parents tacked up calendars and cranked the radio; Edith's parents hung oils and bowed the cello.

Or my mother-in-law, Sabine, did, while my father-in-law, Walter, just paid for it, out of the piles he made supplying buttons and snaps and clasps to the trade, also zippers, studs, and shanks, hook-fasteners for bras, and elastic bands for socks and underwear. Sabine had gone to work for him as his receptionist and quit as his wife, went into psychoanalysis, and was eternally training to become an analyst herself, at some semi-accredited psychoanalytic institute run by a Balkan émigré out of a closet off the Bowery. When the Balkan declared her ready—if he'd ever declare her ready, which he ultimately didn't, before his stroke—she'd go into practice on her own and every time she talked about that prospect, it was usually in terms of her future office, where it would be located (what neighborhood, building, floor), and how it would be decorated ("Oriental"). She fancied herself an expert in fashion, design, and culture in general, and while her taste was good enough, she had the bad taste to work too hard at it. She'd talk about concerts in terms of how expensive the tickets were and how much better her seats were than her friends'. She'd talk about art in terms of how much Walt had bid at auction and who against. She liked sharing her opinions, which were properly those of the critics she read: Pollock wasn't interested in how you felt when you looked at it but how he'd felt when he'd made it; with bebop, the very act of listening became improvisation. When she told this to my parents, after one of Judy's grade-school plays, they thought she was talking about some Polacks from Poland? Bird was a bird, easy enough, but Diz was a dog and Monk a cat? Back in the city, she liked to take Edith to "bistros" and "brasseries" uptown and make her order in French. She had in her this drive to know everything, at least to know everything new and not be caught out, and Judy had this cruel trick where she'd ask her grandmother whether she'd heard, say, the new Levi Woodbury "Concerto for Harp," or whether she'd seen, say, the new exhibition at the Peggy Eaton Gallery, and Sabine would answer sure, of course, though neither existed: Levi Woodbury was the longest-serving Secretary of the Treasury of the Jackson administration and Peggy Eaton was the scandal-ridden wife of John Henry Eaton, Jackson's Secretary of War—I hadn't known that Judy had picked up these and other names from me until she used them to skewer her grandmother.

Judy…maybe the one commonality that both Edith's parents and mine would acknowledge was their love for her, which they expressed through the same question incessantly asked: who loves you more…Oma and Opa? Bubbe and Zeyde?

It was because of this competition that our holidays were vexed. Not spiritually, but logistically. We had to split our time, the tradition being to spend each night of a holiday with a different set of parents and alternating the order year to year: one year first-night supper at mine, second night at Edith's; the next year first-night supper at Edith's, second night at mine. I'm convinced this is the reason why the rabbis made all the major Jewish holidays last not for one night but two, at least in the Diaspora—to ensure that the Steinmetzes and the Blums wouldn't have to mix like spoiled meat and rotten dairy.

Rosh Hashanah 1959, Edith and I decided to inaugurate a new tradition: we weren't going back to New York. This year, our second up at Corbindale, we were staying put and we'd invite our parents up, doing so with the presumption that faced with the prospect of having to drive up from the city or even carpooling together and having to eat their meals and sleep together under the same roof for two consecutive nights, both sets of parents would decline, leaving myself, Edith, and Judy to hold our holiday in peace, observing it, or more likely not-observing it, however. Sure, we'd miss the Manhattan-moments of our down-Hudson hajjes, like trying to fit in a Broadway show, or—this was my preference—browsing for books along Fourth Avenue, when it was still Bookseller's Row, or along upper Fifth at Scribner's and Brentano's. But the effort just seemed too much. We didn't have it in us, especially given how fresh our memory was of our visit the year before, when we'd just gotten ourselves settled and established in the new house and unpacked all our boxes and started school, only to turn around and haul back to the snarled city from whence we'd come. That had been exhausting. And though this year wasn't quite as frantic—after all, this year we weren't moving cross-state and upending our lives—Edith and I wanted to set a precedent, despite Judy's protestations: "All summer I'd been looking forward to going back to the city and now you're finking out? After I made all these plans, I'm supposed to tell the only friends I've ever had, sorry, I won't be coming east for *West Side Story*, count me out for *The Miracle Worker* with Patty Duke as Helen Keller who at least was born deaf and blind, whereas I'm being made that way by my own parents who've turned into total totalitarians?"

"At least Helen Keller couldn't talk," I said.

"At least Mao admits he's a dictator."

Edith sighed. "They're not your only friends, Judy. You shouldn't say that. You've made so many new ones here. What about Mary and Joan and the girl from the literary annual who liked your poem about the lunar surface—aren't they your friends? What would they say? You shouldn't put them down. And what about Tod Frew, who walks you home after every rehearsal? Is he your friend or is he more than that?"

Judy threw up her hands and cried, "Fascists," and though Edith

55

wavered in the decision, I held my ground. I put my foot down. Both my feet. I planted them in the soil. Corbindale was where we lived now, Corbindale was our home, the new magnetic center of the Blumian universe and our city-relatives would have to get in orbit and realign. It was time to prioritize the immediate family, the conjugal unit, the hearth. So we picked up the phone—I had Edith pick up the phone—and declared: All roads lead to Corbindale and you're invited.

But only Edith's parents accepted. My parents passed.

We'd been expecting both sets to pass—I kept repeating to myself in appalled incomprehension—but Edith's had agreed and mine had refused and despite my getting involved now by calling my parents myself and coaxing, they wouldn't reconsider and were even, it struck me, enlivened in their recalcitrance by this unexpected opportunity to distinguish themselves.

"I'll let your father explain," my mother said, after I'd worn her out with my entreaties, and my father was losing patience and snatching at the phone.

"You want to know why we're not coming?" he said. "I'll tell you why, professor. It's because unlike your wife's parents, we're not ashamed to be Jews. And on Rosh Hashanah, you know what Jews do?"

"They get together with family?"

"No, professor, they go to shul. And can you tell me where is the shul in Corbinville?"

"Dale. Corbindale."

"Ville, dale, who cares? There is no shul, did you ever think about that?"

"About shul? No, I admit I didn't."

"And do you know, for all your smarts, where is the nearest shul to you in Corbinvilledale, professor?"

"No, I don't. But I know you know and you're going to tell me."

"Do you hear that? He doesn't know, your son the professor doesn't know," my father said, presumably to my mother but also, not inconceivably, to God.

Then he was back to yelling at me, "Of course I know, I looked it up. You're not the only one who can look things up. The nearest shul to you is in Erie, Pennsylvania."

By this time, it was too late to disinvite the Steinmetzes, according to Edith. They were coming alone, they were stooping to come; disdain was their brand of piety.

This wasn't just the first time they'd be visiting Corbindale, this was the first time any of our parents would be visiting, and a decision had to be made about where to put them. Apparently, the place that made the most sense was my study, or so Edith said, since I already had an office at the College. My study was the house's putative third bedroom, for the second child we were always delaying, and, until we made up our minds, Edith was saying, we should be using it for guests, who might least obtrusively be accommodated on a couch that folded out into a bed, like so, and she unfolded a glossy advertisement: *Don't just dream about that extra bedroom, get one for the price of a sofa . . . Hide-A-Bed, the hostess's secret . . .*

One was being delivered next weekend. That one, Edith indicated it with a cuticle. The model was called The Dromedary. But before she could explain why she'd ordered it with the optional Flounce and in a color called Abyssinian Khaki, I protested. I didn't want her parents in my study; I didn't want them messing up my papers, and I made such a show of resistance that Edith revised her offer:

we'd put the new fold-out downstairs in the den, as a replacement for the old non-fold-out we'd brought from the Bronx, and she and I would sleep on it while her parents would take our bedroom (which Edith always referred to as "the master bedroom," just like she called the downstairs bathroom "the powder room," the side porch the "verandah," and the yards "the lawns")—this was her decision and it was final.

The day the hideous Hide-A-Bed arrived and the old cabriole couch was taken away—the site of so many bouts of our newlywed canoodling—Edith spiffed the kitchen and hoovered the dining-room and then, as if wanting to save the first sit on the camelbacked convertible for a calmer eve, or for someone who'd earned it, stood around in the den sorting through the broken-spined album into which she'd copied my mother's recipes: she was going to make my mother's brisket, she announced. That was how Edith was, always working in fulfillment of deals whose terms had never been stated. She was shrewd in her bargaining and might even have threatened the sanctity of my study only as an opening gambit, as a means of achieving her ultimate goals of getting some new furniture for the den and tucking her parents into our bed.

There was a knock at the door and, before I could get halfway downstairs, they let themselves in, Walter carrying two suitcases— two suitcases for one night—and Sabine, who wrapped me in scarves and a nimbus of bergamot perfume.

Walt, who had no free hand to shake, offered me the luggage instead. "What's this? You keep your door unlocked?"

"Apparently, we do."

"You're sure that's safe?"

"Safe so far. Anyway, we're home."

"That's all the more reason to keep it locked. Anyone can just waltz on in."

"Everyone here keeps their doors unlocked and no one waltzes. They also leave their bicycles out in their yards and their trashcans aren't on chains. This isn't the city."

"This isn't the city?" Sabine said, on her way to the kitchen to greet her daughter. "Tell me something I don't know."

By the time I'd returned from depositing their luggage upstairs, Sabine still hadn't gotten over her startle. That, or she just reprised it now for my sake.

"Ruben, who is this? What have you done with my daughter?"

She pointed at Edith like accusing a witch, my wife conjuring hectically over cauldrons and pans.

"What's cooking?" Walt said. "It smells delicious."

Edith recited the dishes she was making and Sabine repeated them back to her in a rote remote voice as if she were baffled at having to choose the one edible dish from a menu that was otherwise venomous, lethal: brisket, kugel, tzimmes.

"You didn't learn that from me," Sabine said.

Edith warded her off with a spoon. "I know—they're Ruben's mother's recipes."

Sabine sniffed. "I'm glad your marriage has helped you to compensate for the domestic instruction I so deprived you of."

Edith clattered the spoon inside a pot.

"And you have no one else here to give you a hand? You can't possibly have done all this by yourself. You can't possibly have."

And Sabine narrowed her eyes, as if trying to find where the help was stowed, which pantry the maid had been folded into like a bed into a sofa.

Walt said, "How about giving us a tour?"

"I have to watch the noodles. Ruben can take you."

"Yes," Sabine said, putting an arm around me, putting both arms. "Let's leave Edith to her hausfrau's chores and dear Ruben will give us a tour of the establishment."

Forget the campus's mock-Goth charms and partially erected brutalist Students' Union; forget College Drive's quaint commercial strip of ye olde shoppes and grange; forget the half-kitschified craft-stands of the Seneca Reservation and the abandoned utopian pottery phalanstery and even the sappy forests sprawling between them reflected sepia-tinted in the rivers and lakes, my in-laws had no interest in anything in or around Corbindale—they had no interest in anything at all besides the house they were already in. This wasn't because our house was particularly interesting architecturally, or even interiorly, but only because they knew how much it'd cost. They wanted to judge how well we'd made out. They wanted, especially, to judge me—the poor Yiddishy kid who'd married their daughter pretty much straight out of Stuyvesant, knocked her up, and then left for war (as they remembered it)... the scholastic prodigy and upstart who even with doctorate on the wall and published works on the shelf still could barely hold onto an associate post lecturing econometrics at CUNY while failing to get tenure (in their mind, there was a tenure position to be had there)... the economist who couldn't make money (a figure as common as the historian who couldn't make history)... the inveterate luck-bungler who, finally exasperated by his dwindling status and inability to make a dent in the city (which to them was the world), accepted the first tenure-track job he was offered in the middle of the barbarian wastes and absconded there with their daughter and granddaughter, blowing them "Upstate"—but really west, America's direction—like the brittle fallen leaves of pathetic fallacy...This visit, then, was their chance for confirmation. Not for reassessment—the Steinmetzs didn't do reassessment—but confirmation, that Edith had been unwise in her selection of mate and Judy unfortunate in her nonse-lection of father.

As I took them around the rooms—less like the lord of the manor and more like the lord's last bastard descendant giving guided tours for tips—Sabine made little prying inquiries about the provenance of every lithograph and sampler; and the price of every estate auction antique, from the Chippendale buffet and tray-table, to the delicate, spindly-legged Shaker chairs, plainmade stick-stuff fitted together by some regional commune of unmarried ladies back in the coal-black nethers of the 1880s, $36 for the pair. Sabine picked these up, weighing their reedweight in her hands, but then she also tried to pick up the Hide-A-Bed and buffet and tray-table too, as if she were measuring our prospects of returning to the city by measuring the portability of our possessions. Walt, for his part, was in an improvements-mood, with a knack for finding every flaw, from some cracked molding in my study to the loose hatch and lacking rungs of the attic's tug-down ladder. Upstairs, in the hallway just past Judy's room, he bellied onto the carpet-runner to examine an open elec-trical socket and said Manuel could fix it, no problemo. Manuel would come up, he could do it all in a day and wouldn't charge much. He'd been employed by the building for years and was considered very trustworthy. It took me a moment to realize that my father-in-law, a man who'd never offered me a red cent—not that I would've taken it—was offering to send the handyman employed by the co-op association of his apartment-building in Manhattan out to the farthest edge of New York State just to screw in a new plate for my electrical socket.

"And this is your room."

"You mean yours," Sabine said, poking at the bed where I slept with her daughter and then slipping off her ballet flats and settling down on it.

"Make yourself at home."

"And you have your own bathroom?" Walt was curious.

"Yes."

"So you don't have to share with Judy?"

"No."

Walt nodded and went inside and stood at the sink and twisted both taps. Then he went over and turned on the shower. Water shot and howled.

"Walt," Sabine said. "Please don't."

Walt winked and closed himself in with the latch.

"He'll be in there for a while."

"He's got a lot to think about?"

"No, he doesn't, but he'll be in there for a while."

I made to leave but Sabine said, "Wait, sit down," and patted a divot next to her on the bed, but I went to lean against the window-sill. "It's a shame we don't get the pleasure of having your parents up here with us, your mother's recipes notwithstanding."

"They like to go to shul. They like to pray."

"They pray for you?"

"For all of us."

Water growled from behind the bathroom door.

"I'm curious, your parents—are they separate-folks or sharers?"

"Excuse me?"

"Your parents, do they sleep separately or share a bed?"

"My parents? They share. At least they did when I was a child."

"You know, our generation was the last in which couples slept in separate beds. I know it's strange to think of me as being from the same generation as your parents, but it's true. Ours was the last to sleep apart with the little nightstand between with all the little pill bottles." She rolled over to jostle open the drawer of Edith's nightstand and then rolled in the other direction to jiggle mine, making tiny inferring grunts at their emptiness. "Of course, poorer families never had that option; I bet that's why your parents always shared and their parents before them. But my parents slept separately, as did their parents. They could afford two beds and back in Germany they even maintained separate bedrooms. I think they thought of it as French, but the reasoning behind it was English, Victorian in a way, which for a German Jew wasn't a pejorative, but a compliment. The French believe in separation in order to have affairs. The women even keep separate quarters, boudoirs, but a boudoir is not a bedroom. It might include a bedroom, but it is not a bedroom so much as a chamber in which to have affairs and sulk about them privately. The British, however, believed in separation because sharing was dangerous, the proximity to another sleeper enabled the transmission of infectious diseases like pneumonia, flus, and colds, which back then were often deadly. I think my parents' generation was also convinced that sharing, bedrooms and especially beds, resulted in an increase in sex, which in turn resulted in an increase in pregnancy, in an age unprovided with reliable birth-control. Though perhaps the infection-reasoning was invented to obscure the sex-reasoning by women of the past, frustrated at always being pregnant. Regardless, I find it disturbing, don't you? To imagine that past generations didn't think that a married couple could just as easily not be having sex in a bed that was shared?"

Squeaky loafers-on-tile sounds came from behind the bathroom door and a moment later a gaseous hiss was released and faded into the cascading. Sabine just lay on the bed, head up on the pillows, stretched out, staring straight up at the ceiling.

"Are you going to tell me how you are, Ruben? Are you going to tell me something personal?"

"I'm fine. I'm alright. Personally, I try not to think about the sex-lives of my ancestors."

"And Edith?"

"What about her?"

"It's not too much for her, handling all this domestic pageantry along with her responsibilities at the library?"

"I don't think so."

"I knew how difficult it was for me to work for Walt."

"But she doesn't work for me, she works for the school."

"I just meant the proximity. You're always bumping into each other, aren't you? At school and then again at home, in bed. It must be claustrophobic."

"She works in the back of the library, in the stacks."

"And Judy? How is she handling the adjustment?"

"It's already been a year."

"It must've been quite a transition. Whisked away from her friends in the city, having to start a new life at a new school."

"Same as Edith. Same as me."

"But you're not an adolescent girl. At least not physically. Edith tells me all these farm boys are asking her out."

"I wouldn't know. What did Edith tell you?"

"That all these farm boys are asking her out. To go pick apples or something. How symbolic."

"I'm sure the apples they're picking are apples. It's not symbol season. Anyway, Judy mostly sticks to her schoolwork and college applications."

"Of course she does. Getting into some college is her only way out...of living with her parents in a college...but I'm sure she'll get into somewhere better."

"She's working hard."

"With your help and some good recommendations...I was thinking of asking some people I know from some charity boards I'm on to write her some good recommendations."

"I don't know that's necessary."

"It's not necessary, but I'm thinking of asking. Some people I know from the Union Club, the boards of the Met and Carnegie Hall. Anything to help."

"It's appreciated."

"Let Judy appreciate it. She must be excited to leave. I know I'd be."

"You know, the truth is, Edith and I rather like it here."

"I think about you, Ruben, I think about all of you and try to understand your circumstances: as city-people alienated from the college-people, but certainly closer to them than to the non-college-people who are unsophisticated and toothless and spend too much time with animals. I wonder, do they even know how to read?"

"My neighbors or the animals?"

"Don't misunderstand me, Ruben. I'm sure it's a fine school you have here and, I'd assume, in many ways ideal for serious work. But then all the isolation and such that makes it ideal must make it

absolutely unsuitable and even hostile to every other aspect of civilized life. Boredom is the absence of a city, as Verlaine said, or maybe
Rimbaud. Without museums, without concert halls, you have to
become your own entertainment."

"When I lived in the city, I was bored sometimes too."

The toilet flushed, with the sound of someone summoning up
mucus to spit against a waterfall, and Sabine rolled her eyes at the
unplastered bald-spot of ceiling just above her.

"In an environment like this—in an understimulated environment where the only stimulus besides your own blockage is the
mediocrity of your colleagues—survival can be difficult. Ignorance
is a subtler enemy than vulgar xenophobia. Because it's the enemy
within, requiring no demagoguery to stir it up. No uniforms. No
rifles. Nothing incendiary. Just a job, a job title, a college. It's latent
in the college. You dedicate your life to knowledge and your society
can only reward you by placing you in an institution. And yet the
real tragedy is that you yourself regard this as a reward, being placed
behind high stone walls in the midst of the woods, where you can't
hurt anyone, where you can only hurt yourself. Frankly it's a miracle
that not everyone has committed suicide."

"Not yet."

"Instead, they sleep with their colleagues' spouses, they get into
petty arguments over property lines, they nurture grudges like
retarded children and impose their insecurities on one another's
time. They wave from their windows and chat across fences, they
knock at the door and ask to borrow a pint of milk or a pinch of
salt—they ask to borrow your wife or daughter—they can't leave
you alone."

"You're telling me that no one has adultery in New York anymore? Sabine, I'm disappointed."

Sabine tucked to her side, to face me. "The same things happen everywhere. Infidelities and squabbling, pointless parties attended by pointless people who have only the slightest common contexts, and even those are mostly just narcissistic co-dependencies. But you leave a faculty meeting and you're still in Corbinton."

"In Corbindale."

"And I leave an appointment of mine and find myself in a major world city, with all its allures."

"And all its grime and crime and crowds, for which they keep jacking up the rent."

From the bathroom came the soft screech of the toiletpaper roll being unwound, the metal dowel spinning in its socket.

"I think of you up here and become depressed, Ruben. I think of this house out in the woods and all of you huddled together inside like tattered gypsies around a single candle, talking to fill the silence and darkness and ignorance all around."

I flicked the bedside lamp on and off. "We have electricity, Sabine, no need for candles, and as you can tell, we have running water too."

"That's not what I meant. I was speaking metaphorically."

I turned and looked out the window. "Outside, I'll tell you what I see. I see grass, not woods. Non-metaphorically. I see paved streets with cars on them and I see houses with antennas on their roofs that bring in the news from all over and wires connected to telephone poles so that if I wanted to right now I could call up Simone de Beauvoir and ask her about her boudoir; I could call up Jean-Paul Sartre and ask him, Monsieur Sartre, I'm here with my mother-in-law, can you please help me prove she doesn't speak French, s'il vous plaît? And if that's not enough evidence for you that we're not ignorant hicks, you might want to check out where your daughter works. It's a library and it even has books."

"You're agitated...she's still working in the stacks and you're agitated..."

I was tapping the pane, tapping it hard. "And next year, when Judy sends us letters from the college of her choice, which she'll have gotten into without any assistance from you, Edith will make copies on the new copying-machine the library's getting from Xerox and we'll drop them from an airplane onto Central Park."

"I didn't mean to make you agitated, Ruben."

"Then don't."

There were the wet sucking sounds of the toilet being plunged.

"When I mentioned ignorance, I was just referring to your work. All the extra assignments they're making you do because you're Jewish."

I resisted the urge to turn. "What did Edith tell you?"

"Nothing much."

I stood staring at the Dulleses', the vacant tire-swing a hypnotic pendant in the wind, the leaves piled up for burning, and farther up the street, Judy slinking homeward, knapsack-hunched, kicking a pinecone listlessly.

"Sabine, whatever Edith told you, whatever you think she told you, it's not accurate. I was just asked to be on a committee to consider the work of a Jewish scholar."

"And what do you know about Jewish scholars?"

"Not much. But more than most up here."

The plunger gave gasps like wet flatulence.

"You have to admit that this would never happen in New York," Sabine said, "this kind of insult."

"It wouldn't happen because in New York there's more than one Jew. And anyway, to my mind, the true insult has nothing to do with anti-Semitism. The true insult is to the school, the Department, and the candidate himself."

"And you've told them that, I assume?"

My breath had fogged the pane, blurring Judy's crossing. "It's like talking to a window."

"Ruben, you know what I think?"

I cuff-wiped the fog and faced her. "It doesn't matter."

From the bathroom came a final, definitive, throat-clearing flush followed by strong squealing pumps on the soap dispenser.

"I think whether you find it offensive or not, whether the request itself is intrinsically offensive, or whether something like intrinsic offense can actually philosophically exist—I think you're still confused about the situation. If you decide to go and hire this Jew, they'll say Jewish favoritism. If you decide not to go and hire this Jew, they'll say you're trying to avoid the appearance of Jewish favoritism. Wait. I know what you're going to say, the decision's not yours, it's up to everyone. But while it might not be yours, the confusion is, and I think it comes from the fear of having another Jew up here to share the woods with. I think you've gotten quite used to being the only one and you're afraid of losing that special status. With another Jew in town, you won't be the pet anymore ... you won't be the mascot ..."

"Thank you, Sabine, it's a compelling interpretation, but I doubt it."

Just as Judy came into the house—her door slam shaking Sabine into sitting upright—Walt came bounding out of the bathroom, fondling a towel.

"Judy's back?" Sabine said. "That's her?"

"Your towels," Walt said, "they're too rough."

Judy's voice, high, taut, pierced its way upstairs.

"Where's the suitcase?" Sabine said. "Walt, the green suitcase?" And then she yelled, "Judy, come up and say hello already! Judy!"

"Feel this," Walt said and handed me the towel. "That's polyester, or some poly blend. I'd say 300, at most 350 grams. Sheets you count in threads, towels you count in grams. Rough like this, without the looping stitch that makes it absorbent—this tells me it's a kitchen towel, not a bathroom towel. Remind me when I'm back in the city and I'll get a guy to send you some cotton. A dozen top of the line plush terry, a dozen Egyptians. We can even do a monogram. Imagine it: a B, a classy B, embroidered, name the color."

"Walter. The suitcases?"

"They're here," I said. "I put them in the closet."

Judy flew to Walt who hugged her up off the carpet and passed her to Sabine who put lips to each cheek and stroked her hair. "You're so beautiful."

"Stop it, Oma. I'm not."

"So beautiful, like an actress."

"Please stop, Oma."

I stood next to the open closet, pointing at the suitcases, "Which?"

Walt shrugged and Sabine said, "I told you already, the green," and Walt picked up the green suitcase and plopped it next to Judy, by Sabine's lacquer-toed feet.

"Walter, it's a suitcase—you don't put a suitcase on a bed where you sleep. You know how dirty suitcases are?"

"No. How dirty are suitcases? We put our stuff in them, how dirty can they be?"

"They're clean inside and dirty outside, the opposite of you. Everybody knows this. Have you ever met anyone who cleaned the outside of a suitcase?"

"Have you ever met anyone who cleaned the inside of a suitcase?"

"Put it on the floor," and Walt complied.

Edith entered, like a bit player late to the stage: ruddled, flustered, batter-spattered apron trailing strings. A large house, a large consanguineous cast all massed in the same small room: was this theater or Judaism? Or just an unconscious attempt to bring the cramped city-apartment ambience back to our holidays?

"Did I miss it?" she asked.

I asked, "Miss what?"

Sabine, still grooming Judy, said, "We got you some presents."

"Presents? For Rosh Hashanah?"

"Don't be so pious, Ruben. Not for Rosh Hashanah, for her college visitations. Little presents for my big girl Judy. Outfits from the fall collections. I want you to look your best. I know you're going to say that admission is based on your performance, but really, it never hurts to look your best."

"Or to get straight A's."

Edith said, "Hush, Ruben."

"Or a 1600 score on the SAT."

Sabine said to Judy, "You'll give us a fashion show, won't you?" And then to Walt, "What are you waiting for? Open it up," and Walt knelt down and unzipped the suitcase and opened its lid to the aftermath of an explosion: gobs of whiteness, a creamy sheen over darker fabrics.

Sabine shrieked—she leapt off the bed and, knocking Walt aside, squatted on her haunches and dug around inside the suitcase, pulling out clothes from it like she was pulling out tissues from a box to stanch a cry of mourning; dresses and skirts and blouses in sober blue-blacks and browns and pinks all splotched with milky white. "I can't believe it," she was plucking up the garments one at a time, "I just can't goddamned believe it," and holding each up to let it unroll from its folding and show its Rorschach stains before flinging it away. "They're ruined. All ruined. That stupid goo must've leaked."

"What goo?" I said.

Sabine said to Edith, "I told him to pack it separately."

"You can't pin this on me," Walt said, rising from his cower. "I'm not the one who packed."

"I told you when you put the suitcases in the trunk to be careful, but I'm sure you just tossed them in . . . and then coming into Jersey you hit that pothole . . ."

She held a haltered black sheath aloft from its hanger so that it unfurled like the scroll of an old hear-ye, hear-ye royal proclamation and a plastic tube fell out and I picked it off the floor and, holding it close—getting a whiff of its bleachiness—read its label: *slimmer . . . trimmer . . . anti-bump . . . topical-use only, do not insert in nose . . .*

Sabine said, "I'm so sorry, Judy. It's that stupid nose cream your mother had me buy. I wanted to get all these outfits for your college visits, so I called your mother for your sizes, and she told me to also get this stupid special nose cream from this stupid special pharmacy all the way at the end of Chinatown between the bridges."

Judy screamed, "Mom, you told them?"

"I didn't."

"Mom, how would they know unless you told them?"

Walt said, "It was actually an herb store. At the counter in the back, there were turtles and frogs."

"Mom, how could you?"

"But when I got closer, they were just shells and skins. No turtles or frogs left in them at all. It was foul. Your friends sent you there? Or sent us there? I'll tell you this: if my friends had sent me there, they wouldn't be my friends for long."

"Mom, I can't believe it. Why?"

Sabine said, "Your mother was telling us you don't like your nose and you're trying to get them to pay for the surgery."

"Seriously?"

"She said you were snoring a lot and had bad airflow."

"Unbelievable."

"Obstructed airflow, she mentioned, sinus headaches, sinus infections. And you're having trouble smelling."

"Which might be a boon," I said, "because this gunk smells rather harsh."

Judy ignored me, bored into Edith, "I can't trust you with anything."

Edith, softly, with a tremor, "Judith Leah Blum, you ask me to get you this cream they only sell in the city, so I ask your grandparents to bring it up. Tell me, how could I hide what it's for? How could I hide who it's for? Should I have said I want the disappearing-nose-lotion for myself? Should I have said it's for your father's nose?"

"I don't need to tell you how to lie, Mom."

"And I shouldn't have to remind you to say thank you—how about that? How about a thank you? To Oma and Opa. This vanishing-nose potion was very expensive."

"I'm sure it's cheaper than surgery," Sabine said.

"Which as long as she's living under my roof," I said, "I'll make sure she'll never get"—to my regret, that was my vow, and the moment it left my mouth, Judy ran out to the hall and into her room, banging the door.

"It's a horrible surgery, just horrible," Walt put in, defending me to the echo. "I want you should mark my words about this, Edith. A nosejob is one of those operations they tell a woman is safe, but it turns out that after, she can't have a baby."

"Enough, Dad. Nothing you do to a nose can affect your having a baby."

"You'd be surprised, Edith. You'd be very surprised. And I bet those creams cause cancer. I bet they cause nasal cancer and don't even work."

Sabine said, "Is someone going to help me?" She was scrabbling around laying out the blemished garments on the carpet, appraising their damage.

I said, "Whatever it does to noses, it definitely doesn't work on things not noses."

"Ruben," Edith said.

"What?" Walt said, "He's right . . . Rube's right . . . If it works, why should it only work on noses? If it works, why haven't the clothes shrunk? Why isn't the suitcase now like a suitcase for a munchkin from Oz? Or maybe the clothes when we bought them were gigantic and we used a giant's suitcase like for what's his name? King Kong?"

"Dad, please."

"Buying shrinking creams like magic beans! Have I got a bridge to sell you!"

And then he farted.

"You're a pig," Edith shouted and stomped out of the room to stand in supplication outside Judy's locked door. Sabine watched her go, then returned to salvaging the clothes, picking up a suit's top here and a mismatched bottom there and smoothing them out atop the shag, in the process getting the now-hardening, pasty goop on her hands and face and I had the thought that if this miraculous solution were any solution at all, if it worked on anything more than merely noses, then all of this scene in front of me, all of these intruders in the drama of my house, would soon shrivel and wither away.

"What are you doing just standing there?" Sabine yelled. "Start wiping off the excess before it dries."

I realized I was still holding Walt's towel, so I underhanded it back to him shortstop-style, pure Pee Wee Reese, and went downstairs for more, for kitchen towels and paper towels, and it wasn't until the landing that I noticed the redolence of char. I dashed into the kitchen, the stink of cream mixing with the stink of meat, the brisket ashen in my nostrils.

5.

DEAR DOCTOR PROFESSOR Ruben Blum, PhD. [*went the much-scuffed, foreign-size letter that arrived in my box just before Thanksgiving*],

My name is Peretz Levavi and I am a lecturer in Assyriology, Aryanology, and Indo-European Linguistics and Philology at the Hebrew University in Jerusalem.

I would like to apologize for this letter. I was not certain whether I should write to you or not and was in the process of internally debating the matter when I found that I had already seated myself and loaded my pen, and I am sure that I will still be debating whether to send the completed pages even after I have folded them up, addressed and sealed the envelope and queued at the post-office for the appropriate stamps. I am not sure whether I believe in that inner demon à la mode that goes by the epithet "Unconscious," though its existence does seem incalculably more plausible to me than that of Asmodeus or Belial or, for that matter, Satan, the angel who fell when he failed to get tenure. Perhaps I am under the influence of them all. Perhaps I am merely being responsible. I leave it to you, and to your own angels, to decide.

I am writing to you about Ben-Zion Netanyahu, or, as he is now to be called, apparently, Dr. Ben-Zion Netanyahu, PhD., whom I have been made to understand is under consideration for a professorship in History at your institution. This information came to me from Netanyahu himself, who for weeks and weeks has been inundating the faculty here with telegram requests for letters of recommendation, to be sent to you as the secretary of the hiring committee. I do not know how many of my colleagues refused him...I hope I am not the only one who did not refuse him... Doing what research I could on you, I was delighted to learn that you were educated at the City University of New York, which is home to so many old and dear colleagues who knew me back when I was still called Peter Lügner at the Friedrich Wilhelm in Berlin (*Dr. phil. habil.*, 1930). Maybe you know Dr. Max Gross? Or Dr. Eric Pfeffer? They can vouch for me. I tracked down the single article of yours available in our library—concerning the fiscal policies of your President Andrew Jackson, who, I confess, was formerly a stranger to me—and came away from your fascinating examination of the financing of the Indian resettlement convinced that you are a passionate and intelligent man; a man with ears that can hear and eyes that can see as well as additional soul-sensitivities beyond the animal senses. This is why I am not hesitating to write you directly, with full confidence in your discretion.

I will begin by noting that few if any of us here at Hebrew University—including even those who refused to officially support him with a letter—would object to Netanyahu obtaining a position for himself at some American institution of higher learning; indeed, at any institution of higher learning beyond the borders of Israel. Further, many not only throughout all levels of Israeli academia, but even throughout all levels of Israeli government, would prefer Netanyahu's continued employment abroad to the prospect of his returning. Consider, for a moment, these statements of mine, and think what you would do, were you in my position. If you would like a man to obtain a job in a distant land, would you praise him beyond what he deserves and lose your honor? Or would you say nothing and retain your honor? And if he were offered the job, because of your praise that he did not merit, what responsibility would you bear? And if he were not offered the job, because of your reluctance to speak falsely, or because of your insistence on speaking honestly, what guilt would you suffer?

But these are rabbinic questions, and I am no rabbi ... I am merely a lecturer, who to remain truthful in my work must remain truthful in every situation, regardless of the consequences ... Below, I hope to provide you with a reliable assessment. Below, you will find the facts, presented with little agenda and less poison.

By way of introduction to our subject, I would like to call your attention to a certain famous figure from now-extinguished European Jewish life—a figure of whom I am sure you are aware, if only from Yiddish literature—namely, the solitary scholar-sage, the bearded eminence whose intellectual labor is supported by the community. This is the man who studies. The man who lives in the house of study. Surrounded by books. Surrounded by mind. Because this figure has gathered such an aura around himself, an especially holy aura after the tragedy of European Jewry, it has become difficult to ask after his origins. How did this man come to exist? And why? Or, to put it more coarsely, how did he obtain his position? Why was this man elevated above all other men and allowed to sit in the dim corner of the yeshiva and study all day unmolested? Who or what gave him this permission? What special talents did he have, what special intellectual abilities did he possess, that marked him out as exceptional from among the ranks of an already-exceptional people? When I was young and myself a student of religious Judaism, I encountered not a few of these figures and believed that they had attained their positions solely on their merits—I believed that the most intellectually capable man in each community was selected on the basis of his linguistic skills, or cognitive talents, or memory, and accorded the privilege of contemplating the sacred writings on the community's behalf, in order to earn for the community the approval of God and a portion of the kingdom of heaven.

Then, however, I grew up, and, as I entered academia, I discerned the truth: The reason these men were given the honor of their sinecures was merely to keep them from teaching—rather, to keep them from misteaching and corrupting the youth.

What else was there to do with them? What else could be done with these proud, intransigent men, who were unable or unwilling to earn a living? Was not the best course of action to give them some darkened niche and parchment to contemplate, not out of charity, but as a preemptive defense? Because we all know what happens to educated men when they are neglected: they become inflamed by neglect. And we all know what reactions can fester: heresy, apostasy, false messianism. Jewish history is full of men of brilliance whose wounded hubris caused them to turn against the tradition.

Netanyahu is just such a man, afflicted with the hubris of the wounded intelligentsia. His temperament, which might have qualified him for history, disqualifies him from teaching it. Unfortunately, I know of no position in the history field without its share of teaching and bureaucratic duties, both of which Netanyahu feels are trivial and beneath him.

Instead, what his mind and mood are best-suited to is individual scholarship, research without the burden of advisorships and paperwork, without even the burden of publication. Regrettably, that is not the sort of sinecure that academia often provides, except to the engineers and physicists who develop weapons. And it is surely something that should not be expected by an obscure quarrelsome foreigner in the humanities.

Regarding that research: As is frequently the case with a solitary scholar, toiling in isolation, his research is not without flaws. Time and again, Netanyahu has demonstrated a tendency to politicize the Jewish past, turning its traumas into propaganda.

What I mean by this is the following: Let us allow that his facts about, say, the Crusader-era pogroms and Inquisitions are correct; and let us allow too that the interpretations he develops from these facts are useful; interpretations about, for example, the distribution of state power in the Medieval Era, and the ever-evolving triangulations among the monarchy and nobility and ascendant burgher class; or, for example, about the vast numbers of Jews who, delivered from violent Muslim rule, gratefully converted to Catholicism over the course of that Crusade called the Reconquista, and the way that their success in Catholic society caused the Church to redefine Judaism from a religion to a race, so as to justify purging itself of the Jewish blood of converts. Fine. Good. Excellent. But there comes a point in nearly every text he produces where it emerges that the true phenomenon under discussion is not anti-Semitism in Early Medieval Lorraine or Late Medieval Iberia but rather anti-Semitism in twentieth-century Nazi Germany; and suddenly a description of how a specific tragedy affected a specific diaspora becomes a diatribe about the general tragedy of the Jewish Diaspora, and how that

Diaspora must end—as if history should not describe, but pre-
scribe—in the founding of the State of Israel. I am not certain
whether this politicization of Jewish suffering would have the same
impact on American academia as it had on ours, but, in any milieu,
connecting Crusader-era pogroms with the Iberian Inquisitions with
the Nazi Reich must be adjudged as exceeding the bounds of sloppy
analogy, to assert a cyclicity of Jewish history that approaches dangerously close to the mystical.

   As for the source of this politicizing impulse: I will tell you. *Netanyahu* is the Hebraicized, Israeli name of a family called Mileikowsky. There are countless tiny towns and villages scattered like grain
throughout the Slavic lands whose names are some variation of the
Proto-Indo-European root *melh*, "to grind," Mileykovo, Milikow,
etc.: "Milltown." (I am sure there are countless Milltowns in America.) To go from "The Man From Milltown" to "God-Given" (the
grandiose meaning of *Netan-yahu*) is quite a transformation. Netanyahu's father, Nathan Mileikowsky, was born in the violent,
Cossack-bloodied year of 1879, in Krevo, White Russia, near the
Lithuanian border, and studied for the rabbinate at the famed
yeshiva of Volozhin, where he fell under Zionist influences. And
yet, on reconsideration, perhaps this is a misnomer: perhaps "Zionist" has now become a historically incorrect characterization and
the current inflections of the term have become so powerful as to
turn this original usage into an anachronism. The history of Zionism
is so difficult to recount, and all attempts evanesce into metaphysics.
Socialists, communists, anarchists, Zionists—think of how many
identities Jews had to assume over the course of the modern era only
in order to be what they were, to be Jews again . . . but this time, to
be Jews freely . . .

In brief, the Zionism now taught in the textbooks both here and abroad was the creation of Western Europe, a movement of cosmopolitans like Herzl who knew little about traditional Judaism but much about journalism and how to patronize cafés; these were men who spoke no Hebrew or even Yiddish but German, and who came to their political awakenings through the debacle of Dreyfus, and the nation-state rumblings that accelerated the decline of Austro-Hungary. This was also the Zionism that sought Jewish political autonomy wherever it could find it: a Jewish State in British East Africa, in Dutch Suriname, in the Argentine, a Jewish colony in Cyprus or Madagascar or Baja California. However, there was also another Zionism, a separate Zionism, whose adherents would correctly argue was both older and purer—though Jews should always be wary of claims of purity. This Zionism was the creation of Eastern Europe and the Pale of Settlement shtetls, a movement of the religious poor who sought to settle the land that God had promised to their ancestors, the ancient Israelites. Their settling of this land would fulfill that promise and hearken a sort of paradise on earth. This was the Zionism of Rabbi Mileikowsky, an itinerant orator and agitator who published his polemics under the pen-name "Netanyahu." Yes, the name of your candidate, that master of pseudonyms, was once a pseudonym itself! We must take care when we seek to conceal ourselves, for one generation's concealment may be another's notoriety! In the texts Rabbi Mileikowsky signed as "Netanyahu," his position is unmistakable: Unlike the Zionists of Vienna, Budapest, and Switzerland, he refused to wait for the world to "give" the Jews a homeland, whenever and wherever the great powers pleased; God had already "given" the Jews a historical homeland in

Palestine; it was there, it was waiting for them (it was *Netan-yahu*); all they had to do was take it.

The earliest Zionist Congresses were split between these polar-opposite positions—between the "political" "evolutionary" Zionism of the West, and the "practical" "revolutionary" Zionism of the East, whose disagreements centered on geography and method: the questions of whether *a land* or *the land* should be negotiated for or seized. Dissension among parties and delegates was vigorous, and became mobilized by the outbreak of the First World War and the involvement of the British; with political Zionists pressuring His Majesty's Government to support Jewish nationhood in Palestine, and practical Zionists volunteering for the Royal Fusiliers to fight in Palestine. But the geographic issue was definitively settled—and the points of contention winnowed to methodology alone—only after Palestine passed from the suzerainty of the Ottoman Turks, and the British turned immediately from allies into adversaries.

In 1920, or thereabouts, Rabbi Mileikowsky arrived for the first time in British-Mandate Palestine, set up house and left immediately—establishing a precedent for his son's itinerancy. At least our Netanyahu travels with his family in tow, but his father, the rabbi, spent much of the '20s deprived of the company of his wife and nine children, while he traveled the world raising funds for the establishment of a state: funds for land acquisition, immigrant resettlement and retraining, and ultimately for weapons and armaments for the Jewish resistance squads, the makeshift military wing of that practical movement that had begun to be known under the term "Revisionist Zionism" (meanwhile, political Zionism went on to be called just plain "Zionism"). These Revisionists were led by a charismatic

Odessan named Vladimir "Ze'ev" Jabotinsky, who had founded the Jewish Legion with Trumpeldor and fought for the British, before declaring himself their mortal enemy. Rather, as he liked to point out, he did not fight *for* the British so much as fight *against* the Turks. Jabotinsky's entire movement was imbued with this almost militant fastidiousness and rigor; his Revisionists loathing the Arabs only slightly more than they loathed their dithering brother-Jews; coreligionists such as Weizmann and Ben-Gurion, whom they regarded as Marxist appeasers: meek, apologetic weaklings who begged for land they should have taken by force, and who made rousing speeches in lecture halls but refused to get their hands dirty. Revisionists gave no quarter, and made no compromise, with the Mandate—with the Crown, with the Mufti, with anyone. This was the atmosphere in which our Netanyahu grew up: His was a peripatetic and largely fatherless childhood, whose only consistency was ideological. He entered the decade-old Hebrew University in 1929, the year of the Arab riots over the Temple Mount, when the Revisionists—who claimed Jewish sovereignty over the Wailing Wall—engaged in retaliatory violence so severe that the British cracked down on the movement and revoked Jabotinsky's residency documents, effectively expelling him from Palestine. The chaos that ensued is perhaps too complicated to summarize; too complicated, too painful, and too boring. When a family conflict is related to a stranger, I often wonder whom it hurts more, the family or the stranger. Suffice to say that rioting now broke out between rival Jewish factions, and though Netanyahu did not participate in any of the street-fighting, it was not because he was too assiduous in class. Trading in the writing of term-papers for the writing of editorials, he went to work as a columnist for Revisionist periodicals that were routinely censored and shuttered by the British. I translate for you here a few excerpts of his corpus from *Beitar* (which he co-founded) and *Ha-Yarden* (which he co-edited): "The Left has engineered a crisis for the Land of Israel [...] The Left fights every Jew who does not bow down to it [...] Jewish majority in the land must be established, or else the Holocaust that we face today in Europe will be repeated here tomorrow at the hands of the Arabs, the Bedouin, and the Druze. [...] Just as the savages of Arabia hunted down Jewish refugees from Spain in the fifteenth century, so they are now, in the twentieth, hunting down the refugees from the inferno of the Diaspora at the gates to the homeland." Elsewhere, he forgoes the Medieval comparandum and holds Israel up to your own country, correlating the Jews to "Anglo-Saxons" and the Arabs to "the Indians": "The conquest of the soil is one of the first and most fundamental projects of every colonization [...] A member of the Anglo-Saxon race, who was in constant conflict with the redskins, did not content himself with merely establishing the vast metropolises of New York and San Francisco on the shores of the two oceans that border the United States. Rather, having established those two cities, he strove to ensure for himself the route between them [...] Had the conquerors of America left the agricultural areas in the middle of the land in the hands of the savage Indians, there would now be at most a few European cities in the United States and the whole country would be inhabited by millions and millions of uncivilized redskins, as the tremendous need for cereal crops, produce, and other commodities in Europe would have led to the tremendous natural population growth of the natives in the agricultural areas, who would inevitably overrun the coastal cities as well."* I left Germany to embark on my career at the university during this very period and remember it well. As a new arrival to a small colony with a small press in a small but growing language, I would read anything I could find, even these murky publications I would forage from campus benches only to find formulations in them that might have been welcome in the *Völkischer Beobachter* or *Der Angriff*. I instantly knew that the "B. Netanyahu" whose screeds I was reading had to be the same "B. Netanyahu" who was truant from my Akkadian and Sumerian seminars, but it took a while—and some repeated phrases, and some student tattle—for me to realize that he was also "Ben Soker," and "Nitay," and the fulminating Jabotinskyite who went by the Latin letter "N," among other aliases. This prolific rabble-rouser's most provocative column was focused on university life and repeatedly attacked the university's leadership, which it treated as a surrogate for the leadership of the State. Numerous installments condemned the university's Chancellor, the American-born Judah Leon Magnes, and the former Legal Secretary of Mandate Palestine, Norman Bentwich, who upon the occasion of his

---

* I realize that words as charged as these require not just translation, but annotation, and because copies of these blessedly now-defunct publications are difficult to find these days even in Israel, I am enclosing with this letter some of my own—issues from my private collection. I have underlined the quoted passages, to make it easier for an independent linguist to verify the accuracy of my versions. Should you or your committee desire further materials, I would be happy to oblige, and merely ask that a postal order be sent in my name to the Israel Postal Bank in the amount of £3 (or US dollar equivalent). I hesitate to make this request, but would prefer to retain at least some of my originals, and the University still limits the mimeograph privileges of its lecturers and charges us for excess use... though lately there has been some reason to hope that policies might change...

installation as a professor of political science was to deliver a lecture entitled "How Nationalism Is Being Turned Into a Religion." Alas, I never found out how—no one did—because before Bentwich could even get a word out, a bomb was thrown in the hall. I recall the crash—the gasps—the fizzle—from my seat in a middle row— and I recall the feeling of panic, as students and colleagues abandoned their differences and ran like cockroaches for the exits. I remember thinking, in my own hurried egress, that one bomb failing to detonate did not mean that the next would not be a success, and just then, a noxious cloud closed in and I became dizzy and fell and was trampled (my ankle has yet to completely heal). The bomb turned out to be a sulfur bomb; a stink bomb that blisters. The bombthrower was a student named Abba Ahimeir; the bombmaker was a mathematics major named Elisha Netanyahu, the younger brother of our Netanyahu, who was the mastermind of the entire incident (allegedly).

The stench of sulfur was still in my hair and only suit when Haim Arlosoroff, head of the Political Department of the British-approved Jewish Agency, was shot dead on the beach in Tel Aviv. Three men were arrested, including Ahimeir. The case was a sensation; Jews killing Jews was in many ways the fulfillment of Jabotinsky's prediction that a Jewish state would become a normal state like every other only once it had—in addition to Jewish bankers, Jewish carpenters, and Jewish tailors—Jewish murderers too. Netanyahu, under his various pen-names, sprung to the support of the arrested men, as did his father, the aged rabbi, who died shortly after visiting them in prison. According to the son's Revisionist obituaries, Rabbi Mileikowsky died not of any of the chronic diseases that he was afflicted with but from grief that men so dedicated to the cause of Jewish statehood would be so harshly treated. In mourning, Netanyahu's excoriations only intensified, as he broadcast his ire indiscriminately at all Jews who collaborated with any organization recognized by the British, including, he emphasized, the University, whose faculty, dean, and rector he called "monkeys," "rodents," "traitorous cowards," and "Zionists intent on making Zionism fail." I would like to emphasize the madness of this position. Recall that at the time, Netanyahu was still an undergraduate.

No student, however brilliant, would be forgiven this behavior, and Netanyahu was only brilliant by foreign standards—a statement I make with due respect. At any American institution, he would have been "a star," but please remember that historical circumstances have conspired to hold Israel to a higher standard. Each year Netanyahu was at Hebrew University, new refugees streamed in, until, on the eve of the Second World War, the school was a monstrous teeming haven of the best faculties of Europe, all jostling each other for prestige. In the History Department alone we had Baer, Koebner, and Tcherikover, who together were fluent in something like 22 languages; Polak, who liked to say that he could read two books at once, one with each eye, and his mortal enemy, Dinur, who liked to say that he could write two books at once, one with each hand, would jockey for lectures and office-supplies with Shelomo Dov Goitein, who was just starting on his project of deciphering the Cairo Genizah; it was a common occurrence to walk down the hall and meet the dusty figures of Leo Aryeh Mayer and Eleazar Sukenik, two archaeologists taking a break to consult the archives between their excavations of Jerusalem's walls; it was a common occurrence to walk out for some air and have to hold the door for Martin Buber or Gershom Scholem (I once neglected to hold the door for Buber, who walked straight into it). Most of these men were geniuses, but some were also traumatized, broken émigrés content just to breathe a bit, content to be alive. Some of them did not mind the British, and even liked British culture and manners, which were familiar to them, vestiges of European gentility in this warm estranging climate. Others were actually men of the Left, or professed to be, though they were Marxists with the tastes of bourgeois. No matter their stated political orientation, however, their Zionism was basically literary, poetic. They were trying to revive the lives they had dreamed of as youths in Europe and would gladly have stayed in Jerusalem forever under the reign of King George V. These were library-men, who had just fled one carnage they had not requested and could not be expected to foment another. However insufficient their psychology, they were also physically unfit, a tubercular lot totally unsuited for armed rebellion. And Netanyahu, the zealot, could not accept this. He could not abide their political fatigue. And he could not stand anyone more skilled and credentialed than he was. He might even have ideologically rejected the university as vociferously as he did as a type of advance strike against the university's rejection of his talents. Tell me how, in this atmosphere where everyone was a world-historical genius in Tanakh, Talmud, Kabbalah, Hasidut, cuneiform, modal logic, matter, anti-matter, and quantum dynamics; where everyone had a theorem named after them and field-defining publications translated into Esperanto and a dragon's hoard of advanced degrees from the universities of Berlin, Munich, Paris, Basel, Zurich, Vienna, Petersburg, and Moscow—tell me how, in these conditions, a position could be found for an Israeli-educated malcontent with no PhD and no book and a history of inciting terrorist violence? What dark hushed corner could be found for him at our small university in our small country without a budget, where all the corners were already taken?

The answer was none—or none except abroad. The answer was Ze'ev Jabotinsky. Just prior to the invasion of Poland, Netanyahu left academia and threw in his lot with the crazy old Odessan, who ever since his expulsion had been wandering around Europe, like Netanyahu's father, the rabbi, used to wander; frail, shaky, bereft, speaking wherever he could, speaking like an immolating prophet, warning his fellow Jews of an impending genocidal cataclysm and trying to raise a Jewish army to fight the Nazis—trying to raise an army without a country. The Jews had to found an army first and a country second; the country would follow from the army, this was his belief. Jabotinsky's methods might have been strange, but his instincts were correct, the Nazi threat was real, it was real and present, and his old Zionist antagonists were in denial. In retrospect, he might have been the only one who saw the coming slaughter... he and some Yiddish poets, maybe, but then poets are always seeing slaughter... In 1940, Jabotinsky appointed Netanyahu to lead the Revisionists in the United States. In this role, Netanyahu was essentially filling in for Jabotinsky himself, who not only knew what carnage to expect, but also knew that if the Jews were to survive it and flourish in its wake, they needed the help of the Americans. To Jabotinsky, but especially to the younger Netanyahu, Europe was finished—Europe brought death—America was the future. In Britain, foreign policy could be changed only by changing the minds of the hereditary elite who filled the government, whose educations were founded in Jew-hatred, and who had no incentive to betray their class. In America, however, foreign policy could be determined by popular appeal, through advertising and informational campaigns aimed at the common man who voted. This, to Netanyahu's mind, was why America was so crucial: it was the only country in the world in which all foreign affairs were primarily domestic; the only country in the world in which—by dint of its immigrant demography and democratic system—the foreign did not exist. If enough Americans could be inspired by the dream of a Jewish State, they would vote enough politicians into office to make that dream come true, with treaties, aid agreements, protection from the Soviets. This was Netanyahu's plan, for which he went on the road and toured the States— not just visiting American Jewry in its synagogues, but also American Christians in their churches, preaching the gospel of Revisionist Zionism and soliciting funds to help resettle European Jews in Palestine and whip them into soldiers. However, only a short time after Netanyahu embarked on this work, Jabotinsky himself arrived in New York City, made a few public appearances, and then decamped for a militia training camp somewhere in the Catskills of New York State—incidentally, I think somewhere near your institution— where he suffered a fatal heart-attack.

With Jabotinsky dead, Netanyahu lost his patron. He found himself abandoned in a foreign land, with nothing in Palestine to return to but opprobrium. Meanwhile, Europe burned. Netanyahu withdrew into his academic work and arranged to finish his PhD at this odd little rabbinic seminary in Philadelphia, dedicated to preparing odd little rabbis to lead your "temples." You would know more about it than I would. But imagine! During the greatest tragedy to ever befall his people, Ben-Zion Netanyahu was neither in Europe nor in Palestine but in Philadelphia, Pennsylvania, writing about Medieval Spain! Writing about the Inquisition during the Holocaust...writing about the failure of the Iberian Jews to save themselves as a proxy for his own inability to save the Jews of Europe…What insanity! After the war, how could he feel? Even after finishing his dissertation, what could he celebrate? Certainly not the establishment of the Jewish State, which was claimed as a victory by his enemies but had come at the cost of millions dead. A state that had not been taken but given, not freely but guiltily, in reparations for catastrophe. To him, it was a State led by accommodationists, concessionists, barely-Jewish incarnations of Neville Chamberlain: Ben-Gurion, Weizmann, men who spit on the grave of Jabotinsky and would not even let his body be returned to Israel from the earth of Long Island, where it is buried. No Revisionists were invited to participate in the new Israeli government. The movement had no influence in the Knesset. There was only one Zionism now and Revisionism had been revised into oblivion. Regardless, Netanyahu returned here—he had to return here, despite everything—to find a political role, a military role, an intelligence role, any role at all, even in academia. Or perhaps he returned merely to witness Israel fail. But of course, it did not fail. It has not yet. And still Netanyahu persisted, waiting nearly a decade for someone, for anyone, to bring him in from the cold. He was an historian left out of history, the spawn of a frustrated rabbi-diplomat who himself had been written out of the annals of the State. It was tragic. If university colleagues previously avoided Netanyahu for his politics, now they avoided him for his tragedy. For his bitterness, his resentment, his rage. I confess that I avoided him myself. There was nothing to be done. At the time, our university was in administrative shambles; we had dozens of people who could split an atom and expound relativity, but no one who could run an office and balance accounts. Having been forced to move from our Mount Scopus campus, which after the War of Independence was located in a United Nations–administered exclave surrounded by Jordanian territory, we were operating out of an unreconstructed cloister in central Jerusalem whose landlord was the Catholic Church. The only one of my university colleagues who had occasion to help Netanyahu was the generous, and devious, Dr. Prof. Joseph Klausner, who submitted his name to the publisher Alexander Peli, who needed someone to edit the *Encyclopedia Hebraica*. But I do not want you to think that this was a kindness. Or I do not want you to think that this was only a kindness. Because it was also, in its own way, an insult. It was, to be honest, one of the most creative insults I have ever heard of. Imagine being tasked with providing your new country with a new encyclopedia of its origins; imagine being given the responsibility of producing the most ambitious and comprehensive knowledge-project in the Hebrew language since that language was reinvented by Ben-Yehuda's modern Hebrew dictionary, but then, remember this: When you are the editor of an encyclopedia, you can include an entry on almost anything and anyone you want, except yourself. The editor is the one person who must always be excluded. Netanyahu had to edit entries on all of his old foes—he himself wrote the entry on Anti-Semitism—but he could not mention himself. How offensive it must have been, to have to rely on this self-erasure for his support! The Jews invent some truly brilliant vengeance! I had thought that Netanyahu would remain here, working on this laudable and surely interminable project, but perhaps the pain it caused him was too acute; perhaps the reminder it provided him was too shaming. I had heard, from Klausner and my colleague Dr. Prof. Yeshayahu Leibowitz and others who were producing entries for Netanyahu, that he had gone abroad again to seek an appointment, but had received no confirmation of this until the telegrams came: to Klausner, to Leibowitz, to half the historians here, and then to me, begging a recommendation.

If this letter has gone on too long, let its length be a testament to my candor: I have told you most of what I know and too much of what I think, yet none of it with a sabotage's intention. I, a refugee, am well aware that men can change, and that each man contains many men, and that the faces they show can be different; tragic one moment, comedic the next, pitiless, pitiful, bewildered. I hope for your sake that the Netanyahu you meet will be another Netanyahu—I hope that he will genuinely be another, bearing no resemblance to the man I have described. If that be the case, then praise be to God, Who brings about change in its season, and praise be to you, for not holding this letter against me and attributing to my character the very flaws that I have attributed to his. I shall conclude with another prayer that will not be found in the liturgy, but in Heine, I believe: *Mögen Fremde über uns alle urteilen!*: "May we all be judged by strangers!"

With heartfelt wishes, I remain, sincerely yours,
Dr. Prof. Peretz Levavi (Peter Lügner)
Hebrew University
Jerusalem, Israel

6.

For thanksgiving, we had my parents, who insisted on making the ten-plus-hour trip, starting out before dawn in the wrong direction, heading from the Bronx to Penn Station and from there reversing course on the Lake Shore Line, through Albany, Schenectady, Utica, Syracuse, Rochester—my parents were the type too concerned about keeping track of the stops to notice the shifting crops of scenery—to Buffalo, where they plunked themselves on a bus and rode through the dreary dug-up fields, doing a perverse type of penance. Ever since Edith's parents had spent a holiday alone with us, my parents, Alter and Henya, had been determined to have their own, and if they had to settle for a secular holiday, so be it.

The table was laden with the homier foods that were as alien corn to my parents; the foods that Edith had taught herself to cook from the back of the packaging their mixes had come in: "instant" yam-and-marshmallow casserole, "instant" cranberry soufflé, "instant" stuffing, and of course, the quite-far-from-instant turkey, a huge fledgeless knoll of gleaming gravied flesh that I attempted to carve at-table, until my father intervened and took over the knife. Cutting was cutting, whether cloth or bird. An expert was an expert.

My mother and father had arrived so famished from their travels that we'd immediately sat down to eat and given their sense of eating as a chore to be discharged, we were already at the dessert course within thirty minutes—they'd spent ten-plus hours in transit for a supper that was close to over in thirty minutes. The desserts were a pumpkin pie, a pineapple upsidedown cake, and an apple-rhubarb brown betty over which whipped cream was sprayed, was shaken and sprayed from its rocket-canister, in liberal white-petaled florets.

Perhaps the single fact that best characterizes the differences between having Edith's parents and mine over as guests was that even after finishing up their sweets (my father licking the last dollop of cream from the canister's nozzle and my mother spanking his hand)—even after finishing their seconds, they remained in their seats and showed no curiosity whatsoever about any of the other rooms of the house, let alone about mattress firmnesses, appliances' warranties, the surface concerns of formica and micarta, the detarnishing of copper, the restoration of porcelain, or the winterization of sash windows.

They merely sat back, content with the diningroom, content with their view to the contiguous den. To them, the upper floor of the house was another life. It might as well have been another family's apartment or the afterlife, an eschatology.

Edith and I sat with our coffees and my parents sat with their teas, which they still drank in the antiquated style, with compote sugaring the bottom, for which we had to substitute grape preserves, and my father stirred in some leftover cranberry sauce.

I was bored, and I'm sure Edith was too, but Judy, refusing all hot beverage, was the only one who showed it, sighing theatrically as the conversation ranged over whether there was ever a direct bus from New York City to Corbindale (no); whether the trains servicing Corbindale were ever passenger-trains, or had they always been freight (yes, freight); the differences between my job at Corbin and my job at CUNY (my father: "So there are not so many exams you give here, but they make up a much larger portion of the final grade average?"); and Edith's opinions of the library: where its collections were adequate (in the 630s, which in the Dewey system was Agriculture); where its collections were inadequate (most everywhere else, but especially in the 490s, Other Languages); the duration someone could borrow a book for (it depended on the book), and the fines for being late (a penny a day). She—Judy—kept trying to interrupt and insert her voice between my father's proddings, and he every time ignored her, until my mother put a palm to the nape of his neck: "What?"

My mother said, "Judy's trying to say something," and she nodded at Judy, who mumbled, "I was just trying to excuse myself, that's all."

"And what do you have to get to that's so important?" said my father.

"My themes."

"Your themes? What are those?"

"My prompts."

"Your prompts," my father said and sat with the word for a moment, tasting it like a mint. And then, despite the escalating pinch-pressure my mother was applying, he proceeded: "You maybe don't believe me but I speak English, so you should speak English too. And then we could both be two people speaking English with each other together."

Judy relented, "My essays for college applications."

"Aha. These are the essays you have to write for your applications to go to college."

"But really," Judy said, "they're just opportunities for Dad to boss me around. I write pages and pages and give them to him to read and he gives them back to me all marked up in red, showing me how many dumb mistakes I made."

"Mostly they're just suggestions I'm making, not corrections," I said.

"I'm sure they're helpful," my mother said, being helpful herself.

Edith said, "They're most definitely improvements."

"And this is how the colleges decide who to let in, based on what is written there?" my father said, swerving to me, "You're telling me that you can't just call up someone at the college she wants and say to them please, here, I am a professor like you are a professor, and I want you should take my daughter as a student?"

"That's not how it works, Dad, and anyway, Judy doesn't need my meddling. Or anybody's. She does well enough on her own."

Judy said, "Then why do you mark up my pages?"

She had a point. Perhaps I corrected her too much. Perhaps I corrected her for my own erring. I certainly think I pushed her too hard, expecting her to spin Gibbon or Carlyle or even just a Lincoln-Douglas debate out of the most hackneyed of required topics. In the space provided, please write "A Letter to the Past," or "A Letter to the Future," or chew over "If I Were President of the United States, I'd . . ." She'd make her drafts in her sloping, loopy, unmethodically Palmeresque hand and, under the cover of night, slip them under my study door, and I'd stay up late after my own work, or in lieu of my own work, reading through them; reformulating, restructuring, telling myself I wasn't being punitive so much as enhancing, but knowing at some chthonic lake-depth that the more time I put into these edits, the longer I could put off the Jews, which—who—lay heavy on my heart.

"So for example," my father asked, "what is one of the subjects?"

"There are lots of them," Judy said. "Each school is different, but the one I'm working on now, the subject is fairness."

"Fairness?" My father sunk a fist into his cheek. "So what do you have to say about fairness?"

"Ask him," Judy said, indicating me, "he's the one with the opinions."

"I'm not him," I said, "I'm your father." Then to my own father I said, "Do you want her to read us what she's written?"

"No, Dad."

"Come on, Judy, a command performance? A recitation?"

"I don't want to."

My father said, "And I don't want her to read it to me neither. If she can't tell me what it's about just with her mouth, it's not about anything."

This was an essay for Vassar, I think, which was one of Judy's top choices, because it had a higher Jewish quota than most of the Ivies save Cornell and Penn and unlike Princeton admitted women. Of all her essays, this was the most troublesome, though perhaps it only troubled me. "What Is Fairness?" was the exact question being asked, spelled out in that way, with the first letter of each word aggrandized in capitals, and Judy and I had spent long weekend afternoons through that fall talking out her answer: how the theoretical "what is fairness?" differed from the practical "what is fair?" and how fairness could often be at odds with equality (for example, fairness might take individual achievement into account, but equality can never). We looked up "equality" and "equity," I had her look up "egality"; we quarreled about whether it was "equitability" or "equitableness," and what "equatable" might be, and so many other qualities I was failing to embody in the face of her idealism. That's what aggravated me, recognizing in Judy's idealism the degradation of my own. Words—phrases—logopoeic, propaedeutic, patriotic sentiments were emanating from her that I'd vaguely agreed with, or thought I had, until I met them in her voice, in which they gave the impression of being banal and naive, like a girl dressed to impersonate her mother: "Fairness is democracy in action . . . fairness is when women get a fair shake, and when minorities in this country, including the Negro, are treated equally . . . fairness is not considering legacies or family connections when making a decision, and never judging a person but judging the facts . . ."

She did a rendition of this for the table, interspersing memorized bits from her drafts with the extemporaneous, working herself up, self-inspiring and reaching for eloquence, until finally summing up with, "And fairness must also be this: that everyone in this country who can pay for a nose with their own money can have one."

Edith, sitting erect at the edge of applause, suddenly crumpled, and my mother, the quiet and enduring, put her hand on Edith's knee and said to Judy, "You have the nose of my Aunt Zelda. And the man who loves you will marry you because of it, not in spite of it. That is important to remember. Many men found Zelda very beautiful."

Judy snorted.

Silence descended on us like a lid and my father, squinting, said, "Fairness," as if sounding out the dark. "I want fairness too," he went on, after a moment, "and I want to be fair to you, so you must tell me, Judele, because I can't decide myself. Is what you are saying just now about fairness something you have to say for the school because the school will like it or is it something you choose to say for yourself because you actually believe? Because I understand, trust me I understand, that sometimes in work and also in life you have to do things that are not what you want—you have to hold your nose, your pretty nose and do them, because of what's expected."

"No, Zeyde, not at all. I'd never write anything I didn't believe in. These are one hundred percent my opinions. One hundred and ten percent."

"I understand," my father said, tapping his spoon against his saucer. "One hundred and ten percent I understand. I just felt I had to ask you before I argued because it is foolish to argue about something with someone who doesn't believe. But now that you say you do believe and this isn't a formal, a formality, it's different." He shoved his chair back, harder than he'd intended to, perhaps, and as my mother lowered her gaze into her lap and Edith leveled hers at me, I tried to tell myself, Rube, you know what your father's about to do, you know what your father's about to say, and how Judy's going to feel, so butt in now and intervene: tell a joke, spill your coffee, knock over his tea, make like a Catskills magician and strip off the tablecloth so all the cutlery remains; do whatever you can to provoke his attention in your direction and away from your daughter and spare the evening from his temper.

But I couldn't, because he was my father and I was his son and all I could do was sit by and take in what he said and try to remember, strain hard to remember, that this was how I myself appeared to my daughter: overbearing, overcertain, blatant and mean.

"Someone who does only what he believes," my father said, "what do you think that life is like? What to call someone who he follows that behavior?"

Judy said, "Honest? A hero?"

"Dead. I call him dead."

"That's so cynical."

My father flicked his spoon at her. "If I was trying to go to college, I would tell the bosses of the college not what I thought but what I thought they wanted to hear, I would look at them and know what to say to them, and from that I would be picked by them and everyone would get what they wanted: they the opinions and me the college. That is my advice, and it is the best advice, even though the man who gives it never went to a school in this country in his life. Here I worked and in Kiev I went to cheder. You know what is cheder?"

"No."

"It is a school for Jewish children, that is cheder," and he fell again to spoon-tapping. "But that's not the subject. The subject is fairness, not cheder or how I never had a proper education." He met Judy's gaze, "I would not tell a college what I tell you now, what I think about fairness, because I'm not a putz. I didn't have a proper education but I'm not a putz because instead I had my life, where I learned that fairness is just an idea, like the Soviets have an idea, which doesn't work. It goes against nature."

"But Zeyde, that's the point. It's more like a principle: fairness is something we have to live up to. We're supposed to overcome the herd urges and nepotistic tribal ties in this country and learn to live together equally, judging others with an open mind and knowing that helping those who are different from us will actually help us too."

"You think that's true? I've been in factories, I've been in unions, I've been kicked in the ear on both sides of the picket line, but I've never seen it."

"Maybe you have to open your eyes."

This riled him and he dropped his spoon and tugged at his eyes, with a forefinger at the corner of each eye, tugging, "You try to open your eyes, what happens? They only open so far, until they get slanted like a Japanese," and then he stuck his tongue out.

"Immature."

He dropped the act and found his spoon again, his pointer. "Tell me, Judele," his voice deceptively mild with humor, "tell me what's fair to me? You don't have to think about the shvartzes. Or women. All the shvartzes and women in the world. Think about me," and he thumped his spoon against his chest and waggled it at my mother, as if to say that any thought about him must necessarily include her, "or think about my parents, killed in a pogrom, my father at least killed by a man but my mother killed by the man's horse that it ran away atop her, Rzhyshchiv, Yom Kippur 1905. What was fair about that? And then I was in Kiev an orphan, a wanderer of stables. Fair? With no family, no money, nothing."

"That's horrible, Zeyde. But then you came to America for the fairness."

"No, I came to America to run away from the great Soviet revolution of fairness and spent years and years here being robbed of my nothing by everyone I worked for."

"But the past doesn't have to be the future. That's the point of something you aspire to."

"All of us are born how we are born and suffer how we suffer and if even God can't make us equal who are we to think our laws can?" He prodded the spoon against a bunched rill in the tablecloth. "Or maybe God doesn't want us to be equal."

"Maybe." Judy was being flippant.

"So you choose, Judele: can't or doesn't want?"

"I'm not going to choose. I don't believe in God."

"Alter," my mother interrupted, knowing this to be his crisis, but my father blew by her: "Henya, enough, I'm asking my granddaughter a legitimate question . . . Tomorrow, Judele, what if tomorrow the Ku Klux Klan rides through here shooting off guns, what would you do? Stand in the middle of Evergreen Street and scream fairness? No. You will run to people who will help you. You will run to people you can trust. Other Jews, your family."

Edith knuckle-rapped the table and got up and started clearing and he wheeled on her, "What, Edith? Think about it. If the Klan came and you had to run. All of you. Ruben, do you think the other professors at the college would hide you in their barns? Would the History Department, which should know from history? Would they bring you what to eat and drink? Would they come and empty the buckets you, excuse me, pissed and crapped in?"

"Disgusting, Alter," my mother said and Edith, one-handing a tilting stack of dessert plates, tried to take my father's, but he held onto it.

"It's empty," Edith said, "You're finished."

"I'm not," my father said and slapped his spoon onto the plate like striking a gong and, when nothing shattered, let it go. "In America," he returned to Judy, "they tell you to mix with non-Jews, marry non-Jews, run away from your tradition, get a new name, get a new nose, change who you are, eat a turkey like an Indian, and in return you get fairness. That's the deal. And so you change it all and then go to collect this fairness you were promised but all the offices where you make your claim are closed, because this country never holds up its half of the bargain. And even if it does, even if it treats you fair by accident maybe, or maybe only by treating someone else next to you more unfair and you feel better when you compare yourself, there will still always come some problem that fairness can't solve, and the moment it does, everyone jumps overboard from the sinking ship and rushes back to the people they came from."

"But democracy says that the people around you are the people you came from," Judy said. "Your neighbors, your fellow citizens."

"Who said anything about democracy? I'm talking about the real argument against the fair. Even the least frum, the least religious Jews, like your other grandparents, the yeccas, when they're dying, they'll start to pray, they'll start calling up the rabbis. They'll call up a rabbi to come to their bed and pray and then they'll tell him, 'It's not fair!'"

"So that's your argument against fairness? Seriously? That because death is unfair, we can be too? That we can cheat others because life cheats us?"

Judy cackled, my father lunged—he thrust his hand into the slimy remains of the pie and grabbed its server, a bright-polished flatfaced wedge like a fancy mason's trowel with serrated edges tapering sharply and flung off the viscous pumpkin-filling stuck to its tip. "I cut cloth forty years, you don't think I can do your nose, girl?"

That's when I stood, put myself between them. Reminding my father that I was taller than him. I was wider. I'd had the benefit of American abundance; however fair or not, it'd grown my bones. Let him poke me another navel, I wouldn't feel it; I was too full to feel it: poke the pouch and all the meal I'd eaten would just slip out.

Edith ducked back into the diningroom. "Ruben?"

"Alter," my mother was standing now too.

Judy, presenting her face to my father in serene defiance, said, "I dare you."

Edith seized my father's wrist and snatched away the pie-server. She did this so swiftly and deftly, he froze, and it was only the clatter of her dropping the pie-server into the kitchen sink that broke the mood and let my father leave the table with a meekened shrug. He went to the den and sat down on the Hide-A-Bed. He lay down. He wasn't going to help clean up. He wasn't even going to offer. He stretched a bit and yawned.

The pumpkin filling he'd flung trickled slowly down the dining-room wall.

That night, as I took the trash out to the bins penned to the side of the house and passed the pointy conic firs that marked the Dulleses' property, I thought about the Klan.

I thought about the street lit up by a pogrom and batty harmless Ellen Morse, the wife of my boss, taking unthawed TV dinners out to us lying low in their detached garage and lugging away a brimming foul bucket of my and Edith's and Judy's fly-swarmed slop and dumping it to the black-leaved bushes.

With my parents asleep on the Hide-A-Bed and Edith tossing in our bedroom, I sat up in my study guilty and glutted, reviewing the evening. Asking myself what I should've done and why, what I believed and why. Asking myself about fairness. About the impartial, the unbiased, and the dispassionate too, all of English's nugatory terminology for the objective and neutral. The more I thought about the concept, the less convinced I was I understood it, but when I tried to imagine what fairness felt like, all that came to mind was the calm, sober, even-keeled guy on the box of Quaker Oats, the key ingredient in the turkey's stuffing.

I reached for the latest draft of Judy's essay, but couldn't find it. My desk was a midden of midterm papers, half of which I still hadn't graded. They were composed on a level significantly lower than Judy's, but because my students weren't my children—I was never that type—I had to grade them on a belly-shaped curve. Anyway, Judy herself was too proud to hold her work to the standards of a college she didn't respect and wouldn't even apply to—she wouldn't even apply to Corbin as a courtesy to me, and I admit I had the idea of falsifying an application and submitting it on her behalf, just to show my colleagues that we Blums weren't snooty elitists, holding out for what my father, confusing all idioms, called "the Ivory League."

All that stopped me from going through with this, besides dread of my daughter's rancor, was my lack of a plan—I wasn't sure what the fallout would be from Judy rejecting the full academic scholarship that Corbin would almost certainly offer her.

Every few draft pages of Judy's from another of her application essays ("The most difficult decision I ever had to make was . . ."), I'd find another midterm paper, some of them marked in my hand, with tremorous underlinings and circlings and what I could no longer parse as either upright question-marks or slumped exclamations; such as the one I put alongside a sentence about how "the Articles of Confaderation [sic] founded the Confaderacy [sic], which led to the slavery states succeeding [sic]." About as intelligent as these papers got was one by a student named Gary Farrier, who lived up to his nickname of "G-Man" when he wrote, "*All men are created equal* is a famous phrase that implies equality ends with the Creation, and that all attempts to enshrine this equality in our government and enforce it through legislation must be treated as abominations to G-d [sic] that verge on Sovietism". . .

Below that paper was a messy sheaf of cheap stationery creased with uneven folding, its erratic typing smeared with pools of Tipp-Ex and excess ink, clipped to a scuffed envelope whose stamp showed the Liberty Bell, crack out and streaked with cancellations: the letter from the Philadelphia rabbi. And below that was another stack, but of the oversize sheets of Europe, hand-ruled and acquitted with superior penmanship, clipped to a *par avion* envelope covered with gorgeous stamps of pomegranates, a frisky gazelle, and a bristly, disapproving Herzl, who in my fever had become the letter's sender: the prof at Hebrew U.

I was panicking, shuffling through the paper accrual and finding loose pages of tax-research mixed in too—all my work had gotten jumbled.

Reaching out, I swept the whole lot of papers to the floor and sat myself down next to where they fell to start sorting them anew, laying piles into which I separated the student-work from Judy's, and the both of them from my committee-work and my own research materials and manuscripts and, as I sorted, I kept finding pages here and there in Hebrew, a language whose modern conjugations I found so difficult that even trying to spell out a headline made me drowsy...and the pages themselves were slowly turning into leaves, crackling, rustling, rust-colored, as incomprehensible as dream...

...I dreamt that I was out in the brilliant fall foliage of some campus much grander than Corbin's. Think more like Oxbridge, Medieval stone, foreign, fantastical, the trees ablaze. Judy was walking next to me, dressed in one of the fancy suits Edith's parents had gotten her, with a pillbox on her head and another slung as a purse, and in the middle of her rouged face her regular nose-clamp, a type of spring-loaded metal-and-rubber bicycle-clip that was the nasal version of orthodontia: she wore it while sleeping to straighten her nose, and here she was wearing it in my dream, where it seemed perfectly natural and even attractive, like it wasn't a corrective device but a species of jewelry that matched her Oma's clip-on earrings...

...Judy was heading toward a stone building and I followed, along the paths of a vast, neatly mown parade-ground studded with young cadets doing bayonet drills and calisthenics and as we approached the building, they ogled her and whistled...

...Then we were in a hallway, which began like a hallway at Corbin, and then became like a hallway at Corbindale High, lined with lockers and shrieking. On either side of the hall were classrooms and though most were darkened and their doors were shut, others had their doors ajar and cast spotlight shafts onto the laminate. Judy walked ahead and I trailed her, I gave her space and, as she crossed into the lights, she never turned her head; she'd be hit by a beam and just keep herself brisk and rigid and moving forward, like her entire self was clamped, her body a vise. I didn't have that kind of control, however, and as I passed the lights, I peered into them. Each room held one of Judy's classmates, one of her newly made friends surrounded by a few big brown-overcoated guys in dented Homburgs I recognized from certain corners of the prewar Bronx. They were holding the kids captive, subjecting them to interrogative torture. Porcine Mary Busti was hung upsidedown from a hook and being lowered into a boiling oil drum by the guys who used to drop by my Uncle Sruly's grocery to pick up their envelopes. Joan Gerry, little Joan from down the block, was having her skin flayed off with little brushes and combs by the debonair and sleeves-rolled-up Collee brothers. Tod Frew, the plainspun Quaker boy who'd played Judy's Romeo and who kept auditioning to play him offstage too, even as he vied with her for class-valedictorian (his father, Dr. Frew, was Head of Corbin English), was tied to a stake and Paul Manzonetto was saying, "Just tell us—this is all we want to know—why didn't Roosevelt bomb the tracks like the boss told him?" Tod murmured, but only blood came from his mouth, and one of Manzonetto's bagmen wiped it clean and then balled the handkerchief to gag him. Another guy was down on the floor drawing a chalk outline and Manzonetto stooped over him and rasped, "Make him feel it . . . *Mi capisci, si? Non ammazzarlo* . . . but will someone kill the lights?" and just as I was about to step in, the door slammed in my face, and I hurried away to catch up with Judy . . .

. . . The hall ended in a sort of lobby area, where we were met by Edith, who pretended not to recognize Judy or myself, who pretended not to be Edith at all, but a matronly secretary her own mother's age, older even, myopic and hunched and toddling us through a typing-pool and mailroom and leaving us at the door to my office at Corbin . . .

. . . My office, which I hardly used, because I had to share it; splitting the tiny slovenly pigeonhole with a roster of untenured faculty and adjuncts I never got to know beyond the mugs and moldy sandwiches that lingered after their contracts expired—a roster that included Jabotinsky, apparently. He sat behind my desk. Or behind a desk that I had rights to. It was Jabotinsky, no doubt about it. The dark round bakelite glasses, the plastered-down, sideswept, steel-gray, steel-white Hitlerite hair topped with a tasseled mortarboard, the pinstriped doublebreasted suit staved like a tent atop his gauntness, that strong set jaw hiding an inner flicker that might've been a swallowed laugh or his tongue seeking out the gaps of errant molars. He pointed a finger at Judy and then at a chair. There wasn't a chair for me, but it was like I wasn't there … like I was just observing a scene I wasn't in, or they were deliberately ignoring my presence as irrelevant … Jabotinsky picked up a folder from the desk and flipped through it, frowning, biting his lip, and then said, "And what did you do during the war?" … I wanted to yell, "Lay off her—she was just a kid—she was conceived the day after Pearl Harbor," but couldn't find my voice, and anyway Judy had the better response, which was to smile. She, unlike me, could recognize a joke when one was made, and produced a high-pitched, hollow titter due to the pressure exerted on her septum by her nasal apparatus. The sound was birdy and not unpleasant. Jabotinsky pinched a paper from the folder, squinted at it as his glasses slid down and said, "Excellent grades, really excellent. And a well-rounded complement of extracurricular activities … Chess Club, German, French, Camelot, Salmagundi. The Plein Air Aficionados … and your medium is?" … "Watercolor, mostly." … "Excellent. And junior and senior Orchestra—your instrument is what?" … "Flute." … "Excellent, flute." … "I enjoy the arts and foreign languages." … "*Vous avez été très occupée, nicht wahr?* The liberal arts are an integral part of every young person's education, but I'm worried about the lack of physical pursuits. Healthy body, healthy mind. Young people must be healthy, especially if they're to handle the training we provide here. Aren't you interested in sport?" … "I'm just getting into the winter sports, skiing, skating. Back when I lived in New York City, I didn't have much of a chance to be involved in anything physical. But now that I'm living out in nature, I'm taking full advantage, I assure you." … Jabotinsky put down the folder—I got a glimpse of Hebrew letters, but he closed the cover. "Would you mind?" he asked, and, without waiting for an answer, he reached over a shaky swollen hand and gently removed her nose-device and used it to clip the folder shut. Judy kept her eyes open throughout, she didn't even blink. Jabotinsky sat back breathless, repositioned the tassel of his mortarboard out of his face, and cracked some crepitus out of his fingers, recovering from the exertion and regarding her heavily, ironically, not without eroticism. "And are you prepared," he asked, almost panting, "to carry out any order you're given, without any hesitation, even an order that you find repugnant?"…"I am."… Jabotinsky waved that away, or just flicked at the tassel, which had fallen again onto the bridge of his glasses, "And in the event of capture by the enemy, will you swear not to divulge any information even on pain of death?"…Judy nodded…"Good," he said, "I thought so." He opened and closed a few desk drawers, as if to ensure that his own dream was being kept secure, before saying, "I think we're through here," and then he turned to me and finally acknowledged my presence by adding, "unless my fellow committee member has any questions he'd like to ask?"… and while I was sure that he meant I was a member of the committee considering Judy's admission, I had no clue which institution we were dealing with—a guerilla finishing school? a camp instructing in the humanities of Nazi-hunting? I considered asking, don't you know this is my daughter? And then I thought, or are you also testing me? Which of us is being interviewed? Her or me, Vladimir Ze'ev? And then perceiving a sudden opening above my head, I looked up, which is where—as Edith has always told me—I tend to look when I lie, and there instead of the fluorescent-bulbs and ceiling tiles was a vast high gallery like in an operating theater or trial court, and the pewlike benches that lined every cardinality and ascended toward the heavens were filled with my students and colleagues, the others on the hiring committee and

Dr. Morse, the Steinmetzes in a gaudy mezzanine box below my father and mother in the standing-room stalls, and my Uncle Sruly holding the pallid naked body of his wife whom he'd married because she'd gone through Birkenau, which meant she'd had to be kind to him, and who after he'd disappeared gassed herself in the kitchen of their windowless apartment...and they were shouting questions at me...they were shouting and from their mouths was coming fire...

7.

DREAMS ARE INVOLUNTARY. Every tradition believes this, from the neurological to the numinous. Some dreams are held to be prophecy, while others are held to be nonsense, which is prophecy yet unmanifest, but all dreams are to be regarded as forced upon us, even those we have while waking—those waking dreams indistinguishable from yearning...

Judy, our achieving dauphine, our hope-invested, our entelechy-girl, the family's "meek anticipant" and "rose of expectancy"... I walked around for years, thinking she was going to run things. I'd pass one of the snugger old manses of Corbindale patricians and perished canal tycoons and think: one day, Judy will live there. I'd shop at one of the new chain-stores out by the highways where I could never find the caulk or even a clerk to assist me and think: one day, my daughter will own you and straighten you out. I was convinced that everything she ever wanted, everything Edith ever wanted for herself, she would have. A career. In business, in industry, beyond academic politics. A career on Wall Street. Equities and brokerage. She was going to succeed and never struggle. How she was going to do that while remaining unhappy never bothered me. She'd figure it out. She'd stop being unhappy, she'd decide to stop, which was perhaps what she'd decided that Thanksgiving.

In the nearly half-a-century since that morning-after, Judy has still not given any better explanation of her actions than her scream—her siren scream that pierced my sleep and roused me from the papers blanketing my study floor.

I was supposed to be up early to drive my parents to the station and drop Judy off with friends, who were taking a sleigh-ride excursion in Holiday Valley. We were supposed to leave at 6 AM—rather, that was the time my obsessive-compulsively early-rising parents were supposed to wake me and Judy up, but Judy hadn't slept: she'd stayed awake for it.

That, at least, is how I screen it in my mind: Judy staying up sleepless and, if only I'd noticed, unsnoring and staring at the clock until—hearing my parents stirring and packing and folding up the Hide-A-Bed downstairs—she left her bed and got down on her knees on the carpet by her door, putting her hands against the door's panels, putting her slight girl's weight into her hands, and lining her face up with the doorknob so her eyes grazed just above it and she could look down into it and see her brass-yellow distorted reflection.

At 6 on the button, my parents were outside her door. My father was; he was trying the exterior knob, but the door was locked. He knocked. "Wake up, Ms. Fairness. We're leaving." No answer. Somewhat louder now, "Wake up, Fair Judele. Let's get a move on," and Judy said, in a sleepy voice, "Come in." My father rattled the knob. "It's locked. What's she afraid of that it's locked?" Judy said, "I'm pulling, but it's stuck." But of course it wasn't stuck and she wasn't pulling; she was pushing against the door with all her weight. "Try it now, Zeyde." My father said, "OK, just get out of the way"—he always maintained he'd said that and my mother, who was standing at the stairhead, and Edith, who'd come out of our bedroom to stand next to my mother, have alternately corroborated and contradicted his claim, their accounts agreeing and conflicting depending on exigencies, family-weather.

"OK, Zeyde," Judy said, "I'm out of the way," but of course she wasn't, she just stayed where she was, kneeling at the door like some meditating monk or imam salaaming on her carpet, her face up close to the knob, and, with an exhalation, merely surrendered her hands to gravity and let her arms drop limply to her sides, so that when my brute father gathered his garment-worker strength and charged the door, the door flew open and its interior knob slammed her nose as if her nose were a spike to be driven through her face.

That, at least, is how I've imagined it, and I've had to imagine it, because I wasn't there...I slept through all of it, until her final shrieking...

I've dreamed it since incessantly: the stiffness in her knees sinking into the bile-colored carpet, the sweat from her loathed nose dripping onto the mirroring brass knob, the perverse discipline required to wait and hold still for the perfect moment to relent—to let my father damage her in the way she'd so desired.

Rather, Judy would get more than that, because she'd only ever talked about cosmetic rhinoplasty, and—as the doctors understood the instant my father and I staggered her into the hospital wailing and giddy—what was required was a full reconstructive effort.

The blood on the carpet couldn't be cleaned, despite Edith's scrubbing, and despite, when Edith got tired, my mother's scrubbing: the bilious tint merely purpled.

My parents left, I don't remember when so much as how—Edith kicked them out, and then spent days taking her emotions out in phonecalls with local floorers, trying to cajole someone to come out and lay new carpet before Judy was discharged and returned to us. And as with every task Edith took on, she managed it.

The door was my job. It'd gotten splintered and clotted and had to be, Edith felt it had to be, replaced. I took it off its hinges myself—aghast at how proud I was of that accomplishment—and Judy's room gaped.

Tying the door to the top of my car, I hauled it around to Chautauqua Lumber and Bemus Windows & Doors and about a dozen other places and was told by all that a replacement would have to be ordered and wouldn't be in until after Christmas.

They had other models in stock, obviously they did, but Edith insisted on the same model: a single mismatched interior door would betray the tragedy behind it. After putting in the order, I drove around for a while, considering the woods, considering construction sites, trying to find somewhere inconspicuous to dump the old door so I wouldn't have to leave it out in front of the house as evidence for the garbagemen and neighbors. I ultimately decided just to leave it slanted in a dumpster behind the Corbin cafeteria, hoping some kid would find it and use it as a sled when the snows came down from the mountains.

I went by Corbindale High and got Judy's assignments and brought them home and completed them and brought them back. Worksheets on scansion, acids and bases, and calculus: the calculus gave me trouble.

While Edith slept in a chair by Judy's hospital bed, I stayed home and mooned around her room, snooping through her shelves, noting the color most used in her watercolor set (black), and the trill-fingering most scribbled above the staves of her etudes (C to C#). The satiny corner of a nightie stuck out from under her pillow and

I cursed myself for having missed it earlier—for not having realized that the Judy I'd taken to the hospital had been fully clothed. Her face gored with blood must've kept me from noting the outfit she was wearing below it, one of the unsalvageable, already-smirched suits from her other grandparents, which in my dream had been unwrinkled and spotless. I tugged the nightie out and found swaddled within it the nose-apparatus. It'd been advertised in the back of a beauty guide and Judy had snipped out its coupon and sent away for it and ever since it'd arrived in a plain brownwrapped package, shortly after Yom Kippur, there hadn't been a night she hadn't worn it, save the sleepless night before . . . when Jabotinsky had used it to hold together his foldered dossier on her . . .

I put it in a bag with the stuff Edith wanted—books of crosswords, other puzzles—and drove over to the hospital, where I pressed the quack calipers into her hand.

"Judy's nose-device? What am I supposed to do with this? What is she supposed to do with this? She doesn't need it anymore."

"She wasn't wearing it."

"So?"

"When we brought her in. When it all happened. She wasn't wearing it."

"Which proves what?"

"Which proves that what happened wasn't an accident."

When Edith stopped crying, she got up and walked me to the elevators and tossed the pincering contraption into a bin. "Let me ask you, Ruben—was my pregnancy an accident?"

"No."

"And do you consider our marriage an accident?"

"No, not at all."

"But do you have any proof?"

"I don't besides you. My only proof is what you say."

"Your only proof is what we both say together and in this case, we both say that Judy had an accident."

"Understood."

"And if we say that enough, someday we might even believe it."

Every time in my erranding when I opened a door, I'd think of Judy on the other side; I'd think of every time I'd opened a door too quickly and Judy's face had been there ... had she been rehearsing this stunt or even trying to make me responsible? What about those times she'd wanted to borrow multi-volume reference materials or some other weighty, hardcover tome—what had she wanted with Marx's *Capital*, except to drop it from atop a ladder and then climb down fast and let it whack her in the septum hump in the middle of her stunned expression? And what about that once she'd gotten a bit too close to the gaps between the retractable slats that doored the garage? Were all these just attempts aborted? Back in the adolescent Bronx, there'd been a kid on my block who claimed that a certain masturbation technique aided by rubberbands had enabled him to elongate the skin of his penis, recreating the foreskin that'd been clipped from him at one week old. I wonder if it worked. I mean, he showed me, he showed all of us in the alley, but I couldn't tell, not really. The last I heard of him he'd made a fortune in insurance, reinsurance, and consumer credit. Anyway, I think that's what I'd need, some sort of jerry-rigged Medieval stretching rack, but for my mind, to understand my daughter.

After tossing her drawers, I went through my study, deciding on the final drafts of her essays and typing them up, putting together her applications and signing her name to them. Then, on the day

Edith was bringing Judy home, I went out to the post-office. What a pretty simple building in the December dusk. A pretty simple building of clement brick. A fir wreath already hung over the counters. Returning home, star-tipped tapers were blinking on and miniature lawn ornament burros adored an infant cradled in straw.

Over break, I still went into school daily, if only to rubberneck on the way the pulled curtains, the washed windows, the interiors lit up with tinsel-swaddled trees. It was like every home was a commercial—*and now, a word from our sponsor . . .*

Our house was the one house darkened. If last year our undecorated windows had declared—to our neighbors, but more to our inadequacies—"Jews Live Here," this year they added "Sadly."

We didn't even remember when was Hanukah.

Inside, while Edith and I punished each other, Judy exulted, staying in bed and between the sheets, tucked in tightly under the covers as if she'd broken every bone, though all that was wrong with her was some soreness and bruising, a bit of panda about the eyes. Her head propped princessly atop the pillows, she watched TV from around the obstruction of her splinted bandage, which jutted up from her face like a gauzy antenna.

The TV was new, just purchased. I'd never have sprung for so lavish a gift if I hadn't been so weak. It was a gift for all of us, from all of us, together. This was what I'd told myself: we needed some laughter in the house, we needed something bright, and the newest models on the market were showing color. I picked out a hulking Philco "Miss America" whose blonde pine console was like a pine tree's stump, which I had the deliverers haul up to Judy's bedroom before Edith could object or even knew about the purchase.

I made sure to mention, to Judy then, and to Edith when

she came back from the library, that the arrangement was only temporary.

Once Judy had recovered, the TV would come back downstairs where it belonged.

Game shows were what she liked, and it was heartening to hear her laugh and yell out the answers in the jags between her Percodan.

From my study, I couldn't hear the questions clearly, I could only hear the answers Judy yelled and from them—if they were correct, and they almost always were—I'd have to guess the question. Vasco da Gama. Which Portuguese navigator discovered the sea-route to India? Willem Barents. For whom is the Barents Sea named? Judy yelled out her answers and yelled at the wrongness of the answers of the contestants onscreen and then, when she was shown to be in the right, she clapped. She applauded herself and cheered. It was disturbing. The change was almost manic, at least on the bloodied mummy surface.

It was as if by the mere flick of a switch or turn of a dial, or just by a door slamming her face in, some pleasure-circuit had been tripped and she was smiling like she used to as a child, or as much as she could tolerate the aching of smiling.

Explorers and Exploring was a favorite category, but she also liked Inventors & Inventions, Anatomy, and the Solar System. She liked the suspicion that these quizzes were rigged, because even with everyone cheating, she was winning. She kept her own tallies and one day proudly announced that she'd won—not could've, but had won—$32,000 and a San Juan cruise for two: "Which one of you beach-bums am I bringing?"

Edith and I waited on her hand and foot—rather, Edith brought the hand and foot and I the fractured heart. We tiptoed up the stairs toward her room atop new carpet that lay lumpy and pouched and not yet sun-faded.

We knocked at her jamb and stood there at the threshold that still awaited its door bearing Percodan and Canada Dry on a tray and confining our patter to game show pleasantries: *I'm good, I'm great, I'm so excited to be here . . . I just want to say a big big Hollywood hello to all the folks back in Peoria . . . I'm just raring to play the game . . .*

Downstairs, Edith and I conferred like a maid and butler who'd had a failed affair, trying to put their differences aside for the sake of an ailing mistress. We whispered together about Judy's meals. We whispered together about whether she'd eaten and how much she'd eaten of what. We whispered about whether it was already too late to send out a family Christmas card, which, as we'd been made to understand the year before, was pretty much obligatory for members of the Corbindale Women's League, the Algonquin Heights Neighborhood Council, and the Evergreen Street Mutual Aid Association. We whispered even though the TV blared and in the kitchen, the dishwasher was churning.

When we had real things to say to each other, we convened out on the porch.

Judy had walked into a door (was the story we'd told the doctors); Judy had slipped and fallen into a door (was the story I'd told Judy's teachers at Corbindale High); Judy's grandparents were coming down the stairs when she was coming up "and the oldsters took a frightening tumble and I had to dive to break their fall" (was the story Edith overheard Judy tell her friends on the phone). Edith and I stood out on the porch and whisper-debated which story to stick with should anyone ask, and whether we should send the doctors some flowers, or would flowers be too much? And why not bring Judy to a specialist in the city—a specialist in the city meaning a Jewish doctor—just to make sure that everything on the inside of her was healing because sometimes, nose damage can do brain damage?

"How?" I asked. "What doctor told you that?"

"Dr. Doolittle. Dr. Zhivago. It's common knowledge. If the nose bone is bumped back into the brain, it can damage something."

"Judy's nose bone didn't go into her brain."

"How do you know?"

"Or if it did go, it made her happier."

"It made her even crazier. To the point that I'm afraid of her. I'm afraid of what she might do if we leave her alone."

This was Edith showing concern but also trying to get out of our Christmas engagements, telling me I'd have to make our social rounds myself. And if I couldn't handle them alone, I should just skip them. I wasn't sure which was worse, though: for a faculty member to show up to a function wifeless or not show up at all. Not showing up at all would've suggested a snub and been religiously interpreted; but showing up solo implied trouble in the house. Kitchen drinking. Pill problems. A professor on the prowl.

"What should I do?"

"I don't care. I don't want to go. Not this year."

"What should I tell them?"

Edith paused. "Tell them your wife's afraid of your daughter being left alone and hanging herself from a curtain rod, or suffocating herself in plastic bags, or sparking the stove and leaking out some gas."

"Edith, stop, you're being irrational."

"We're standing whispering on a porch in winter outside a mostly empty house. We're both irrational. But I'm the one who's going to stay home to make sure nothing happens."

"Like the people who don't step on cracks or open their umbrellas inside. Like the people who can't let themselves fall asleep or else a meteor will crash into earth."

"Like that, exactly. Tell them I'm sick."

"What kind of sick?"

"A cold. Isn't it the season? And who knows, maybe I have one? Maybe standing out on the porch without a coat I'm developing one right now?"

The phone rang and Edith dashed inside. She had to pick it up in the kitchen before Judy could pick up the new extension phone upstairs, which we'd had installed on her nightstand for her convenience—again, a temporary measure.

If Edith managed to get to the phone before Judy, and if she managed to stay patient and silent, she'd be able to listen in, once Judy had satisfied herself that her mother wasn't on the line by yelling, "Mom, hang up! Are you there, Mom? If you're there, hang up!" as if her voice had to carry from the upper floor on its own and wasn't already being amplified.

I came back inside, shutting the porch door behind me cautious for quiet and doing all I could to prolong my preparations, slowly putting on my shoes and coat and hat and ducking back into the kitchen to wave goodbye to Edith, who ignored me.

This was the domestic scene I took with me into the chill: an eavesdropping woman leaning against the counter, the phone to an ear, one hand over the mouthpiece, the other hand's fingers entwining in the phonecord, the porch window behind her channeling into the kitchen's stillness the last dust-catching light of the sun.

I was late to every party I went to that season. I didn't drive, I walked and walked slowly and took the long way and took a long time at The Blooming Flour Bakery picking out a treat—the store-bought yule logs that made Edith's sickness credible.

"She has a nasty flu," I told Dr. Hillard at the Department Christmas party.

"Dr. Morse said you'd said a cold. But it's a flu now?"

"She's not sure."

"The poor dear. You'd better be careful it doesn't develop into pneumonia."

At the all-faculty Christmas party, Dr. Morse said, "What a pity she's not out and about yet. The library must miss her. And I do too. A hale Edith would've baked."

"And I hear Judy's under the weather too?" said Mrs. Morse.

Dr. Morse said, "But I'd heard it was some sort of tobogganing accident?"

"She took a tumble and smashed her nose and then, while she was resting up at home, I guess she caught whatever's plaguing Edith."

"That's terrible," said Mrs. Morse.

Dr. Morse said, "Don't you catch it yourself, Rube. Or by the time it gets to you, it'll be incurable."

"That's positively terrible," and then Mrs. Morse grinned. "But shouldn't you be getting into your Santa costume?"

Dr. Morse draped his tweeds around his wife and reeled her close to him, "Rube isn't playing Santa for us this year."

"He isn't? Oh, isn't that a shame?"

"I think Rube's busy enough as it is, dear."

"So who's going to play Santa?"

"I'm afraid we'll have to make do this year without him."

Mrs. Morse turned and showed me a sweetness that would've hidden me from the Klan, that would've hidden my whole family and never turned us over, on the condition that I annually donned the costume and slid down her chimney bearing gifts.

"I really liked when you did it, Dr. Blum, because you had the proper spirit. Some people just don't have the proper spirit, but you know what people want and don't mind giving it to them...you aren't above that..."

I was about to thank her, but she kept on, "And here I was just assuming you were going to be our Santa again and continue the tradition because you grew your beard back...I'm such a fool... Anyway, I'm glad it's back. A beard suits you."

My hands shot up to my face, but one hand held a cup of nog, which sloshed onto my tie. I excused myself, put the cup down atop a water-fountain and left the creped gymnasium for the cinder-blocked halls. I followed the stripes of Corbin scarlet that coursed along the walls. I raced the stripes past the corkboards whose tacked announcements flapped like tongues. I stopped in front of a display-case, glassed up front, mirrored in back, and filled with bright gold and silver trophies, tiny idolized men with balls. And I looked beyond them, to the back of the case, to my reflection. I looked at myself, at the exhaustion, the ruined tie, the unexpected and disheveling pelage. Edith hadn't mentioned it and I guess I hadn't gawked into a glass in a while. I couldn't remember the last time I'd shaved. I tried to rub the hair away like it was crusted cream, but it was sharp

126

and bristled. Around my mouth was a frozen field of stalks, black and white like television static, gray like television static, with a slightly longer wisp at chin that I realized I'd been, I was now, absent-mindedly curling, like Edith had twirled her phonecord, and there beyond the trophy idols a bedraggled rabbi stared back in disgust.

Home again, my neck sliced and wadded with toilet paper, I took the rare step of skipping my study and getting into bed with my wife, who couldn't have been sleeping. There was no way to sleep with the TV's sign-off seeping in from the hall, test-patterning our room with its shrill tone and spectral bars. Either I had to get inured or get up and go into the hall by Judy's doorlessness and pull the plug from the plateless socket.

"Don't," Edith said.

"We won't be able to sleep."

"If she can sleep this way, then we can. Don't disturb her."

I got back into bed and reached for my wife, but she rolled away. "You're drunk and you smell like smoke."

"I'm sorry."

"And you put too much pressure on our daughter. Always saying nothing's good enough. Her essays, her grades, her new friends."

"I'm sorry. I know."

"And so to get back at you, Judy took it out on your father."

"I know." And then a moment later, "Your mother told you that? This is her amateur analyst's interpretation?"

"She did. It is."

"And what did you say to her back?"

"It isn't fair, Mom."

On New Year's Eve, the TV was suddenly off and the house was filled with a live studio audience, which Edith and I had invited. All of Judy's new friends from the Plein Air Aficionados and half the woodwind section of the Orchestra, her Gilbert & Sullivan co-stars and Romeo, Tod Frew, and Mary Busti and Joan Gerry, whom I'd dreamed of too and who, to my relief, had shown up unscathed from their tortures.

They were here to pick Judy up and whisk her away to some dance-formal, and while they were waiting for her to descend, earnest Tod Frew inquired after Edith's health ("I'm glad you're feeling better, Mrs. Blum, my father told me you'd been ill lately"), and after the health of Judy's grandparents ("Elderly folks, taking a spill like that down the stairs, they're lucky they're intact, Mrs. Blum"), and whether Edith and I had any plans for the evening ("I'd imagine that you're both feeling rather cooped up?").

Then, carefully, Judy came down the stairs, resplendent in her mother's heels and the blueblack sheath dress that had just arrived for the holidays, sent by Edith's parents as a replacement—a college-visit dress she evidently wasn't saving—and, atop it all, held proudly up in the air, an unbandaged bumpless nose. It was still slightly bruised, and from straight-on still slightly swollen, but from profile-angle it was impeccable, and whatever yellowish lividity remained, and whatever whitish patches that'd been under the tape had yet to fade, she'd rosily smoothed over with concealer and blush and set off with mascara and eyeliner and crimson lipstick, half the contents of Edith's vanity.

Tod Frew turned to Edith, "She takes after you, Mrs. Blum." And then turning to me, "She takes after your wife."

"I heard you, Tod," I said and squeezed Judy's hand.

And Judy said, "I take after my mother? Jesus Christ, I seriously hope not."

Edith wilted.

Judy was cruel. She had that smart cruelty to her of someone who'd gotten what she wanted. And she'd gotten it the fairest way, through suffering.

8.

THIS WAS THE WEATHER with which we began 1960: cold. All I wanted was to stay in my study, sitting in front of my typewriter atop my newly gained eight winter-break pounds, grading finals and trying to make some thoughts about antebellum deficits and debts. But unfortunately, I had a visitor coming. January is no friend to the social.

Judy went back to Corbindale High on Monday the 4th, but the college term didn't start up again until Monday the 18th, when the snows started up again too, intensified through Tuesday, and by Wednesday had piled up to half-a-foot.

There was no point in shoveling except to rid myself of the headache I'd woken up with, so I bundled myself and, beginning curbside, did the dig, kick, scoop, dumping wide margins past the dead flowerbeds that lined the walk. By the time I got to the stoop, heaving, steaming, the curb was once again enrimed and I slunk inside to shower.

Coming downstairs flagrant with aftershave, the casement clock was chiming noon and I checked the window. The walkway was once again pure white.

In the kitchen, Edith had the knives out. Her apron strings cinched tight, she was wielding steel through cheeses, carving apples into broken swans.

"It's bad out there. Maybe he'll cancel?"

It was almost distressing, the size of the spread she'd put together. Who, after Christmas, could stand another calorie? Who had an appetite for anything, up to and including even banter? I wasn't sure what Edith was trying to prove, or to whom: whether she was going overboard to prove her wifeliness or my, or my Department's, unreasonable demands. There was a crudité tray, dainty bowls of brittles and marzipan from the Amish, and some jiggly pâtés from that strange gourmet Scandinavian chalet out on Route 394.

"'Hosting guest prospectives at a faculty-residence is a time-honored Corbin tradition,'" I said, repeating what Dr. Morse had said to me, in a remark I was hoping would become a new private quip between Edith and myself. "Or was it 'entertaining prospectives at a faculty-residence is a time-honored staple of Corbin hospitality'?"

Edith wasn't smiling.

"When I came up here to interview, you know where they invited me? The cafeteria."

I went to pick up some type of blistered cracker, but Edith turned and flashed a blade and I relented.

I sat in the den with a book on Jackson's destruction of the national bank, mostly staring out the window at the white page of lawn. Every time I thought, I should get up once more and hoist the shovel, I'd hear a car come down Evergreen and get woozy.

I felt like Judy waiting for a date, except that Judy never waited by the window. She had the dignity to wait up in her room.

Conventional wisdom makes Andrew Jackson out to be a hick Indian-slayer whose backwoods buddies stormed the capital for his inauguration and trashed the White House, tromping their muddy boots across the damask and vomiting all over the flocked wallpaper. The truth, however, is that Jackson wanted to redecorate the executive mansion, but, lacking the funds, he invited guests he could count on to wreck the place and then in the hungover light of the next morning staggered over to Congress to beg for help with cleaning up the mess and buying new furniture, in a subterfuge reminiscent of Judy's...

After Jackson's censure by the Whigs, but before that crazy Englishman tried to kill him—that's where I'd left off... my page bookmarked with Netanyahu's sole communication with me prior to this visit, a "Merry Christmas" card:

Expect me on 20/1 by noon. Dr. Morse provided the address.

Yours, B. Netanyahu

P.S. Forgive the card.

His handwriting was pygmy, and the date wasn't just written backward but its zero was slashed, as is the practice in Europe, where the women grow out their hair and go without underwear and the children all smoke and drink wine.

A car came chunking down Evergreen, chunking slow and near the curb, the better to look out for street numbers. We had a bronze 18 on the lintel out front and The Blums on our mailbox and the mailbox's post wasn't gussied up North Pole–style... and our door was visibly unwreathed... Those are the directions that should've been given to Netanyahu: keep a look-out for the one house that isn't Santa's workshop.

The car was a desert-colored, rusted-out Ford of the '40s, ponton and streamlined and, it must be said, slick for its day, which, by the time it skidded down our street, had already long been over. It was one of the first model cars they started making after the wartime hiatus and one of the last model cars with a face. By which I mean the front of the thing, with its widespaced high-socketed headlight eyes and grille bullet-nose, was almost like a person. It came at you with this sweet stupid human look. This pitiable dependent look that almost made you forget that its maker was a Nazi. This specimen was especially poignant, because the face it presented was smashed. Its grille was missing and its dented chrome fender was half hanging off and kind of flicking the snow ahead of it like an impotent plow.

But maybe this wasn't Netanyahu. For one, there were too many people inside. More than one person inside was too many. In Netanyahu's card, he hadn't mentioned coming up accompanied and yet this clown-car heading toward me appeared to be so crammed that—through my window and the car's windscreen—it wasn't clear to me how many passengers there were or what they were doing: fighting or getting dressed?

There was a fad at the time, especially popular among my students, of trying to figure out how many of them could fit into a phonebooth—for a while, this seemed to be among the most pressing concerns of the Eisenhower Era: "Will we obliterate the planet through thermonuclear war?" was right up there with, "How many co-eds can we stuff into this phonebooth, this clothes-closet, this refrigerator's cardboard box?" Photographers and film-crews would show up wherever a stunt was staged and record its hormonal-hilarity for TV, film, and the pages of the yearbook. This persistent effort among my students to accommodate as many of their young bodies as possible into a single cramped space was as much an

attempt to exorcise the age's confusing combination of stifling con-
formity and unrestrained consumption as it was a rationale for sexual
touching, in a sort of unconscious dress-rehearsal for the revolution
to come: I'm not tit-grabbing for the sake of tit-grabbing, I'm just
trying to set a new world-record . . . for how many of my friends I can
fit into a package of Cracker Jack . . .

This cramming-craze had also made it to cars, especially to old
Fords like the one outside, which was of a model that many students
owned, handed down to them by their parents; and, as I was shrug-
ging on my coat, I had the idea that Netanyahu had broken down
somewhere and hitchhiked and some students picked him up . . .
and then on the way to campus, the students had gotten into an
accident . . . which would explain the Ford's hood puffing Los Ala-
moses of popcorn-cloud smoke and its busted fender sagging as it
rattled past the Dulleses' and stopped, blocking our driveway.

I stepped outside just in time to catch the car's rear door opening
and bodies pratfalling out—not clowns in full bozo regalia honking
horns and juggling plates, but close enough: shearling-clad kids, one,
two, three of them. It took me a moment to count three of them:
small, medium, large. Their identical sheepskin coats, and, especially,
their suddenly unconfined energy, made them seem more numerous.
They were chasing each other between the sidewalk and street and
tossing snow, as two larger, adult forms slid out from the front door,
curbside. The doors on the far side must've been jammed. These
two adults at first seemed indistinguishable and completely androg-
ynous, as they were bundled up in bigger version sheepskins of what
the little ones were wearing. Five identically furry toggle-clasped
coats, hopefully bought in bulk at a substantial discount. As the kids
firedrilled around the car in a riot of snowballs thrown and dodged,

one of the adults raised a hooded head to the sky and screamed out in that language that in my youth had been spoken by God. She— because the scream was a woman's—must've been telling the kids to stop running and shut up already. This was my first encounter with the Netanyahus, the whole family: *die ganze mishpocha.*

As the wife wrangled the kids, the husband tugged back his hood to show the face I knew, or thought I knew, from the passport-size snapshot haphazardly glued to the upper-right-hand corner of his resume: he'd aged. He was about fifty years old then, his face a tough nut of vaguely Mongol features, tiny olive pit eyes and absolutely enormous and fleshy oyster-shell ears, strong nasolabial folds that I'm not going to call "smile lines" or "laugh lines," because the mouth itself was humorless, tightlipped. His head was topped with a Bactrian camel's two humps of hair, the dome risen between them a luminous egg of freckled baldness. The first words he addressed to me were, "Dr. Blum, I presume?"

"Pleased to meet you."

"Dr. Ben-Zion Netanyahu."

Yes, he insisted on using titles at first and, yes, he shook my hand without taking off his linty mitten. His accent was stronger than I'd expected; it was gritted, but later I had the impression he was purposefully stressing it: Ben-*Zion.*

"You can call me Ruben. Or Rube. Shalom."

We were standing on snow over what might've been the sidewalk or the lawn, impossible to tell, and he pursed his lips and nodded thoughtfully, as if he didn't recognize the salutation, or was resigning himself to it. "Shalom, Rube."

I led the man up the powdered path to the house, followed by his wife and kids whom he hadn't introduced yet.

135

It was only once they were up the stoop and inside that the stocky, quiffhaired wife said, "My name is Tzila," but she said that while staring at her husband, who said to me, "Her name is Tzila, my wife," and I stuck out my hand and Tzila took it and drew me to her and offered her cheek. I pecked it. She offered her other cheek. I pecked that too.

Her cheeks were cold.

Edith, freshened, flashing teeth, came to greet us. "And Tzila, Ben-Zion, this is Edith," and Edith said, "Oh lovely...you brought your children...what a nice surprise, Ruben didn't mention children...here kids, let me take your coats..."

The kids and parents shed their identical skins and mittens and scarves and hats and, piling them, turned Edith into a coatrack.

"Would you mind"—her voice a muffled chirping from under the layers—"please taking off your shoes?"

But the parents had already passed over the interior mat without even wiping and on into the den, tracking snow across the wood, the parquet puddling with the melting runoff.

The boys burst out into screeching. Apparently, the tallest of the three had smuggled a snowball inside and was busy shoving it down wherever he could into the middle boy's clothing, his shirt, his pants, inside the waistband of a wedgie.

Tzila reprimanded them in Hebrew, as the middle boy chased the oldest boy around the piano and the youngest boy howled. More snow went to water on the floor, shoeprints soaked into the faux arabesques of the faux Persian rug and Edith tried again, "Would you mind, please? Your shoes? I'm afraid we run a rather Asian household."

Tzila said something again, something that sounded too terse to have been a translation, a single word impatiently and densely packed, tensed, declined, and gendered, and the boys all at once froze and plopped down where they stood, the two older boys on the rug, the youngest on the parquet, and started tugging at their overknotted laces. "You folks too, if you don't mind," Edith said to Tzila and Netanyahu, who looked quizzically at each other and then sat down on the Hide-A-Bed to take off their footwear as well.

No one in the family, I realized then, was wearing boots or galoshes or any type of shoe even remotely appropriate for winter: Netanyahu had bluchers, Tzila had flats, and the boys were in cheap canvas sneakers. Tzila's stockings were soaked and one of Netanyahu's socks had a hole and a big toe thrust through with a gnarled untrimmed nail.

Tzila handed her and her husband's footwear to Edith, who went around collecting the boys'. As each handed his pair over, Tzila named them: the eldest Jonathan, the middle Benjamin, the youngest Iddo, and Edith said, "Thank you, Jonathan, thank you, Benjamin, thank you, Kiddo," and Tzila said, "Iddo," and Edith said, "Kiddo," and the older boys giggled and whatever Hebrew they spat at the family's runt, it ended with "Kiddo."

As Edith set their shoes down to dry on the mat, Tzila gave their ages as 13, 10, and 7, respectively, and I remember noting that spacing and thinking that was just about the only disciplined and orderly thing about them—about these Yahus, which was immediately how I began referring to them in my head; these uncouth and rowdy Yahus who'd charged into our home and snowed up our floors and were now upright again and wandering the den like they were casing it for a burglary; Jonathan and Benjamin making an inspection of the mantel, examining its Mayflower and Speedwell ships-in-bottles,

manhandling the tin wind-up toys of Hamilton and Burr, and over-
loading the pans of the antique pewter balance scales with weights
that kept clattering. Iddo was between their legs, poking at the and-
irons and digging in the hearth, and then rubbing at his face and
smearing it with ashes.

"Ruben," Edith said, "we're going to need some extra chairs . . .
ground-control to Ruben Blum: you're going to need to bring a few
in from the diningroom."

Tzila, perhaps misconstruing, said to the boys something that
must've meant sit down, and they went scrambling for perches;
Jonathan and Benjamin taking the delicate Shaker chairs facing the
Hide-A-Bed before Edith or I could stop them.

Iddo, who was chairless, tried to get up on Jonathan's lap, but was
pushed off, and then tried to get up on Benjamin's lap, but was
pushed off from there too, in an alarming shaking of Shaker joinery
and basket-weaved seats, and Iddo—who'd tumbled to the floor
dangerously close to the Chippendale tray-table—crawled off crying
to wipe his wet blackface on a flank of the Hide-A-Bed and nestle
between his parents.

I went to the diningroom and brought back two of the table's
sturdy, aluminum-framed chairs and positioned them at the gathering's fringes and sat in one and stared at the other and tried to
think of the politest way to get the older boys to switch.

"I put together a bit of a smorgasbord," Edith said, "a lot of savo-
ries, but I guess I should get some treats together for the kiddies?"

Tzila didn't respond, just kept stroking the head of the bawling
blackfaced boy, so Edith tried again, "Would you mind if I served
your boys some c-o-o-k-i-e-s?"

Tzila, confused, repeated the spelling, "C-o-o-k," but Jonathan

138

interrupted his mother, "Cookies, she's spelling cookies." He said to Edith, "We speak English."

Benjamin said, "We're not idiots."

"And what about him, then?" Edith said to Iddo, "What about you?"

"He's an idiot," Jonathan said. "Right, Iddy? Am I right? Iddy, are you an idiot who doesn't speak English?"

Iddo, voice thick with sniveling, reached for his mother and said, "Cookies."

Tzila hoisted Iddo and smelled him and then laid him atop the tray-table and, without laying a towel, proceeded to pull down his pants and peel off his diaper. "The boys can eat anything," she said, as if she were addressing the mess. "Really he doesn't need these pampers anymore except at night and whenever we have a long car trip."

Edith, shutting her eyes, disappeared into the kitchen. As Tzila dug in her bag for a roll of toiletpaper and wiped Iddo, I asked, "Ben, Jon—you want to switch seats?"

But Benjamin was leaning over his younger brother's ashy nakedness and flicking at his penis. Tzila slapped his hand away and Iddo howled. "Chocolate chip poop cookies," Benjamin said, pointing into the diaper, "chocolate chip brownie fudge poop cookies."

"It's not poop," Tzila informed me, "it's pee-pee...pish..."

"Urine," Jonathan said and picked a petal off a poinsettia.

"And who is this?" Netanyahu asked, pointing at the sidetable's display of family portraits from Sears and picking one up and examining it. "Your daughter?"

"Judy. Judith."

"Yehudit."

"She's in school all day, high school, I'm afraid you'll miss her."

"That's the Hebrew name, Yehudit, whose book is accepted by the goyim but excluded from the Jewish canon for reasons of prudery. Yehudit, the heroic Jewish woman, pretends to seduce the Assyrian general Holofernes, plies him with food and drink until he's in a stupor, and then she takes a knife and slices off his head."

"She's named after Edith's grandmother, the wife of a grain merchant from Trier, who became a zipper merchant on 34th Street."

Netanyahu replaced the photograph on the sidetable, propping Judy, Edith, and I against the lamp upsidedown.

"Iddo was a prophet, who wrote books we know existed, but now are lost. And Jonathan is Yonatan, and Benjamin is Binyamin. Those you surely know from Tanakh, the canonical Bible."

Tzila handed him the balled-up diaper, but he didn't take it. He just said, "Yoni, Bibi, and Iddy…I hope I don't regret having brought them along…"

Tzila dropped the diaper in his lap and said something in Hebrew, something needling—the only word I caught, which she repeated, sounded like "kettle" or "fettle" to me—and as she went on, his gaze dropped lower, to the hole in his wet webbed sock and his jutting toe, which he wiggled the louder she got, until he stamped his foot and blurted, "English."

Tzila said, I assume to me, "I regret already that we came with him."

Her English was choppier than his, more limited but with a better accent, which I heard as Midwestern with a guttural Levantine tinge: "The boys were supposed to stay with our—woman," she said, "our woman who stays with them."

"The babysitter," Netanyahu said. "The babysitter canceled because of a fire."

"She had a flood in her house from pipes that are freezed."

"I thought it was a fire."

"It was a flood from pipes that are freezed and a fire."

"How can you have both a flood and a fire? Wouldn't the fire put out the flood or thaw whatever's frozen?"

"How would you know? I'm the one who talked to her."

Netanyahu turned to me. "As I was saying, it was an emergency: the babysitter couldn't stay with the boys and Tzila didn't want to be alone with them."

"Tzila is right here. Tzila is right here in front of you. And no, Tzila didn't want to stay home with the boys and the boys didn't want to stay home with Tzila," and then she lapsed into Hebrew, directed at Iddo, and then came back to English to say, "Who would want to stay at home with a mother who forgets her son's underwear?"

"Isn't there a pair in the car?" Netanyahu said, "in the glovebox?" and Jonathan said, "I can get it," and Benjamin said, "I go get it with you."

"No," Tzila said. "I don't deal with the car," she said this to me, "the car is my husband's problem, not my problem." She ripped off a square of toiletpaper and wetted it in her mouth and stuck it to the tip of Iddo's nudity, "That should be enough for now," and pulled up his pants and picked him up and set him back standing in front of her between the Hide-A-Bed and the tray-table and poked him in the stomach, singsonging in a heliumated tyke-voice, "We all wanted to come with your father! We just can't get enough of him! The moment your father leaves the house, everything collapses!" She picked up Iddo's sweater and the identical sweater beneath it and the undershirt beneath that and leaned down and Bronx-cheered into his belly, until his howling turned into hysterical giggles: "What would we do without him?...pfffhhh...Yes yes yes yes what would we do without him?...pfffhhh..."

"I'm the same way," I said, to placate. "Without Edith, I'd fall apart."

Tzila frowned and straightened Iddo's clothes. "What we all wanted was a vacation in New England and it was only after we left and were on the road that we discovered from the map that the great genius of our family was wrong and Upstate New York is not New England."

"It is," Netanyahu said. "It's New England."

"What do you think, Rube, is Upstate New York New England?"

"I don't know." I was hesitant.

"Be honest, Rube."

"Maybe it's Mid-Atlantic. But I don't think that New England is an official designation."

"But it is," Tzila said. "It means Maine, New Hampshire, Vermont, Massachusetts, Rhode Island, Connecticut: those are New England."

"Certainly."

"The map is wrong," Netanyahu said.

Tzila said, "New York is Mid-Atlantic, below which is what?"

"Many states," I said.

"Below the Mid-Atlantic is Washington DC, and below Washington DC is the Dixie South."

"The map is out of date," Netanyahu said.

Tzila said to her husband, "You think it changes? You think the states move around? Call the AAA," she said each letter. "The American Automobile Association. You can explain to them geography after you call to Edelman."

That was the word I'd heard her say, the name: Edelman.

Netanyahu shrugged.

"Can my husband have—can he use your phone, Rube, to make a call? He needs to call to Edelman."

Chaim "Hank" Edelman, the "Philly" rabbi, I realized.

Netanyahu spoke in Hebrew.

"So now you want to speak in Hebrew? Call!"

"You call him."

"Not me. He's your friend. You. Go call to him and throw that out. The pamper. You make it smell in here."

She leveled a look at him and wrinkled her forehead, until Netanyahu grabbed the diaper and sprang to his feet, "Where's the telephone?"

I led him into the kitchen, where Edith was spooning cocoa mix into mugs. "Our guest has to use the telephone."

"You know where it is," she said and spooned tense-handed. There was cocoa powder all over the counter.

I picked up the lid of the trashcan and Netanyahu dumped the diaper inside and then I led him over to the phone, wall-mounted by the bathroom, and retreated to the stove, where Edith was whisking milk at the edge of boiling.

"Stop neglecting your guests. Take that in."

She'd arranged stale stocking-shaped cookies along the rim of a plate, at the center of which, behind its candycane fence, was the stale gingerbread house we'd received from a pair of her library coworkers, the widowed sisters Stunodsky, who every Christmas prided themselves on making for each of their colleagues a gingerbread house that resembled, or at least resembled to the widowed sisters Stunodsky, that colleague's actual domicile.

I pried a gumdrop loose from our icinged roof and, coming up behind Edith, tried to flirtatiously pop it in her mouth, but she resisted and twisted her head away and refused to open up and the red sugarcoated jelly fell to the floor and Netanyahu, who was in the midst of dialing, had witnessed all of it. He had to hang up and dial again. I bent down to the linoleum to pick up the gumdrop and left it in the sink, from which Edith retrieved it and threw it in the trash, scowling as the burped-open lid spread the stench from the diaper.

"Edelman, nu, Edelman," Netanyahu was saying and the rest was Hebrew, his accent labent and Slavic: Warsaw, I recalled.

I took in the plate, and the older boys attacked the house before it even hit the table. They swarmed the yard and knocked over the walls, stuffing their faces with sugar-wafer doors and marzipan dormers with licorice shutters, spilling nonpareils, sprinkles, and crumbs.

I headed back into the kitchen for napkins, but Edith met me in the diningroom and thrust at me a tray of sloshing mugs topped with bobbing marshmallows. "This is the kind of cocoa that doesn't stain, right?"

"That's right, Ruben—and yours is the kind of humor that's droll." She turned to the kitchen again. "The adult spread will be out in just a moment."

I carried in the mugs, for Jonathan and Benjamin, and when Iddo gave a yelp of deprivation, Tzila asked me to pluck him "one of the mint sticks"—a candycane, I figured, a barberish picket I picked out of our fence and gave him to suck.

Glasses, wine, crackers and cheeses and dull daggers to smear and stab with: the adult spread. The olives and nuts. Edith made one trip bringing out the olive bowl and another trip bringing out the nut bowl and then again separate trips for the bowls for olive pits and nut shells. She was making as many trips as she could, and it was only after I couldn't conceive of her bringing in anything else from the kitchen unless she intended to bring Netanyahu himself and the phone he was on, along with the entire contents of the fridge—the butter, the eggs, the leftover meatloaf from yesterday, the chicken à la king from the day before, the jello molds, the spätzle maker, the mixmaster, the blender, the refrigerator itself—that she finally sat down in the diningroom chair across from me and forced a smile.

Then she slapped her thigh and rose again, "Forgot the napkins."

This was Edith's way: she got her emotions out through busyness.

She handed the napkins around, paper ones the older boys didn't unfold onto their laps, but tucked into their shirtcollars like bibs, which protected their flimsy Disney sweaters but not our rug from dribbled cocoa.

"Paper napkins," Tzila said, "and paper towels and even paper tablecloths. Paper, paper, paper. This is what I like about America, the disposing things."

"Disposable," I said.

"The disposing cups and plates and bowls. The disposing pampers. No more cloth. It's so much easier to raise kids in the States."

"It is?" Edith said.

"Washers, dryers. The machine for the dishes. When you want warm water, when you want hot water, you just turn on the tap and it's there so it burns you, no tanks you have to wait for, and in the summers, an air conditioner, not a fan. In Israel, these are luxurious goods and no one has them. But here in the States, you have it so easy."

"But even our generation in the States has it easy compared to our parents," I said.

Tzila sighed. "You would not believe it, how lucky you are. You would not believe it if I told you."

Edith said, "How long have you been in Philadelphia? A while now, no?"

"Philadelphia—even a day there is a while—a day there is forever. It's a city not possible, impossible, to leave. You go out driving and driving and ask to yourself, is this still Philadelphia? And the answer is yes, it is still Philadelphia. You drive through suburbs, you drive through farms where even the horses go faster, you drive and drive and ask, also Philadelphia? Yes."

"The trip must've been draining, especially in this weather."

"Forget just in this weather, also in summer. And you only know you left when you get to Allentown. Wilkes something, like the man who shot Lincoln."

"Wilkes-Barre," I said.

"No, that's not it."

Jonathan, sleeve-wiping cocoa beads from his sparse Puerto Rican moustache hairs, said, "Wilkes Booth."

"Yes, Wilkes Booth."

"Wilkes-Barre," I said, "near Scranton."

Jonathan said, "The actor John Wilkes Booth shooted, shot President Avraham Lincoln, the sixteenth president of the United States who gave to the slaves their freedom in 1865 at the end of the American Civil War."

Edith said, "Try a cookie, Rube," as a way of getting me to drop

146

it. And then she said to Jonathan, "Your history's as good as your English."

Benjamin said, "Mine is gooder," and Jonathan said, "Better," and Benjamin said, "But Iddy is an idiot and didn't shooted anyone."

"And Scranton," Tzila went on, "what an ugly city. You go through Wilkes Booth and you think how ugly can a town get? Is there anything uglier? And then you leave Wilkes Booth and go through Scranton and there's your answer."

"Coal country," I said, lamely. "Pretty barren, pretty desolate."

"It's bleak," Edith said, "but if you don't want to freeze, you need coal."

"Is it cold in here? Should I make a fire?"

Jonathan said, "I want to make a fire"; Benjamin said, "Rebecca Gratz she made a fire"; Jonathan said, "Rebecca Gratz made a flood."

"Is Rebecca Gratz your babysitter?" Edith said.

Benjamin said, matter-of-factly, "Before now she loves Ronnie Edelman but now she loves Jonathan but Jonathan just loves her boobies."

Jonathan spat a marshmallow into the air and it peaked and fell and he caught it in his mouth and chewed. "Not just her boobies."

"Everything's broken, everything's black," and Tzila licked her thumb and, with Iddo on her lap, went about rubbing his face white again. "Even in daylight, it's black in Scranton. You drive through it and say, Is the sun still shining? You can't tell, you really can't. What happened to the sun? And then you see a sign, Entering New York State and you think OK, great, OK, New York is a civilized country, everything will again be better, but it's not. It's not at all. You know what happens when you cross the New York border?"

"You're in New York?" I said.

"Yes, and it just gets worse."

"At least it's forest," Edith said.

"So boring, forest and farms. And if you open the window to get some air you get wind and snow and from animals the smell of pampers," and Tzila held out her wine-glass for a refill, and I grasped the bottle and poured her again and poured Edith again and then was about to pour myself when Tzila shook her glass at me, chiding.

I filled her glass just shy of the brim.

Netanyahu's voice suddenly boomed in a forlorn Hebraic foghorn, "Edel-man . . . Edel-man," and Jonathan cupped his hands and mimicked it and Benjamin cracked up and from his lips sprayed a Vienna-finger chimney and candy-corn shingles.

Tzila, gulping at her glass, raised the volume on her lutefisk English to tune her children out, "All along the highway 81 we took until we came to," but I missed the word, "and then we went up along the," and then there was the word I missed again, "crossing the bridge at Great Bend when the great genius of the family I'm married to, the true expert driver with the map goes too fast when I tell him to slow, to slow down, near to Hallstead is the town where we go off the road like a fat person slips in the tub and almost into the," and again the word and I looked to Edith to fill it in but she was staring in horror at Tzila's claret-colored mouth, "and it's not even our car but we had to borrow it from Edelman."

"Oh my. Oh my."

"He'll be so angry, Edelman, but it's not my fault . . ." and Tzila went to set her glass down on the table and splashed some wine on Iddo's head, "it's my famous husband's fault, so he's the one who has to explain it to Edelman that he almost killed his entire family by driving too fast in the snow at Hallstead and almost making us drown in the," and then that word again, something like the Saksallah or the Sachsvalhalla.

Edith said, "The Susquehanna."

"That's what I said," and who knew—maybe Tzila was correct? Perhaps she knew the native pronunciation? After all, as she'd later tell Edith, her parents had moved from Lithuanian Poland to pre-State Israel via Minnesota. In about a decade, I'd hear the same English again in speeches by Golda Meir, who'd grown up the daughter of immigrant parents in Wisconsin. That odd mixture of Israel and the Northwest Territories.

There was a yell and a bellish bang from the kitchen and Netanyahu stalked back into the den, where the older boys had left off imitating him, but sat rocking back and forth and creaking their chairs in an attempt to contain their hilarity like a bathroom need.

Passing them, Netanyahu told them to put down their cocoa—he must've told them that in Hebrew—and they did, they put down their cocoa, and then he palmed their skulls, one in each hand, and bonged them together so that, if the scene were any more animated, little dizzy cartoon birds would've flown around their heads in haloes.

"I apologize for my boys," he said, as they whimpered. "If they don't behave themselves, this will be the last vacation we ever take."

I thought: some vacation being a six-hour drive through cow pasture and despoiled coal country, the anthracite-black stripped-bare wilderness? And I could see, or thought I could see, that Tzila thought something similar, but held her peace.

"They're wonderful boys," Edith said and picked up their mugs from the table one at a time and set them down again atop coasters.

Tzila said, "I forgot the English word for those."

"Coasters."

Netanyahu said, "In real English, they call them mats."

Tzila said, "British English now is real English?"

"To some people."

"To the same some people who think New York is New England."

The clock chimed one and Netanyahu consulted his watch, the time he trusted.

"It's one," I said. "New York New England time."

"Down to business," Netanyahu said. "We have the class, the interview, the supper, and then the lecture with reception to follow?"

"That's the schedule."

"And the committee will be at all events?"

"I believe so. Though maybe not the class, because that's not our Department. And of course, the interview is committee-only. The supper will be committee plus spouses. And the lecture's open to the public, so I'm hoping folks show up. There was an announcement in *The Corbindale Gazette* and I know Edith put up fliers in the library and I've been talking about it to everyone I meet and made it an attendance-requirement for my students. It's always an ordeal to get people out to these things, as I'm sure you're aware, but it's especially tough after Christmas, with everyone all hibernating, so we're trying extra hard."

He nodded, disinterested. "And the committee is made of Morse, Galbraith, Kimmel, Hillard, and yourself, yes?"

"That's us. Indeed."

"I have researched everyone, but of some I couldn't find much.

You will have to tell me about them. For example, is Galbraith as stupid in person as he is about the Vichy regime? And Kimmel—is he German?"

"I think Dr. Kimmel once spent a sabbatical summer in Wittenberg. And Dr. Galbraith's from Louisiana."

"I understand. You will tell me more in private."

"And between the interview and supper I was supposed to bring you to the Corbindale Inn to check in, but I'm realizing now that the school probably just booked you a single room and you're going to need another... I don't think anyone was really expecting kids, so we should probably..."

Tzila turned to Netanyahu and said something in Hebrew and he said something back, terse and brittle. "I can't believe him," Tzila said, "I told him to call ahead and say we're coming and make the booking for another room."

"I forgot," he said.

"Ajointing, I told you, an ajointing room."

"Adjoining. I forgot."

"It's OK," I said. "I'm sure it's OK. I'll talk to someone in the Department or... Edith, you know what's her name there at the Inn, the innkeeper's wife?"

"Mrs. Marl, yes, she volunteers at the library for the children's reading hour."

Tzila said, "You will call to her, please?"

Netanyahu said, "We don't need another room, if the school won't pay for it. We'll be fine with extra beds, with cots like in the army. Or even just with space for the kids to sleep on the floor."

Tzila said, "Don't be cheap. You'll sleep on the floor. You'll sleep in the tub." She said to Edith, "You will make the arrangements?"

"Of course. I'll call Mrs. Marl."

"Tell her the school will pay for it," Netanyahu said. "Now, Rube, there's only one issue still outstanding."

"Which is?"

"Edelman, the man I called who loaned the car. He wanted me to ask if you knew a good mechanic."

"I don't know... I could try..."

"I'm not finished... let me finish... he, Edelman, wanted me to ask if you knew a good mechanic in the area, but it's my opinion that this car of his is fine. Absolutely fine. Any damage that occurred on our drive here is not just purely cosmetic, but completely the fault of Edelman himself. It's simply a fact that the car was in disrepair before we drove it and Edelman was being irresponsible by loaning it to us in that condition. It was a very dangerous risk he was taking. Somebody could very easily have been injured or killed."

"What do you think is wrong with it?"

"As I said, nothing is wrong with it and it's not our fault. Edelman is to blame and I told him so. Still, he made me promise to ask you about a mechanic and I promised and have asked you, and now you will answer me no, that you don't know a good mechanic in the area, or that all the mechanics in the area are crooked thieves, or no one here does immediate service because of the snow-day... something like that..."

"You want me to tell you what?"

"If you want, you can call Edelman and tell him yourself. Or if that's too much to ask, maybe when we go to campus we can just stop by your office and write a letter."

"You want a letter?"

"*Dear Dr. Netanyahu, In reference to your question of January*

20th, unfortunately there are no good mechanics currently available in the Corbindale area..."

"A letter addressed to you?"

"So I can show it to Edelman... or maybe you can address it to Tzila, so it's less suspicious... *Dear Mrs. Netanyahu, I am sorry to report that all mechanics in the Corbindale area are already committed to other projects...*"

"You can't be serious. You want me to lie?"

"I am not asking you to lie about the condition of the car, merely about the availability of those professionally capable of assessing it. Though if you would like to independently render your opinion that the damage is only cosmetic and the car is fine and will be able to make its return to Philadelphia without incident, who am I to stop you?"

"I don't know what to say."

"Don't worry if you can't remember the wording. When we get to your office, I will dictate it to your secretary."

"My secretary?"

"Or you can type it yourself. I leave that to you."

I made a show of consulting the clock. "We have to be on campus within the hour. I'm not sure we have the time."

"So maybe Edith can do this too?"

Tzila tsked. Edith sat grim, stacking bowls.

"Tzila can help," Netanyahu went on. "You two will be friends."

"Of course," Edith said, "you'll excuse me." She took a tray with her into the kitchen and Netanyahu turned to the older boys, who were conspiring in murmurs: "And you boys will behave for your mother and Mrs. Blum and Devorah, when she comes."

"Devorah?" Tzila said.

"Deborah?"

"Judith," I said. "Judy," and I righted our upsidedown family photo.

"Yehudit," said Netanyahu.

"But she has school. I think you're going to miss her."

"Great. It seems we have a plan, then."

"If you say so." And as Netanyahu went about rummaging in his briefcase, I stood. "You'll excuse me too, for just a moment?"

I'd also heard what Edith had—the disconnect sound—Netanyahu had left the telephone off the hook and, as I came into the kitchen bearing the remains of our ruined house, she was hanging up the receiver. Stricken-faced, pale, she said, "*Ikh ken nisht*."

It was always bad when Edith turned to Yiddish, the language we spoke to each other like children, when we didn't want Judy, or gentiles, to understand us. But Yiddish wasn't going to be of much use to us here.

"Shush. You don't think these Yahus can understand Yiddish?"

"Who?"

"Our guests."

"Oh Christ, what was I thinking?"

"Edith, whisper, please."

"The Yahus, that's funny, that's rich ... Ruben, I wish we both spoke, I don't know, Swahili. We both should've studied Swahili." Yelling was coming from the den, yelling and thumps. "They're so horrible, so pushy."

"I bet you say that about all the Jews."

"Ruben, you're always so obliging. It's unattractive."

"Edith, I want to apologize. I want to say thank you. I'll make it up to you. I'm sorry."

"*Freier*," she said, or that's what I thought she said, Yiddish for pushover, or doormat, foot-wiping-surface, as she turned her chin and I kissed the air.

I came through the diningroom to find Iddo banging the piano and the older boys screwing with the TV, Benjamin twisting its dials, Jonathan yanking its antenna.

I'd had Tod Frew and his father Dr. Frew help me bring the unit down to the den on New Year's Day, at considerable cost to my spine.

"*In farbn*," Netanyahu said, which is Yiddish for "in color." He'd put on his shoes and was walking smutty prints over the rug and winking at me and nodding at the TV and saying, "*Sheyn*," which is Yiddish for "beautiful."

I don't think any of this was ironic, except the choice of language. The Yiddish itself was a dig at me, but the words were oddly admiring.

Iddo was bashing out some atonal accompaniment, cluster chords for a looming monster, or for the villain about to enter the frame— his father, who scooped him up from the piano bench and set him down on the floor, where he considered crying until struck by the light, and then he calmed and sat crosslegged like an Indian, hunkering close to the campfire, hypnotized by sparks.

No one reading this, in the third millennium of Christendom, can have any idea—none at all—of what it meant to a kid in 1960 encountering not just a TV but one in color. First off, in 1960, owning a TV wasn't anti-intellectual, or some surrender to the hivemind, but modern. Owning a color TV was more than that, it was fancy, it was elite, so much so that I was almost ashamed: it was a profligacy of Steinmetzian proportions.

I'm ashamed too to think of how entertained I was by the programming, whose lack of options, whose lack of range, is boggling by today's standards. Game shows and westerns, that was all, game shows and westerns, which were essentially the same to the American mind: zero-sum scenarios of winners and losers, mettle tested by luck.

"*Gunsmoke*."

But I guess I was wrong, because Benjamin, sitting lotused now too, said without tearing his snake-eyed gaze from the screen, "No, *Bonanza*."

Jonathan, sitting meditatively rapt himself, explained, "*Gunsmoke* is black & white, *Rawhide* is black & white. *The Cisco Kid* and *Bonanza* are color."

Edith held Netanyahu's coat out for him and he awkwardly armed into it: he was unaccustomed to the help. I booted up and put my own coat on.

Consider these stories: A band of across-the-border desperadoes threaten a ranch and a lone gunslinger is warily hired to dispatch them, paid a bounty with the last of a sweetheart prostitute's dusty nuggets...a tribe of savage Apache attack a wagon-train of honest Christian missionaries who must compromise with violence...I'm not saying these stories had an outsize influence on the future direction of the Netanyahu boys, so much as I'm saying they had an outsize influence on everyone, at the time. And anyway, when I put on my galoshes, blew a kiss to Edith she refused to lasso in, and left the hacienda amid the giddyups and crack of gunshots, the association I had was with the father himself, Ben-Zion, and frankly with visiting lecturers and guest professors of all kinds, those solitary marksmen who wander as strangers from town to town, itinerant in habit, itinerant in mind, burning with the need to live down their pasts and prove their strength to the cruel and hostile locals.

This was the story of the Yahu striding next to me, the Yahu striding ahead of me, even though he didn't know where he was going—an uncompassed loner in the snowy wastes, a solitary quick-draw artist in hood and beaver hat, thumbless mittens, unraveling scarf and floppy bluchers whose soles flapped loose like a horse's lips.

9.

THE CORBIN THEOLOGICAL SEMINARY (since renamed the Hussein-Gupta School of Divinity and Comparative Religion) was the first of the College's constituent institutions to be founded and it had churned out ministers in the Puritan/Congregationalist mold for well over a century. Its cluster of sere stone buildings was centered around the Chapel, where weekly attendance was still mandatory for students and faculty alike, though the students were expected to derive spiritual benefit, while the faculty was just required to take roll. Back in those days, each Department had to furnish its most junior member to discharge this duty on a regular rota and I was assigned the Monday/Friday crowds, the surnames W–Z. That year, Mondays began with the usually absent Mr. Wabash (the baseball star) and ended with the usually crapulous Mr. Zych (an agronomy major), and Fridays began with the unbearably chipper Mr. Washburn (who went on to run the Corbin Laundromat), and ended with the pimple-visaged Mr. Zoll (who went on to Vietnam). Given that W–Z was, alphabetically speaking, the lightest load, I'd typically finish with my list before the students had finished their prayers, though I couldn't leave my station pewside or do any schoolwork to pass the time—such were the rules dictated by the Rev. Dr. Huggles, who headed the Seminary and led the worship. Though I initially resented those rules, not to mention the worship itself, I gradually came to find Chapel Duty soothing. It was the only time I had to evacuate the mind. Or to ponder the paradox contained in the benediction: *Let us go forth to class and pursue the truth, in Jesus's name, Amen.*

We were bound for the Rectory behind the Chapel, for the Bible Studies class that Netanyahu had agreed—he'd had no choice—to teach. If Corbin would decide to offer him a job in the History Department, he'd also have to teach in the Seminary, at least one class per term. This would be his humiliation, which apparently he'd only been informed of the previous week? In a phone conversation with a Dr. Huggins?

"Huggles ... Dr. Huggles ..."

"It's absurd," Netanyahu said, as we turned off Evergreen, against the wind. "To have historians teach religion. Why not have priests teach history?"

"It's beyond our control. It has to do with the hiring budgets. We only get you in History if Huggles gets you in the Seminary, or someone gets you somewhere else. It's about getting more mileage. More bang for the buck. Dr. Morse doesn't like it either."

"But he does nothing to stop it?"

"I've been reading your work on the Medieval Jews who opposed the Church, and let me tell you, we here in Corbin History are in a similar predicament: we're at the Church's mercy. I don't even want to think about the fate that awaits us should we have the temerity to oppose the will of the all-powerful Corbin Theological Seminary."

Netanyahu paused at the snowmounded corner of Dexter and Wolcott, an intersection of conflicting winds. "You're making a joke, but now for a moment, be serious: You were angered by this man's presumption—Dr. Morse's—am I correct?"

"By which you mean what exactly?"

"You, an Americanist, were asked to take around a Jew, because you yourself are Jewish. That must have annoyed you. But can you imagine how you would feel if you were asked to guest-teach a class in Bible for the very same reason?"

"But maybe that's not the reason. Maybe you were asked to teach a class in Bible because of your Hebrew."

"You split hairs. Hebrew is the language of the Bible because it is the language of the Jews, whether or not they speak it."

I left that remark hanging in its chalkcloud of breath and led us on toward campus.

Netanyahu huffed behind me, then next to me, and then, as the campus gates swung into view, a step or two ahead, his words blowing back, "What is the Bible? Signs and wonders, pillars and plagues, and I'm qualified for this because why—because I'm a legitimate historian? And even if it were just a linguistic issue, where I'm supposed to impart to the youth delinquents and future sheep breeders of New York State the language of Solomon, Ezekiel, Jeremiah, and Moses—tell me, would you be qualified to teach a class on Shakespeare or Chaucer solely on the basis of your ability to order a hamburger or read the traffic-signs?"

"Stop . . . Dr. Netanyahu, stop . . . I'm not joking . . ."

But Netanyahu plunged ahead, scorning the sign and stepping high across the piled whitefall and crossing at a run, trying to beat the plow that was making its own lane down the middle. And it wasn't slowing, but bearing down—so that Netanyahu panicked, flung his briefcase, and launched himself atop the soiled matterhorn of the opposite curb.

I waited for the plow to pass and got sprayed mildly. Netanyahu, however, was covered.

I retrieved his briefcase and knocked it free of encrustation against the campus gates. "That driver was a lunatic," he said and snatched it back.

As we entered onto campus, I started babbling the tour, "So over there's the theater for tonight. And over here's the library, where Edith works, and that just past it, is Fredonia Hall, which houses all of History and the humanities."

But Netanyahu's mind was elsewhere. "On the way to teach religion, a famous historian is killed... who's to say that I don't deserve it?"

"You have to understand, Dr. Netanyahu. Corbin's a small college, so we all have to double up. At least the new hires will have to, and I'm sure that'll be the case for the rest soon enough. Take the committee members, for instance. We're all expecting to be asked to pitch in. Dr. Hillard, a historical geographer, is convinced he'll be teaching surveying. Dr. Kimmel and Dr. Galbraith are already preparing to teach elementary German and French. There's even been talk of me teaching double-entry bookkeeping."

"It's a scandal."

We passed on through the Quad; passing hurrying bundles of down and fur that at their overheated cores were students; passing a snowman whose proboscine carrot had become a phallus; passing a snowwoman with freakish breasts and twigs sticking out as nipples; passing the icicle-throned statue of Mather Corbin, industrialist and eugenicist, whose verdigrised and weather-pocked head showed a splotchy phrenology of pigeon droppings.

Netanyahu walked straight past all this impervious.

He stared down at his floppy-treaded bluchers and slapped along the paths, but then somehow missed a turn and walked directly into

Quad-snow and forged his own path through it, cutting corners. He was either scattered or trying to make his earlier frolic in the powder seem purposeful. He must've been freezing.

"I once read this thing about the kibbutzes in Israel."

"The kibbutzim, please. Not kibbutzes. I can't stand these English plurals."

"The kibbutzim, have it your way. I read a thing about how everyone there has their roles. In Minsk you were a violinist, in Pinsk you were a painter, in Lvov a poet, a streetsweeper, or an aeronautical engineer, it doesn't matter; on a kibbutz, you're a laborer. Everyone takes their turn in the fields, hoeing, tilling, whatever. You can't get out of that responsibility. You have to take your shift."

"That's Marxism for you. Shoveling the shit of—what are they called, the tiny horses?"

"Donkeys?"

"No."

"Mules?"

"No."

"Shoveling the shit of tiny horses, the ones that in the Bible talk ..." and he stopped and dug in a shoe, "not in the Bible, in Torah ..." he dug in between his shoe and sock, or between his sock and skin, and scooped out some hoary clumps.

"Dr. Netanyahu, when we get to a phone, maybe I'll call home and get you something better for your feet? Maybe Edith can run some other shoes over?"

But Netanyahu grunted and plodded on.

"I'm sorry I didn't think of this earlier. But please, I have an extra pair of galoshes. Or even just some rubbers. You must be freezing."

He stopped, heaved around, and spat Yiddish at me: "*Farvas?*"
Why? "*Vayl irre kalt, zol ikh tsiter?*" Just because you're cold, should
I shiver? "Our people have short legs and small feet and yet still we
can walk in the snow better than anyone. You think they have better
shoes on a Leftist kibbutz? On a kibbutz, they have only left foot
shoes and walk in circles. And in the Nazi camps, where there was
more snow than on Mount Hermon, what did they wear but rags?
And yet they made do. And some survived. By wrapping rags around
the toes that were missing. So just imagine that we're in a Nazi camp
in Poland...up there," he mittened at the steepled clocktower of
the Chapel, "is the machinegunner and searchlight and over there,"
he pointed his exposed thumb at the walls of the Seminary complex,
"it's all electrified wire and here," and he pointed wildly, but couldn't
find anywhere to point, so he just shrugged, "imagine that's our
situation and you'll feel better about my feet."

We'd stopped at the entrance to the Seminary complex, a snow-
patch as vapid and gray as the sky and he squinted up at the plain
personless cross that towered among the trees as if he were considering whether to climb it, if only to escape me.

"Dr. Netanyahu, I was just trying to do you a favor."

"A favor? It's embarrassing. It embarrasses me. Your fixation. This
is all you've talked about since you met me, my feet. I walk into your
house and it's like God to Moses, take off your shoes, for the ground
beneath you is holy."

"It's not holy, it's just a nice rug. But I do sometimes think of
Edith as God."

"You think we profane your house, but we are respectful visitors
and do what you say, and then you laugh at our socks."

"No one laughed at your socks." I noticed, over Netanyahu's

shoulder, a stumpy figure waddling out toward us in an Eskimo parka. "And anyway, I'm not talking about the desert. Or about my house. I'm talking about how cold it is."

"You don't think it gets cold in the desert?"

"The bush was burning. It was on fire and fire is warm."

"What ho, Dr. Blum?" Dr. Huggles huffed up to greet us, a small round man with a pigsnout face popping out from behind the cinch of small round bifocals. "What theological issue could be so pressing that you have to debate it outside?"

"Dr. Bart Huggles," I said, "meet Dr. Ben-Zion Netanyahu."

"A pleasure," and Netanyahu glared at me and thrust out a frayed-yarn hand. "How foolish of Dr. Blum and I to be having this conversation when a true Bible expert is among us—perhaps, Dr. Huggles, you can come to our aid?"

"I can try."

"I was quoting Dr. Blum some of my favorite passages in the original Hebrew and he asked me the source of one, chapter and verse, and I'm humiliated to admit I don't have the answer," and then he proceeded to pronounce in sly Yiddish a line I knew from the Bronx, "*Mayn fis zenen nas, aber er layd* . . . I think it's Exodus 3, is it not?"

Dr. Huggles approved vigorously, "I believe so, yes. Exodus 3."

"Or is it Exodus 4?"

Dr. Huggles blinked behind his bifocals, utterly lost.

Mayn fis zenen nas, aber er layd, meaning: My feet are wet, but he suffers . . . my feet are wet, but he's complaining . . . my feet are wet, but he's the one it bothers . . .

As Dr. Huggles conducted us inside his stoneclad domain, Netanyahu kept nattering in evil Yiddish: "This is the man who teaches

Bible *(Torah)*? This ox *(bulvan)* who thinks Yiddish is Hebrew and pretends to understand me?"

"*Genug,*" I said, enough.

"To expect to learn anything from a man like this is to expect to have an egg from a cow…hello, cow, lay one for me…"

"*Shvayg,*" I said, shut up.

"Rube, I'll shut up when you tell me: is this man a fool *(narr)* in a college of liars *(ligners)* or a liar in a college of fools?"

And though I was tempted to say, And which would you be, if you ever wound up working here?—instead, I just responded in English, "I'm no Hebrew scholar, unlike Dr. Huggles here, so if you wouldn't mind, let's stick to English."

"*Gewiss,*" OK.

"Out of courtesy to my own limitations."

Dr. Huggles smiled and clapped my back. As we entered the classroom, he clutched me, as if holding me back, begging me not to betray him.

There were no empty seats, so we stood, as Netanyahu went to the front. Dr. Huggles, still tugging at me, settled us up against the rear blackboard.

As the two-dozen souls of the Bible class swiveled their heads between us and their guest, I imagined the backs of our coats getting frosted with unerased gospel.

This was perhaps the most mixed class I'd yet been in at Corbin, with about half the attendance women, Sunday schoolmarms-in-training and a forbidding older nun seated ramrod up front in the immaculacy of her habit—the class's lone Catholic, perhaps a commuter from the convent in Dunkirk, and the only student who didn't turn around.

Netanyahu set his briefcase down on the teacher's desk and put his hat and mittens and scarf on the chair. He took off his coat and hung it on the classroom's flagpole, swaddling the stars and stripes in sodden shearling.

Dr. Huggles inclined his head toward me and muttered, "It's mortifying...to put in so much work to bring this great man to campus, only to find out I've been getting his name wrong. All this time, I've been saying it incorrectly. To myself, to the administration. Even to the students. Thank God you said it first, before I could make an ass of myself."

"I'm sure he's used to it," I said. "Mispronouncing."

Netanyahu raised a brow at me. Water from his coat pitpatted to the floor.

"Can you say it again for me?" Dr. Huggles said.

I said it.

He leaned closer. "And again?"

I said it again.

And even closer, "And once more, so I'll retain it?"

I obliged him, and Netanyahu heard.

He lifted his head and yelled, "Present!" and some chuckled.

"As Dr. Blum has so perspicaciously remarked, my name is Dr. Ben-Zion Netanyahu and I am a teacher of history, not of the Bible. But I understand that here at Corbin College, teaching Bible is part of an historian's job. I would like to think that this extra work is expected of me because I possess special skills, the way if you had a botanist on staff who could also pitch like Koufax or hit like Greenberg, you would ask him to coach the Corbin Crows. But the truth is, I possess no special skills in the Biblical; my exegeses tend toward the eisegetical; and in my tradition teaching the Bible means teaching young children and it's typically the work of the last unmarried son of a minor rabbi from the provinces. I try to tell myself that it is honorable work, though it is also grueling, wearying, and frankly unrewarding. Incidentally, this is what is usually told to people in order to convince them to do difficult important jobs that are poorly paid, like trash-collecting, or fighting wars: they say to them, but it is honorable."

He paused and the radiator, which had been clanging throughout, seethed steam.

"So I was thinking: how best to spend this sample class? If any of you besides the sister here were Catholic, we could have ourselves an old-fashioned theological disputation, at the end of which, the loser would be murdered. Though history teaches—again, history, my discipline—that no matter what arguments I'd advance, I'd be the loser and murdered and that would very much interfere with my evening's lecture, which will be engaging, I assure you, and the reception to follow should be ample ... Can you hear me back there, Dr. Blum?"

"Yes," I said, and then, swallowing phlegm, "loud and clear."

Netanyahu nodded. "Most if not all of you grew up so believing in the Bible's truth that you chose to study it in college, and yet the way it's usually studied in college—especially under historians like myself—almost always undermines that belief by challenging the Bible's veracity. And I don't think that's very fair. Do you, Sister?"

She stammered. "Professor? I'm afraid ... will you repeat the question?"

"I asked whether you think it's fair that by making a study of your faith, you lose it?"

"I don't know ... do you have to lose it? Does everyone?"

"Or are you just risking it? Or testing it? Answer her...you, the boy who looks like he does farmwork...the stable-boy with the braces, the suspenders, you...what do you think—is it inevitable that you end up eroding belief by subjecting it to scrutiny?"

"For some people, sir."

"But what about for you?"

"I believe the Bible is the word of God, sir."

"Why? How? Because God said so?"

"Because God said so."

"God told you?"

"Not me. God told someone."

"Yes. Excellent. God told someone. And that someone told someone who told someone else. So once it leaves God's mouth, there's a provenance. God told Moses who told Joshua who told the Elders who told the Prophets who told the Men of the Great Assembly, the Sanhedrin. This is the line of transmission. In other words, God's words were written down in the Torah, which you call the Bible, or the Scriptures, or the Old Testament, which precedes what you call the New Testament in the books you put in the bedside drawers of your inns. The Torah is interpreted in the Mishna. The Mishna is commented upon in the Gemara. The Mishna and the Gemara together make the Talmud. Are you with me? Do you understand what I'm telling you, which my father told me, which his father told him? There is an unbroken line of descent, when the word of God enters history."

He looked out the window, and the students craned their heads in that direction, seeking some manifestation in the burgeoning storm. "From this perspective," he continued, "history seems like something you can believe in, a belief that will not disappoint you.

There is no waiting for revelation, no waiting for a miracle. By contrast with religion, the discipline seems reliable. History makes no promises or covenants beyond telling how something from back there arrives at here. At us in the present. The front of the room, where the teacher is. But history, I have to tell you the bad news, is not always reliable. And Jews, whose life was the communication of God's words from generation to generation, and from faith to faith, knew this better than most. This was because they lived under foreign rulers. Their history in Christian lands was a Christian history; their history in Muslim lands was a Muslim history; written by non-Jews under the patronage of despots who insisted on being flattered, or at least who insisted on the centrality of their roles. It was the Jews who first understood the impossibility of a truth shared by all people. They were the first who understood that all that was possible was a truth shared by the dominant people, the group or subgroup or family in power. Universal truth, if it could exist, could only be found in the Bible, whose claim to divine provenance and authority demanded its accurate preservation. This realization resulted in a firm distinction being made in Jewish culture between preservation and interpretation, which is the psychic adumbration of the trauma that results from a fanaticism of accuracy. Once the Bible had been commended to other faiths, it's the interpretation that interested the Jews. Interpretation was, in many ways, their only freedom. This interpretative capacity allowed them to remain outside history and dwell in myth, which instructed about morals and ethics and structured the calendar and community life. The Jewish preference for the instructive and aesthetic story over the accurately documented history was a direct outgrowth of the circumstances of Diaspora, in which Jews were exiled and oppressed and denied the right of self-rule. In exile, where non-Jews made the history that Jews had to suffer, could the details matter? Why care about the facts, when you can't create them? What would be the point of recording the name and coordinates of every city that kicked you out and the exact specific date of your every misery and slaughter? When it came to chronicling Jewish life, what difference could there be between Rome and Greece and Babylon? Weren't they all just ultimately variations on Egyptian bondage, and all of their rulers essentially incarnations of the Pharaoh? Through this process of repeatedly relating the Bible to the present, history was negated; the more these stories were repeated—every weekly recurrence of the Sabbath, every annual recurrence of a holiday—the more the past was brought into the present, until the past and present were essentially collapsed and each next year was rendered identical to the last, with all occurrences made contemporary. This collapsing of time imparted a certain messianic quality both to the daily lives of individual Jews and to the collective spiritual life of the Jewish people. In other words, through interpretation these preservers of God's word were preserved themselves. Take, for instance, Zion, a historical kingdom that in its destruction was transmuted into myth, becoming in the Diaspora a story and poetic trope that reigned supreme in the Jewish imagination for millennia. The world is full of real events, real things, which have been lost in their destruction and are only remembered as having existed in written history. But Zion, because it was remembered not as written history but as interpretable story, was able to exist again in actuality, with the founding of the modern state of Israel. With the establishment of Israel, the poetic was returned to the practical. This is the first example ever in human civilization in which this happened—in which a story became real; it became a real country with a real army, real essential services, real treaties and real trade pacts, real supply chains and real sewage. Now that Israel exists, however, the days of the Bible tales are finished and the true history of my people can finally begin and if any Jewish Question still remains to be answered it's whether my people have the ability or appetite to tell the difference."

10.

THE INTERVIEW WAS HELD in the main reading room of Fredonia Hall, which students didn't read in so much as nap in and during Department meetings was closed even to that and blocked-off with a velvet rope. Unhooking it for Netanyahu and ushering him through, we entered into gloom, misted windows, a round table of my colleagues.

This was the first time the entire hiring committee had ever met, and I had the sense that I was interrupting something; the sense that my colleagues had already been here for a while, or perhaps had even held other meetings here without my knowledge, at which they'd discussed not Netanyahu's case, but my own. Evaluating my competencies. Rating my aptitudes as chaperone. Scoring my performance on a scale of acceptable to menial. Determining whether I was capable of bringing someone from one spot on campus to another vaguely on time and fetching caffeinated beverages, should Ms. Gringling be indisposed.

As the members of the committee rose unsteadily from their padded chairs to offer blandishments to the candidate, Dr. Morse gave me a sort of signal; a raised forefinger I took as a cue to raise the room temperature—no—a flutter of fingers I thought meant close the drapes—no—I couldn't decode it, if it was anything.

But once Netanyahu was seated and the upholstery squelched,

I realized it: there weren't enough chairs at the table; there wasn't one for me; so I went to drag over a reading-bench, grunting, straining, but it was bolted to the wall.

"Are you settled?" Dr. Morse asked and I was about to answer when he added, "I trust Dr. Blum has been taking care of you."

"Quite," Netanyahu said, suddenly a Britisher.

He sat chap-cheeked in his chair, with beaver hat in his lap and his peeled mittens balled up with his scarf inside like an odd tartan gourd.

He was still wearing his shearling, which just in the trek over from the Seminary had acquired a new pelt of snow, swiftly liquefying.

"Wonderful." Dr. Morse shuffled some index-cards out of their rubberband. "We're very glad to have this chance to get to know you better."

"Naturally."

Dr. Morse fanned the cards face-down on the table and dealt them to himself, one at a time, now pulling from the stacked edges of the deck, now pulling from the middle, and reading aloud: What do you see as the relationship between your teaching and research? Would you involve your students in your research? Why did you choose this field? How well do you take criticism? Do you hold more stock by essays or exams? What do you feel is the most important skill a History Professor should possess?

Dr. Morse asked these questions one after the other, like a gambler discarding, folding a hand, without pausing to let Netanyahu answer.

I'd been pretty proud of these questions when I'd put them together at Dr. Morse's request, but upon hearing them now being asked aloud and out of sequence, they struck me as a touch too light, or just overly inspired by Judy's game shows . . . and now, playing for the measly annual salary of $5,700 after taxes, give me three words your students would use to describe you? Angry, angry, angry . . .

I could've played this game with everyone at the table. Dr. Kimmel, the Germanist: dull, tedious, repetitive. Dr. Galbraith, the historian of France: repetitive, chubby, and short. In my own more-than-three-word-estimation, both were "Ivory League" failures turned ivy-smothered idlers; genteelly lazy, slumming Brahmins; Kimmel actually from Boston, I think, and Galbraith from some outer parish of New Orleans, crumbling and hateful. Kimmel's one publication was a study of a single letter from Luther to Melanchthon, which turned out to be a forgery. Galbraith wrote on the not-so-famous Napoleons, II and III, the son and cousin. Between them sat Dr. Hillard, who came from no such privilege: he was a hardscrabble up-from-the-fields type, the rangy, resentful son of localish farmers who'd clawed his way into academe as an expert in chronology, historical geography, and the history of Viking relations. He was a stale-suited string-tied bachelor, and a sour-breathed harbinger of the perils of meritocracy.

"My greatest weakness?" Netanyahu repeated, and his lips took on a superior curl. "Ask my wife and I know what she would answer: my greatest weakness is a tendency to overwork, which for her is a vexation, but for me is a joy."

Dr. Morse smiled as he shuffled the cards again and Dr. Hillard cut in: "About that work, Dr. Netanyahu, it's almost alarmingly diverse. So I was wondering, would you care to sum it up for us? Or at least define its major subject?"

"Certainly. Most would say I deal with the Jews of the so-called Middle Ages."

"But which Middle Ages? Early? Late? The period is vast."

"Between the fall of the last great Christianizing Empire that ruled the Jews and the Iberian Expulsions."

"So all of the Middle Ages?"

"Even the Middle Middle Ages."

"Only about a millennium, give or take."

"Roughly a millennium. Though if you want, I can pinpoint a tighter range. Say, the roughly eight hundred years that Muslims and Christians fought over the Iberian Peninsula, or the roughly three hundred years between the founding of the papal and regnal Inquisitions. Speaking frankly, the specific period doesn't matter to me as much as do the Jews, who for me are chiefly a vehicle for the study of how history is written."

"How?"

"The study of who writes it, why, and how."

"I know the Jews are the chosen people, Dr. Netanyahu, but why choose them for this? What makes them the best vehicle, as you say, for such an undertaking?"

"Because of all the peoples of the world, none is less historical, or less historically minded. Which is curious, given Judaism's antiquity. As Dr. Blum can surely confirm for you, it's a common enough quip among contemporary American Jews that Jewish parents would rather their children become pediatricians or litigators than, say, the messiah. But I would submit that even messianism, even false messianism, is more Jewish a discipline than history, whose allegiance to sublunary powers such as regents and facts was traditionally regarded by the rabbis as idolatry."

"You're against regents and facts?" said Dr. Kimmel.

"What about deans?" said Dr. Galbraith.

"I'm not against them," said Netanyahu. "I'm merely interested in the antagonisms."

"Between?" said Dr. Hillard.

"So many things."

"Such as? Could you give us one example?"

Netanyahu sighed. "Such as the antagonism between Aristotle, who believed the world would never end, and Plato, who along with Origen and Augustine and Aquinas, believed that, because the world was created, it could also be destroyed . . . and speaking of Augustine, the antagonism between his Six Ages and the Four Empires of Cellarius in the Catholic and Protestant periodizations of apocalypse . . . and saying that, I realize I'm not providing these examples in any order of my own, for which I'm going to have to beg your forgiveness . . . the antagonism between Jewish messianism, which was political, and Christian messianism, which was religious . . . the antagonism between human and divine governance in Abravanel's political philosophy . . . the antagonism between religious and racial identity both among the Christians regarding the Jews and among the Jews themselves, that's an important one . . . and what else? what am I forgetting?" and he grabbed the table's curving lip with both hands, "perhaps I should just conclude with the antagonism between the belief that history never repeats itself and the belief that it always repeats itself, in the very circular eternity of this table."

Dr. Morse smiled. "Apologies if you were going to cover all of that in your lecture."

Netanyahu didn't yield. "Dr. Morse, I assure you I'm not the type of scholar who merely cites the ideas of others and calls it a lecture. You have my word that all the material I'm going to deliver tonight is original."

"I don't doubt it."

"So let me ask you something else," Dr. Kimmel said, "not about your research so much as about the response it's gotten."

"Please."

"As you yourself have openly admitted in some of your papers, so much of your work dissents from the work of your colleagues, and you've explained this contrary stance not as a product of your personality but of your sources—Jewish sources, which most historians don't have access to, linguistically. Anyone so proficient in the internal materials of their own people should also be familiar with their people's reactions to how those materials are used—the reactions to the way they've been interpreted."

"My work is different because my sources are different, yes. But I'd attribute that difference less to my own abilities than to the ignorance of my colleagues. What you call a linguistic barrier, I'd call anti-Semitism."

"Fair enough," Dr. Galbraith put in. "But that's not what's being asked. What's being asked is simply how your work has been received by your own community?"

Netanyahu sputtered, "My own what?"

"We want to know whether other Jews feel as anti-historical or as a-historical as you do?"

Netanyahu wriggled in his coat. "I'm not sure how to answer. I'm not sure I can speak for the opinion of every Jew."

Dr. Morse tried to placate, "Maybe you can give us just the dominant opinion?"

That's when Netanyahu pulled his chair out and turned to me on the bench: "Maybe we should ask Dr. Blum. He might be more qualified for the dominant Jewish opinion."

Dr. Morse said, "How about it, Rube?"

"Two Jews, three opinions," I said from afar. "I don't speak for all Jews any more than Dr. Netanyahu does, or any more than he speaks for all Israelis, or you, Dr. Morse, speak for all Department Heads... not to mention all cartography buffs, gin enthusiasts, and pipe collectors..."

Dr. Morse grinned.

Netanyahu said, "An excellent answer, Dr. Blum. An excellent nonanswer, and so a very Jewish answer. I admire it. Among all people, there will always be those who live by their passions, and those who live by the facts. This is as true among the Jews as it is among Americans. But there's a further point... Dr. Kimmel, let me ask you, if you went about defaming Zwingli, what would be the response of the Swiss? Or you, Dr. Galbraith, if you slandered the aims of the Cochinchina campaign, would de Gaulle give you a call? And you, Dr. Morse, if you would ever dare to write a challenging reassessment of British policy in India, would they burn effigies of you in London, or in Madras? I don't mean any of this flippantly: I am in the same situation with regard to my own subject. The work we do, gentlemen, is so separate and removed from ordinary life as to approach the priestly. And if this is true in the calm and prosperous States, then it's certainly true in my home country, whose ordinary life has been too preoccupied lately with survival to take note of me, let alone to read my footnotes."

Dr. Morse was stretching the rubberband that'd cinched his cards. He said, "Survival must come first," and Drs. Kimmel and Galbraith nodded.

"And furthermore," Netanyahu went on, "this idea that Jews and history are somehow anathema to each other is perhaps one of the least radical of Jewish ideas, if we include in that category Christianity and Marxism. It's not even radical in a Christian context, where belief in such things as reincarnation is common. There are men who teach at this school even now—I met one today, just prior to coming here, when I taught his Bible Class—who believe in such things as the virgin birth...but I don't mean to cast any aspersions...I assure you that these beliefs are no more outlandish than those professed by some of my own teachers at Hebrew University, who believe they've identified the precise year of Creation and the precise locations of the Garden of Eden, Mt. Sinai, Mt. Horeb, Sodom, Gomorrah, and the river of fire that flows for six days and rests the seventh, the Sambatyon. I know archaeologists who've organized expeditions to dig up the mythical kingdom of the Khazars and who regularly petition the Israeli government to pressure the Vatican for the return of the Ark of the Covenant. I've had colleagues who claim to have found the Ten Lost Tribes among the Druze, the Samaritans, the Kurds, the Pashtuns, the Ethiopians, the Kashmiris, and the Lenape Indians, and colleagues who assert that the original Jews were the Africans brought over to the Americas as slaves and that the white people who today call themselves Jewish are involved in a conspiracy to deny those black people their true inheritance. I've worked with supposedly reputable academics who thought that only comets could explain the parting of the Red Sea; that Noah's flood could only have been caused by an earthquake, or by Jupiter or Saturn emanating electromagnetic radiation that changed the orbit and axial tilt of the earth. The European Jews weren't deported and exterminated; they were just kidnapped by aliens and flown back in time to Ancient Egypt, Mesopotamia, and Mesoamerica, where they were coerced into divulging the mysterious

179

techniques of pyramid-building: This was the thesis of a former classmate of mine, who later revised it and announced that the Jews themselves were the aliens. The history of every people is also a history of its craziness, and the more science becomes a religion, the more religion must pretend to be a science, desperate for all logical explanations. In this light, my thesis about a Jewish resistance to history couldn't be saner."

Dr. Morse leaned back, thrusting his gut. "Fascinating, thank you." I'd been watching him throughout and he'd been watching the snow, twisting out the windows. "So if there are no further questions . . . I think we can . . ."

"Just one more question, if I may," Dr. Hillard's voice glided loud and high. "I would say there's another reason for our curiosity about your work's reception, and it has nothing to do with our lack of access to the Jewish, or Israeli, position. No one here is afraid of being denounced from the pulpit—at least we're not afraid of being denounced by anyone save Dr. Huggles. But then he'll be the one to judge you on religious grounds, not us. Dogma is a concern for the Seminary, not the History Department."

"Agreed," said Dr. Morse, who was judging the dusk: cocktail hour.

"To be blunt," Dr. Hillard went on, "the reason I'm getting at is political. Because your belief that different peoples have such different relationships to history as to constitute entirely separate histories, instead of some unified common history that can be agreed upon through facts, frankly smacks of what's been called revisionism; one of the more pernicious of the new academic trends that back when I was a student, my teachers would never have tolerated. Nowadays, however, we're quite a lenient bunch, and it can only be distressing to an honest man to witness the ranks of his distinguished profession being infiltrated by Reds who seek to pervert what must be taken as history's purpose, which is the reinforcement of our government and political institutions. It's obvious by now how this perversion occurs; in a way, it's like a formal procedure: the Red professor seizes on some fine point of history and—under the pretense of scholarly stringency—attempts to refine it, and redefine it, until the heroes have become the tyrants and citizenship just victimhood. This type of scurrilous undermining is becoming the norm today in higher education, but not here at Corbin History, where we are dedicated to improving the proud Americans of the future." Dr. Hillard paused and lowered his voice to a confidential murmur. "I should like you to understand, Dr. Netanyahu, that I would never ask a man directly about his political affiliations. I am too much of a patriot in that regard, mindful of each man's private liberty of choice. That said, if you'd be amenable, I'd be quite interested in having your opinion on this subject of revisionism..."

Netanyahu approved with his chin. "I thank you, Dr. Hillard. And I'd like to show my thanks by candidly answering what you've been too polite to ask. I'm certainly no socialist or communist. If I were, I would still be back in my home country, where those politics are welcome. More than that, they're encouraged. My mere presence here, seeking work in the States, should be proof enough that I share your concerns."

"Though it could equally be proof of your being some type of subversive or infiltrator."

"Granted. And I've been called those before, and by stronger men than your McCarthy. I've been called a subversive, an infiltrator, an agitator, and certainly a revisionist, by everyone from British lords to lowly Bolsheviks, actually, which epithet I don't invoke in the American style as invective, but in the Russian style as an identifier: real Bolsheviks, veterans of the Winter Palace. It's a strange word, this *revisionism*. A useful, flexible, truly international term. In the revival of the Hebrew language, we've had to come up with a whole bunch of new vocabulary, but most of it we borrowed, we imported, monstrous modernizations like *auto* and *supermarket* and *revisionism*, none of which were mentioned in the Bible. There is no such thing as a telephone in the Bible, but there is in Israel, where the verb is *l'talphen*, and I *metalphen*, and my wife *metalphenet*, often. When I first heard the word *revisionism*, I thought it meant something akin to revising, like what you do after you write. You edit, you make changes. Of course, the true meaning of the word is nothing of the sort. The true meaning of the word is that it has no meaning. It merely takes on the meaning of all who employ it, each to his own agenda. This I came to learn in time. Originally, the Latinate *revisionismus* was anti-Marxist jargon, a philosophy that rejected the pursuit of socialism through world revolution and advocated, instead, for its gradual introduction through legislative reforms, state by state and sector by sector. It held that the bourgeoisie must recognize the materialist aspirations of the proletariat, who in turn must make not enemies but allies of the bourgeoisie, seeking compromise instead of slaughtering them. Trotsky revised Kautsky who revised Bernstein who revised Marx. And all of them were revised by Lenin. But with the emergence of the Soviet Union, *revisionism* was required to change. It now had to mean any deviation from communist, or, better, Soviet ideology. *Revisionism* became the charge leveled at any attempt to change the history that Lenin or, later, Stalin wanted. Today, in America, I suspect that *revisionism* means much the same, only within the context of another power structure: the insistence on writing history in such a way that unsettles what's called a ruling-class and interferes with the functioning of government and business. I admit I find this shift of meaning to be inspiring: a word that originally meant a tempering of radical doctrine for purposes of compromise went on to mean a dangerous threat to established order. But then, doesn't this always happen when you compromise? You lose, your cause is lost, and your weakness is held against you? In another sense, the versatility of the word *revisionism*, its applicability, really, to any political end, reminds me of the use and abuse of another word: *Jew*—another word that can be, and has been, hurled at anyone and anything. Revisionist and Jewish: both descriptors do so much, though ultimately they might describe nothing at all save the intolerance of the person who speaks them. Revisionist history, Jewish history... revisionist science, Jewish science... the words can be exchanged, they can be traded around, they are what the economists might call fungible currencies. In that sense, I think they are, like myself, essentially capitalist. In fact, just earlier today, I was at Dr. Blum's lovely home, admiring his new color television set... pretending that I was happy to let my children watch it, when the truth was that I was happy to be watching it too, and I would gladly have stayed behind to see the end of *Bonanza* because *Rawhide* was next and I'm always curious to find out how the great Rowdy Yates will manage to get out of trouble once again... but of course I had that class to teach and this interview here with you..."

11.

My sharpest memories of that Netanyahu-day are of being outside in the weather, whose bluster stirred up so much anxiety inside me—rushing cross-campus between buildings whose locations I wasn't quite sure of, buildings I knew by name but not sight or by sight but not name, anxious about being late, anxious about taking a tumble on the ice, and above all—after the interview—anxious that my temper wouldn't hold and I'd lose my patience entirely.

As we came off campus and headed through town in the gloaming, Netanyahu lagged behind and howled in the wind's language, Hebrew. I was getting the gist: he felt underestimated, condescended to, demeaned. He felt insulted, he who'd delivered the insults and had come seeking favor. All in all, a familiar scene, reminiscent of Judy coming offstage from a school play complaining that if her performance was bad it was only because the other actors had ruined it; they'd botched their cues; they'd declaimed over her lines, and I'd have as much chance of convincing her otherwise as I had of convincing wounded, heavy-shoed Netanyahu that he hadn't been ambushed. Both my daughter and Netanyahu were natural overactors whose best roles were in assigning the blame they deserved to others, and demanding to be applauded for it, and pitying themselves when they weren't.

"I'm sorry," I said, once he'd caught up with me waiting at the corner of College Drive, where the streetlights were on. "I missed what you were saying."

"You and the rest of the committee." He spat. "Morons, Imbeciles, Idiots. That's the classification I remember, the trinity of defective mental categories. Not Father, Son, Holy Ghost, but Morons, Imbeciles, Idiots."

"Drs. Galbraith, Kimmel, and Hillard? Or Drs. Hillard, Morse, and myself?"

"What do they know? Who are they to challenge me?"

"Colleagues. Prospective colleagues."

"Only an expert can judge an expert," and he swung his briefcase into the back of my knee, "only a Jew can judge a Jew."

"It wasn't that bad." I rubbed my leg and watched his spit sink into the frost.

"It was the Corbin Inquisition."

"And you survived it."

"Tell that to the other committee members. Tell that to my wife."

"I doubt that my opinion would hold much weight with either."

"Regardless, you have an opinion. You must have one. You'll have to tell them something. But what?"

"I don't know—I don't know why I should answer you. If you were in my shoes, what would you say?"

"If I were in your shoes... That's the smartest question you've asked all day..." and he looked at my shoes and then looked at his, sheathed in friable snow, "That's the smartest question he's asked all day."

"Talking to your feet now?"

"Because they listen."

"If they start talking back, we'll know you have hypothermia."

He stomped to free his toe from a snowclod and then dragged on, taking slow heavy steps that ground the sidewalk's salt.

"The History Department must decide upon a Jew and so enlists another Jew for help. Their own Jew. A Jew who is known to them. A Jew they at least partially trust."

I matched his stride. "That's me."

"This is a venerable historical office. You don't realize this, but it is. Usually inherited, a patrimony. *El judío de corte*, *der Hofjude*, the Court Jew. The protected Jew. The useful Jew to keep in your pocket, as a consultant on your taxes. Sometimes an intermediary, sometimes an intercessor. Always balancing competing interests. The Elder of the Judenrat who when the Gestapo says, we need to kill one thousand Jews, he's the one who picks which one thousand. The *shtadlan* who when the emperor summons him and says, we need more money for our treasury, he tries to bargain down the price while averting a massacre. A tenuous duty, susceptible to all corruptions. Powerful, but never the most powerful, and only partially trusted by both sides, belonging entirely to neither."

"As Edith and Judy are constantly reminding me. You aren't describing academia so much as what it's like to be the father in a family of women."

"I'm speaking of something ancestral. It doesn't matter whether it's the Politburo of the Central Committee or your committee here, you doubt you're an equal member. This is your insecurity. You have the sense that something's expected of you. Something more. Because otherwise, your seat is only a reward for having been forced to take me around."

"Asked. Requested. More polite than forced."

"And so if history is augury, the committee will reach its decision either by disproportionately discounting or relying on your counsel."

"One or the other?"

"One or the other, and you can't control which. They'll be equally suspicious of your vote, pro or con."

"But still you want to know which it is—pro or con?"

"No. I'm merely saying what I'd do in your position."

"Which is?"

"Nothing."

"That's it? Nothing?"

"Just be their ornament. Like the snowflake that hangs from their holiday tree."

He'd stopped again, outside the hammering and screwing elves in the window of Maclee's Hardware. "I'd only ask one favor."

Here it comes, I thought, here's where he compromises me. "Only one?"

"It's not much of a favor. I want you to find out when I get my honorarium."

"What?"

"I want to know when and how I'll be paid my honorarium for this evening's lecture," and then he was off again, trudging, and I was at his side.

"This isn't exactly something I'm in charge of."

"So I won't get paid tonight?"

"This isn't your bar mitzvah—they don't hand you an envelope of cash. The payment has to be processed. A check comes in the mail."

"And you're sure of this?"

"Are you broke? What are you worried about? You could lecture tonight in praise of Castro and against private property, the imperialist accumulation of capital, and the very concept of money itself, and still they'd pay you. There's nothing personal about it. No grudge, no animus. It's automated. It's in the system."

"And what if it isn't? What if it doesn't come?"

"You signed something, didn't you? You gave your information? If you did, the money will come."

"But if by some chance it doesn't, I can call you and you'll make sure they pay me?"

"You're exasperating."

"Do I have your word?"

I turned us off College Drive to cut through the lot of the A&P, slipped atop the crystalled asphalt and would've lost my footing, but he caught me. His arm was around my waist and then his threadbare mitten was shaking my glove. "Thanks." I slid a bit, but he held me steady with his handshake. "You'll note that I haven't asked for special treatment. I'm not asking and I don't want any. I understand your pressures. Perhaps you don't know it, but I'm educated in politics. I know what to expect of a Jew, who when dealing with another Jew in the context of goyim can only act in the greatest solidarity or the greatest betrayal."

"Those are the choices?"

"And though I'll never know which you'll choose, I want you to know I'll still respect you."

"Thank you, I guess."

A car was trying to turn into the lot and we were blocking the way and there was honking. "You can let me go now." But he wouldn't release me. "I'll be fine." But he kept me grappled and brought his chapped face near to mine.

"And if the situation were reversed and your feet were in my shoes and you came to Israel, I'm not positive I could get you a job, but I'd do absolutely everything to find you a good apartment, and in a war, I'd die for you."

About half a block from the Corbindale Inn, we ran into a pep squad ziggurat in the middle of the street: many underclad cheerleaders trying to stand atop one another and going sprawling in the drifting hyemal. A petite duffeled woman was walking away from them porting a camera mounted on a tripod; she was walking backward, toward us, stopping now and then to gauge whether she could get all of them and the Inn within her frame. She spiked her tripod into the snow and exhorted everyone to smile, but then a crouching boy at the bottom collapsed and the girls above him toppled, and—after Netanyahu strode into the shot and didn't shrink from the jeering—I followed, through a gauntlet of the drunk and jolly.

Alums, fathers and sons, crowded the sidewalk, flush with the revelry of their reunions. In foxfur coats and coonskin caps, they thronged the Inn's stairs and wraparound porch, welcoming us, or hazing us, or just waving their pennants on dowels.

Inside—I had to let my glasses defog, before I was able to make out anything: a lobby still in its full Christmas glory, ruddy couples bric-a-bracked in mismatched and shabby Victoriana, quaffing from tankards of grog.

One couple played checkers with chess pieces motley and missing and another snuggled together in a book-nook paging through volumes on etiquette and sexual hygiene, pointing out passages and laughing.

Netanyahu joined the line at reception, while I hovered by the fire—let him find out for himself what rooms his wife and children had checked into.

The line was slow because only one woman was behind the desk and everybody, apparently, had a problem and was lightly intoxicated.

The history of the Inn, which was noted on not a few state and federal registries, was also accounted for on some calligraphed vellum above the mantel, as well as on the back of the restaurant menus, and, in abbreviated form, on the matchbooks handed out at the bar, and I reminded myself to bring that up. I thought it might make for a neutral topic of conversation: Washington counted sheep here, that kind of thing.

Mounted above the vellum was a tattered crow leaking stuffing—ostensibly a taxidermized iteration of the school's mascot, though I think it was a raven.

It was frozen in the screech of complaint, a scarlet beanie askew on its head.

But the voice I heard was Netanyahu's—his gutturals unmistakable; his head twitching, searching me out. I had the instinct to hide myself inside a dangling stocking, but he caught me with his stare and I came over. The intermediary. The intercessor.

"This lady," he said, "can't find the reservation."

"Netanyahu?" I said, fidgeting him aside and spelling it out for her.

"Oh, now I understand," she said. "You must be Edith's husband, the professor… And you," she said to Netanyahu, "you must be the other professor…" and she turned again to me, "I didn't understand the name when he said it. I understood the name when you said it, but not when he said it. It's been a busy day."

"Not a problem."

"So everything's in order and there's no need to worry, Professor Blum, you won't be billed."

"I won't be billed? What do you mean?"

"The school won't. But I'm guessing you need to give them some confirmation?"

"Of what?"

"That the reservation's been canceled."

"What do you mean canceled?" Netanyahu said. "By whom?"

"Not by me. Or I?"

"This is an absurdity."

The woman was older, gray of perm and sniffly, with a palsied mouth. I said, "You're from the library?"

"Mrs. Marl," she said.

"Yes. Mrs. Marl from the library. Edith speaks of you often."

"Edith speaks of me often, but she didn't tell you that she canceled the reservation?"

"She didn't."

"Or not her, but that mean foreign lady."

"I don't know what happened. But we'll just have to make a new reservation."

"I'm afraid you can't, Professor Blum. We've already given the game away because of the room … I mean, we've already given the room away…"

"Because of the game?"

"Don't you follow the athletic program? We're playing Iota. Or Iota's playing us."

"I see."

"Iota's our major rival? My nephew's the halfback? Clymer?"

"I see."

"Davis Clymer?"

"Certainly."

"Football?"

The line behind us grumbled, sour with booze. A tabby was shedding up against my leg and then dashed away when a pug leashed behind us barked.

"I tried to help her out," Mrs. Marl said. "Edith and that mean foreign lady with the accent," and she glared at Netanyahu. "But as I was trying to tell Edith, I just don't have anything available: no doubles, no adjoining rooms, no other rooms anywhere; and now I don't even have that single twin from the original reservation."

"Because of the football game we're playing against Iota."

"We're full up. We just don't have a thing."

"No room at the inn."

"None at all...but you'd better talk to your wife, Professor Blum—she's over in the taproom, I think, sitting with that mean foreign lady with the accent."

Netanyahu was already bounding across the lobby, knocking into gridiron fans, and I slunk after him, passing through the swinging doors into the muggy uproar of the taproom, which was centered around a four-sided brass-railed bar of burnished cherry.

Edith and Tzila were seated opposite the entrance, dressed up, and with drinks in front of them. Netanyahu was trying to get them to move; he was trying to horn in between them, but the bar was swarmed and they couldn't scoot far.

Noticing me, Edith got up and surrendered her stool and came around the bar and hauled me into the bathroom vestibule. She leaned with her drink against the cigarette machine, leaned and listed, avoiding my embrace.

"What happened, Edith?"

"These people, Rube, they're unbearable. You wouldn't believe it."

"What I don't believe is that you're drinking. You're tipsy."

"Just a little, Rube. I need it."

I went for her glass, but she wouldn't relinquish it; she just tilted it to my lips and let me taste. A martini with an olive at bottom like a sightless eye.

"What happened to the room, Edith? You canceled it?"

Burly lettermen lumbered past us toward the bathrooms. I pressed myself into Edith to let them by and she elbowed me off.

"When I called to sort out the arrangements for an additional room, Mrs. Marl said they were fully booked, so I asked her to hold the line and told Tzila, who grabbed the phone out of my hand and tried to bully the poor woman and when that didn't work, Tzila yelled that she didn't want to stay at such a fleabag dump any-way… and told Mrs. Marl to shove the reservation; actually, she told Mrs. Marl to shove the reservation up her *tush*, or what she really said was *tukhes*, and hung up and told me they were staying by us."

"What?"

"Such presumption. Not even asking me, telling me. She had it all figured out. She walked all over the house dictating terms. She and her husband will be staying downstairs, she said, and the kids will be taking the floor of your study. It was all decided," she slammed her drink down atop the cigarette machine, "just like that."

"Just like that."

"And I'm angry... or I'm drinking to not be too angry. She's sort of an amazing woman in her way. That bitch strength she has. Maybe I'm jealous. But if being strong like that means being a bitch, count me out."

"I'm sorry."

Edith sipped her martini. "You're sorry? Did you hear what I said? I said she and her husband will be staying downstairs and the kids will be taking the floor of your study and what did you say? You said you're sorry? What you didn't say is where are the kids right now? Because you never think about things like that, Ruben. Things like that just drop out of your head."

"Where are the kids right now?"

"The Yahus? They're at home with Judy. Tzila decided that Judy was going to babysit them."

"You're serious?"

"I'm as serious as a door to the face. I tried inventing all kinds of excuses, that Judy had some sort of rehearsal or club. I tried thinking of ways I could get in touch with Judy at school and warn her not to come home, but Tzila wouldn't leave me alone, and the kids were screaming in front of the TV they're watching so loud, so I don't have the chance, and the moment Judy comes home, the woman pounces on her."

"How did she react?"

"Judy? Overwhelmed. She was overwhelmed because Tzila starts in right away with the flattery; starts in right away telling her how beautiful she is, how smart she is, and Judy's just standing there by the door with her muff still on and doesn't know what hit her. This strange Israeli woman's laying it on thick, saying she hardly ever gets the chance to hear her husband lecture, never in English, and I don't think Judy has any idea what husband she means or remembers anything we'd told her about us having guests and suddenly to save herself she's agreeing to spend her evening taking care of the three wild nutty Yahus."

"Maybe it'll be good for her, the responsibility."

"Except she calls them the Three Stooges. They were crawling all over her, feral. Groucho, Chico, and what's his name?"

"Manny, Moe, and Jack. What are they paying her? It's good she earns some money. What did she get from the Dulleses, a buck an hour?"

"You think they're paying her? Are you out of your mind? These people don't give, they take."

A greasered guy swathed in a whole buffalo of leather swayed over to the payphone and crammed in a coin.

"But that's barely the half of it," Edith went on, "because the moment Tzila decides she's coming, she also decides she has nothing to wear, so she's dragging me upstairs and going through my closet, trying on my jewelry."

"I thought I recognized the earrings."

"It's the necklace that's mine, Ruben . . . and the dress: she's popping out of it, but she keeps insisting it's her size."

The guy held the phone to one ear, stuck a finger in the other. "I'll take the Crows over the total to make $40, give me the spread on Syracuse at $25, and let's do Penn State to make $50 straight . . . you bet your precious berries I'm good for it . . ."

Edith was sputtering, "And meanwhile, now that she's wearing my clothes, she puts her own clothes in the laundry and before I know it, I've got the board out and I'm doing her ironing...and I couldn't resist, I couldn't say no...what's wrong with me that I can't say no...I just let myself get led on and started drinking..."

The guy was making a jerkoff gesture.

"Let's go back in."

Edith laughed. "You think that guy's your student."

"Keep your voice down."

She didn't. "You think that guy's your student, but he's not. You think everyone's your student. A man who's only taught somewhere a year but who's so scared of not recognizing his students that he compensates by recognizing everybody. And it's all because you're so eager to please. All because you're too accommodating. And it rubs off on me."

"Someone should make a case study. You should tell your mother."

She jammed her glass into my chest. "Get me another while I fix my face, will you? I look like I've been crying."

"Another martini, really?"

"I'll be out in a jiff." The guy was bludgeoning the phone against the phonebox to hang it up and Edith squeezed her way to the toilets.

The bar was even busier and I had to shout my order over some heads, pass cash up, and grovel for change. By the time I had a pair of martinis, Edith was back with the Netanyahus, standing. Her stool hadn't been returned to her.

Netanyahu raised his glass, "To our true bosses," meaning, I guess, to our wives. "And I also want to toast you, Rube, for having had the wisdom to marry a true woman of valor who so embodies all the virtues of hospitality."

"And also to your daughter," Tzila said, "who is a gorgeous one but also with a brain and so sweet to take our kids from us for the night so we can be together with new friends, who I know so much will help my husband to get the job here..."

Netanyahu, wincing, precipitously clinked Tzila's glass into splashing wine onto Edith's dress—the dress of Edith's that Tzila was wearing.

"I'm sorry," she said, "I'm so sorry for him."

"For me?" Netanyahu said. "It's you who's clumsy."

Tzila quibbled with her husband in Hebrew while Edith dabbed her dress, smutted now with the local plonk.

I wondered whether she'd managed to get the blackface out of the Hide-A-Bed.

"When I drink I'm losing all my English," Tzila said, "and my husband, he never tells me..." and she turned to me, with napkins plastered to her bust: "so you, Rube—you'll tell me how was the interview and class? What do you think are the chances?"

"Do you mean our chances against Iota," said Dr. Huggles, coming up from behind, "or the chances the games is delayed, or canceled due to weather?"

"Does everything here get canceled?" Netanyahu said.

Dr. Huggles cheersed with his beer but made no contact. "Your lecture won't be. Blessedly and to our profit."

Dr. Kimmel and Galbraith joined us unwived, along with the congenitally unaccompanied Dr. Hillard. "For humanists rush in where athletes fear to tread," he said. "Is that not true, my theological colleagues, Dr. Huggles, Dr. Netanyahu—that the pursuit of wisdom knows no inclemency?"

"And I know nothing about football," said Netanyahu, "and only slightly more about theology."

"You're being modest," said Dr. Huggles, and Dr. Hillard said, "but not regarding football, whose field appears to be the only field that stumps you."

"It's perhaps the most violent game that's also the most strategic," said Dr. Kimmel, "or perhaps the most strategic that's also the most violent."

"Many have compared it to battle," said Dr. Galbraith.

"I doubt that," said Netanyahu, "unless what's meant is one of the old gentlemanly battles whose time and place and even weapons were negotiated in advance and when the combatants met to annihilate each other, the opposing generals sat together over supper on the bluff."

"And what do you think they talked about?" asked Dr. Morse, just arriving with Mrs. Morse, who was asking Edith to feel how cold her hands were.

"Football," Dr. Hillard said, "that's what they talked about. I suppose the generals looked down at the battle and said, 'This reminds us of our football days' and talked nostalgically about their youths before the forward pass was legalized, before helmets."

"Or soccer," Dr. Huggles said, "what about soccer?"

"Which only non-Americans call football."

"American football we call football, or *futbol*," Netanyahu said, "but we have a different word for what you call soccer."

"Which is?"

"*Kaduregel*."

"Meaning?"

"*Kadur*, ball. *Regel*, foot. So 'football.'"

"Just so I understand this: American football is called *futbol* in Hebrew because Hebrew football is called something else."

"The literal meaning of which is football," said Dr. Hillard, and turned to Netanyahu, "but do you know what we call the ball itself? We call it 'the pigskin.' But 'the pigskin' isn't made from pig. The exterior has always been cowhide. The reason for the nickname is that back in the age of the platoon, when one line was both offense and defense, the cowhide was filled with a pig bladder, which could be inflated like a reputation."

Tzila, peeling the soaked napkins off her bust, asked, "You'll excuse me because I know nothing of this, but in football... in their football..."

"That's Tzila," Edith said, pointing her out to Mrs. Morse.

"In your American football, you can throw also... but when do you kick?"

"The kicker kicks and the quarterback throws," said Dr. Kimmel, "and there are two types of kicks, field goals and punts."

"And a down is a play," said Dr. Galbraith, "and you have four plays to score or gain ten yards."

"Do you like her dress?" Edith asked.

"I don't know," said Mrs. Morse. "Do you?"

"Ten yards," said Dr. Huggles. "What is that in your metric? How many yards in a meter... or meters in a yard?"

"I used to like it," Edith said. "It's mine."

"And here I was," said Dr. Morse, "thinking I was in for an erudite evening's discussion of Cavalry or the future of the Suez. But no."

"Dr. Morse," said Dr. Huggles, "don't think I'm stopping you from discussing Cavalry."

"You can talk about that with my wife," said Dr. Morse. "I need to speak with Rube," and he walked me toward the kitchen and trapped me up against a shelf laden with steins and flagons and stemmy clay pipes and handed me a folded paper.

"My introduction to this evening's lecture," he said. "Humbly submitted for your review."

"Now?"

"Unfortunately, Ms. Gringling isn't available for retyping. She has her quilting tonight, so please be legible."

Neither of us had a pen, so he went requisitioning, and while he was gone, I read Netanyahu's cover letter. Or a version of it. And I should say I reread it. The cover letter he'd sent with his resume, his application. Dr. Morse, in putting together his introduction, had done little more than turn Netanyahu's first person to his third, re-pronouning through dictation; so that not only did "I am considered a foremost authority on" become "He is considered a foremost authority on," but also "I believe my perseverance to be among my most important" became "he believes his perseverance to be among his most important."

What could I check? Wasn't all of it in error?

Dr. Morse came bearing a pen, a surprisingly attractive bauble. "Dr. Hillard's," he said. "Only a bachelor can afford such pretensions."

Edith was ordering again at the bar; Dr. Huggles was gathering his woolens.

"When you finish up, Rube, we'll repair to the Treaty Room for supper."

After spotting a pentimento "myself," and with the excellent pen recensing it to "himself," I went to save Edith from another round.

But she'd already ordered another round for all the women.

"Not martinis," she said. "Martinas. They're martinis for women. They're the same as martinis for men, but they're for women."

"And also for Dr. Morse," said Mrs. Morse. "At least I hope he can have some of mine. He always drinks whatever I can't finish."

In the Treaty Room, we stood around the table waiting for a placesetting to be added for Tzila, who'd made her husband take off his shoes and socks and put them by the woodburning stove. Plates, cutlery, glasses: I was looking down at his bare white feet, his white pruned toes.

Netanyahu had been directed to sit at the head and Tzila was seated to his right, on the more crowded side of the table; I was seated to his left and Edith was next to me and across from her was Dr. Hillard. It'd been a bit of a jostle to get out of the standard staggered-gender arrangements that were then in fashion, whereby couples at dinner parties were always split up. I'm certain that some of my colleagues had wanted Edith down by them, but they hadn't brought their wives and I'd held firm, worried about her drinking.

Dinner was served and the smell of bread mingled with the smell of feet. A bread basket of white hot wafting feet. Between stabs at her salad, between failed attempts at stabbing a fleeing pea, Edith put her lips to my ear: "It's strange," she said. But when prodded to say what was, she didn't clarify. She just said it again, when the mutton came, leaning toward me, leaning against me until almost falling into my lap: "It's strange."

"What?" I moved away her martini.

"Don't touch that . . . don't treat me like a baby . . . I'm just trying to say it's strange that I can be so embarrassed by people with whom

I feel no connection, in front of some other people with whom I feel no connection either."

"I'm sorry, who's embarrassing you in front of whom?"

She retrieved her martini and sipped. "It's strange. I don't feel connected to anything or anyone. Usually, in order to be embarrassed you have to feel some type of connection."

Netanyahu wasn't eating much, if at all, and kept rolling his napkin into a cone and unrolling it again. The napkin resembled a snow-shaggy spruce out the window; it resembled a pointy capirote, a Klansman's dunce-cap.

"After the lecture," Dr. Morse was explaining, "there'll be a session of question and answer. But if people are too shy to ask a question, Dr. Blum will break the ice. He'll ask one to start us off." Dr. Morse turned to me, "You'll ask one, Rube? You'll start us off?" and then to Netanyahu, "So if there's any question you want asked, just say so."

"I appreciate the opportunity," Netanyahu said, as he pulled on his damp steaming socks and wormed his toe through its hole.

Dr. Morse, out of tact, checked his watch. "We should get a move on," he said, and went to help his wife with her stole.

"So?" I said. "Any questions?"

Netanyahu was pulling on a blucher. "Ask me if Corbin will hire me—that's the question—ask me and I'll give you an answer."

"What are you, a prophet?"

"You tell me."

I bundled Edith into her coat, hoping to send her home to get some sleep or keep Judy and the boys amused, but wobbly Tzila took her by the waist and commandeered her for a crutch.

We came out into the evening and headed back to campus, a stumbling herd steering toward the lights and against the wind, which mixed the bone-colored snows until none could tell what was still falling from the sky and what had already fallen and was now being blown up from the streets and whirled ghostly around us.

12.

ASSUMING THE LECTERN after Dr. Morse's introduction and waiting for him to resettle his bulk at front-row-center, Netanyahu expressed a hint of regret; reminding all of us—Corbin professors and Seminarians and Corbindale Rotarians and Shriners and their wives and students who might've been mine and some dazed Korean exchange students who weren't, shifting in our squeaking seats in the overheated theater—that this was a lecture open to the public and so its contents would have to remain fairly generalist, even popular.

"Tonight I'm going to speak about my subject in a way that all in my audience can hopefully relate to," he said, in a statement that should've been promising, but from his mouth was more like an apology twinged with contempt.

He explained that his field, or one of his fields, was the Jews of Medieval Iberia, which, he admitted, might not strike a hall of gentiles in present-day America as pertinent. That said, his objective this evening was to dispel that notion, and to do so in an entertaining fashion. And then he smiled, and the effort was evident. Ingratiation was a strain on him.

For the purposes of this lecture, he said, he was going to bookend Jewish Iberia between two depredations—one by the crescent, and one by the cross. The first occurred in the 1140s, when a fundamentalist Muslim Berber dynasty called the Almohades defeated another dynasty called the Almoravides for control of al-Andalus, or Moorish-ruled Iberia, and attempted to forcibly convert its Jews, who refused and fled to other domains in Europe as well to the Maghreb. The second occurred centuries later, when the Jews who'd returned to Iberia over the course of the Reconquista were expelled by the Catholic monarchies—expelled from Spain in 1492, coinciding almost exactly with the date Columbus left on his first expedition, and expelled from Portugal in 1496, the year Columbus returned from his second.

That, at least, was the traditional history, which Netanyahu acknowledged might not be entirely accurate by the standards of those who suffered it. Because unlike the Jews of nearly every other expulsion of the Medieval period—unlike the Jews expelled five times from France (by Philip II in 1182, Louis IX in 1250, Philip IV in 1306, Charles IV in 1322, and Charles VI in 1394); unlike the Jews expelled from Bavaria in 1276, from Naples in 1288, from England in 1290, from Hungary in 1360, and from Austria in 1421—the Jews expelled from Iberia toward the end of the fifteenth century might not have been Jews at all, or might not have regarded themselves as Jews, or as anything but Christians.

This was because they'd converted—or their ancestors had. The descendants of Jewish families that had resisted forcible conversion to Islam in the twelfth century, and that had returned to Iberia with the Reconquista a century later, started converting to Christianity of their own free will, with tens of thousands if not a hundred thousand and more Jews Christianizing over the next two centuries. This was the first and only mass Jewish conversion movement in world history and, most importantly, it was not compelled, but voluntary.

The reasons for it were manifold, ranging from a desire to take advantage of the new social and material advancement on offer to converts under Christian rule, to an apocalyptic attitude inculcated in Jewry by the constant centuries of Muslim-Christian warring, which manifested itself at the precise point at which the tide appeared to turn in Christendom's favor (after the Battle of Las Navas de Tolosa, 1212, which left the Muslims with no Andalusian holdings save Granada). Mass societal conversions such as these depend as much on the strength of the newly assumed identity as on the weakness of the identity it's replacing, he said, and Judaism throughout Crusader-era Europe was already considerably weakened by anti-Semitic legislation, oppressive taxation, and the mayhem of pogroms. For these reasons, and for myriad more, he argued, Jews in Iberia flocked toward the Church, converting—especially at the turn of the fifteenth century—at astonishing rates that bespoke a messianic fervor, with some considering their conversions vital not just to the re-Christianization of Iberia, but to the salvation of the Jews, or of the world. This much is clear, regardless of stated motivation, or justification: these converts were sincere and their conversions were intended as multi-generational, permanent and lasting. These Jews lived as Christians and tithed to the Church and produced Christian children who were baptized in the Church and knew no other identity. They made confession and took communion and believed that Christ, the son of God, was their redeemer.

This, Netanyahu said, was historical fact. It was inarguable. But it begged a Jewish Question that for ages went unanswered, even unasked: If so many Jews became Christians willingly, what need was there for an Inquisition? Or, to put it another way, what was the point of convening a body dedicated to promoting the Christian faith, if the Christian faith was doing just fine promoting itself without it?

This was the problem that Netanyahu set out to solve, and it involved, he said, cutting through all manner of deliberate obscurity and drivel, not least from the Inquisition itself: texts that claimed that the conversos (as they were called) were only Christians of expedience and still practiced Judaism in secret; texts that claimed that the conversos' conversions were invalid, because they'd been bribed to convert, or forced to at swordpoint . . . none of which made much sense. Why was the Inquisition attacking the very people it was supposed to be supporting? The very people it was supposed to be creating? Why go through the expense? Why go through the trouble? The Inquisition was bent on punishing the very converts the Church was always evangelizing for, and it was this paradox—an almost Jewish paradox, Netanyahu said—that caused him to reconsider the institution's nature.

His conclusion, he said, which he could only partly summarize now, lay in the origins of the institution itself. Put bluntly, the Iberian Inquisitions—the Spanish and later the Portuguese Inquisitions—which had been charged with rooting out heresy, were heretical themselves. They claimed, by their name and by their charters, the mantle of the Medieval Inquisitions of the Catholic Church, but while those bodies answered to the Pope, the Iberian Inquisitions answered to monarchs. This was a crucial distinction: it meant that the Iberian Inquisitions were not religious but political institutions, founded to mitigate the tensions between the monarchy and the nobility—between the heads of kingdoms and the rulers of provinces and cities. When Isabella I of Castile and Ferdinand II of Aragon sought to join their kingdoms and unify Spain in the image of their own union of 1469, their chief opposition was nobiliary, the princes, grandees, and hidalgos who resisted having to cede their local authority. What resulted was a struggle in which the monarchy attempted to systematically impoverish and disempower the nobility, but because a direct attack on the nobility was inadvisable and tantamount to civil war, the monarchy decided that the best approach would be a sort of proxy: They'd get at the nobles by oppressing the Jews, who managed the nobles' estates and farmed their taxes. Having decided upon this method, they realized that full subdual of the nobility could only be accomplished by oppressing the Jewish converts to Christianity too, because while so many had changed their religion, they'd retained their familial professions and ties in the realm of international finance. At the same time, the monarchy sought to arouse the intrinsic anti-Semitism of the commoners and parlay it into anti-converso sentiments as well, instigating libels and riots that disrupted civic order and depleted the resources of any nobility that sought to quell them.

Depriving the nobility of the services of the Jews was easy: the Jews could always just be slaughtered. But depriving the nobility of the services of the conversos was a different matter, because the conversos were, officially, Christians, and any attempt to disenfranchise them and invalidate their conversions would have threatened the integrity of the Church. The Spanish Inquisition was founded to provide a way out of this bind, and a justification for converso-oppression. It did so through offering the monarchy a simple redefinition: Judaism had always been defined, and defined itself, primarily as a religion—as a set of tenets, and a set of practices—but the genius of the Spanish Inquisition was to insist it was a race, with the implication that even a convert to Christianity, even a fervent new Christian, was still a Jew at heart, because Judaism inhered in the blood. Once these new Christians were racialized back into a Jewish identity, they could once again be oppressed: they could be exorbitantly taxed; they could have their property and assets seized; and, with the nobility rendered too impotent to protect them, they could be expelled from the country entirely.

That was Netanyahu's thesis, in reckless synopsis: that Iberian Jewry was perennially caught between a native host populace that rarely changed and an absentee host rulership that changed constantly with conquests. Whenever tensions arose between these bodies politic, they were taken out on the nobility-enabling Jews, whose oppression restored civic balance. The main requirement of this process was merely that the Jews stayed Jewish, which was why when they began to convert—willingly, for the first time in their history—they were punished and admonished that they could never be other than what they originally were.

This restatement marked a pivot in his lecture, to a different mode in which the academic prose fell away and I could make out the wrath of the veteran propagandist, the touring public-relationist touting his own delusions as definitive.

As his voice changed—got louder, looser—Seminarians and Koreans shifted in their seats; Edith reached for my copy of the evening's program ("Presenting B.Z. Metayahu") and started tearing it into strips as if in mourning.

Tzila lolled her head and appeared to drowse.

The revolutionary influence of this redefinition must be insisted upon—Netanyahu insisted, launching himself into this new mode with a podium-slap. The Spanish Inquisition, he claimed, introduced the idea that a person could not essentially change or be

changed, but was in fact defined and determined by corporeal factors, by how many degrees tainted they were from that prelapsarian
or just pre-miscegenated state the Spanish called *limpieza de sangre*:
blood purity. In promulgating this idea, the Spanish Inquisition
became the first institution in world history to treat Judaism primarily as a race, as a sanguinary quantum and heritable trait that
could not be lost or abrogated; setting the precedent for subsequent
genocidal and quasi-genocidal regimes so numerous and notorious,
he said, that I don't have to name them. And then he named them:
Nazi Germany, the Soviet Union, and the Arab Ummah, the latter-
most of which had expelled nearly all of its Jewish population in
only the last decade, sending refugees coursing from Morocco, Tuni-
sia, Algeria, Libya, and Egypt into Israel.

Thinking about this turn of rhetoric now, I find it poignant,
though at the time it struck me as strident. And I knew, somehow
I knew, that this new pitch he was making in this new firebrand style
was the one he'd perfected in countless "addresses" and "orations"
and "public chats" in heartland synagogues and chapels and schools
on Jabotinsky's tent-revival circuit—that the only way out of gentile
history was through Zion.

He banged the dais full-fisted, leaned over it, and with all the
gross abstraction of fanaticism spoke of Poland, where he was born
and grew up during the first of the century's two great European
wars, at a time of fracturing empires. The decline of Austro-Hungary
caused, or was caused by, or both—in his frenzy, he seemed to say
both—provincialism, parochialism, and a rise in desire for nation-
state autonomies. This was always the case with marginal identities
in the context of empire: identity on the racial or ethnic or religious
or merely linguistic level is what you revert to after the transnational

project fails; only after you can no longer conceive of yourself as a citizen of Austro-Hungary, and as having been dignified and elevated by that citizenship, can you begin conceiving of yourself as, say, a Pole, a Czechoslovak, a Romanian, a Bulgarian, or a Zionist Jew. Now, after the second of the century's wars, with the new European empire being Asiatic-Soviet, the same thing would eventually occur, sooner than anyone thought: socialism, communism, would fragment back into its tribal constituencies. This was also why an Arab League would never survive, because no people were more clannish than the Arabs, whose basal loyalties weren't even sectarian but familial. It was the function of empires to furnish a common identity to disparate peoples and whenever they couldn't, they failed. This would even be true with America, where everyone if they're asked who they are answers Irish, or Italian, or preposterously three-quarters Scottish, half-Belgian-Dutch, and at most one-drop Mexican black, anything but American. If the American empire couldn't persuade allegiance to democracy over origin, it would fail. He said that while staring at me, unblinking: It would fail. He might even have been pointing at me: You will. What was true for Europe at the emergence of Zionism will one day be true for America too, once assimilation is revealed as a fraud, or once it's revealed that the country contains nothing to assimilate to—no core, no connate heart—not just for the Jews, but for everyone. This, at least, was his implication, the text behind the text of his lecture, which he continued to speak to me with his hooded steppe eyes even after his prepared remarks were finished and he was making his acknowledgments and bowing to the light, deferential, and relieved applause: This is what I think of America—nothing. This is what I think of American Jews—nothing. Your democracy, your inclusivity, your exceptionalism—nothing. Your chances for survival—none at all. You, Ruben Blum, are out of history; you're over and finished; in only a generation or two the memory of who your people were will be dead, and America won't give your unrecognizable descendants anything real with which to replace the sense of peoplehood it took from them; the boredom of your wife—who's tearing her program up into little white paper pills she'd like to swallow like Percodan—isn't merely boredom with you or her work or with the insufficiency of options for educated women in this country; it's more like a sense of having not lived fully in a consequential time; and the craziness of your daughter isn't just the craziness of an adolescent abducted from the city to the country and put under too much pressure to achieve and succeed; it's more like a raging resentment that nothing she can find to do in her life holds any meaning for her and every challenge that's been thrust at her—from what college to choose to what career to have—is small, compared to the challenges that my boys, for example—whom she's been condemned to babysit—will one day have to deal with, such as how to make a new people in a new land forge a living history. Your life here is rich in possessions but poor in spirit, petty and forgettable, with your frigidaires and color TVs, in front of which you can munch your instant supper, laugh at a joke, and choke, realizing that you have traded your birthright away for a bowl of plastic lentils . . .

. . . or at least for another glass of blood-red plonk, which Dr. Morse invited everyone to partake of, once the applause had faded . . .

Thankfully, there was no mention of a Q&A session. The lecture had gone on long enough. People were milling up out of their chairs and making their way out of the theater and into the reception area, digging into slices of jambon and manchego and gummy paella with hard white rice—as close at it came to tapas in 1960s Corbindale, a spread co-sponsored by History, the Seminary, and the Hispaniola Society.

The cheese was a large solitary block that everybody put their hands on. The ham sat on a carving slab next to a big sharp knife with an antler handle. The wine wasn't Iberian but that same sugar-fortified Niagaran vintage the Netanyahus had been drinking for a while now, pour-yourself out of fiasco-basketed jugs.

I felt false. My suit, my tie, my pipe, my skin all felt a costume.

Netanyahu, glorioled in sweat, stood with Tzila behind a wall of compliments, Seminarians, and Dr. Huggles. Tzila had a wineglass in each hand. Netanyahu caught my eye and winked.

"I said I'm tired," Edith said. "Are you even listening?"

"I'm listening. I'm tired too."

"I want to go home."

"Let's. I guess our guests will find their way back on their own."

"I wouldn't count it a tragedy if they didn't."

"I just don't want you walking alone."

"I don't care about walking, Ruben. I care about having to fold-out the couch on my own...You could at least help with that..."

She looked exhausted. She'd gotten drunk and almost sober again, sitting through a lecture. She'd made small-talk and now was done. She'd done her spousal duty. The rest was just tucking in sheets. "I'll get our coats," she said, but on the way to the coatroom was buttonholed by Mrs. Morse, who was curious about paella.

So I went and found Dr. Hillard going through my pockets. "Did you lose something?"

"Just what you took from me." He reached into an inner pocket and extracted his excellent pen.

"I must've just put it there from habit."

He handed me my coat. "An interesting habit."

I took Edith's coat off its hanger and took my hat down from the shelf and, for the promotion of levity, held it out to him. "Want to check inside here too?"

He peered down into the dandruff and said, "Even when you're wearing it, it's empty."

Dr. Morse came in to get his own bundles, and his wife's. "Dr. Hillard, have you heard—we have even more to thank Rube for than we were aware of?"

He gathered up the Netanyahus' shearlings—"the Blums are putting up Dr. Netanyahu and his family"—and heaped them atop Dr. Hillard. "That's a mark of true dedication, Rube, stepping in where the Corbindale Inn so sorely let us down."

"You have Edith to thank, believe me."

"I do believe you."

Dr. Hillard walked out muttering under sheepskin.

"We're very grateful, and I think the least we can do to demonstrate our gratitude is to provide an escort home . . . a lot of football brutes abroad this evening . . ."

So that's how we set off: as an audience, exiting together through the connecting corridor into the tenebrous halls of Theater Arts; Edith's brisker clip already putting distance between us as we headed for the coldening.

Sometimes the halls of the college can feel endless, like you'll never get out, and sometimes, because so many of the halls look the same, you can feel like you're lost and often you'll come out of an accustomed exit and suddenly not recognize the world. It'll take you a moment to get your bearings. Especially in a blizzard.

I crooked my arm into Edith's and tried to support her, tried to slow her, as she rushed us ahead through the snow, booting holes into the whiteness.

Quiet reigned over the Quad. A Gothic quiet. The stone buildings were distant hills. I leaned over to my wife's cold ear and asked, "So what did you think of the lecture?"—the obligatory post-lecture, on-the-way-home-from-the-reception question that usually wrung a laugh or at least a smirk from her, but now: she shrugged my arm off.

Approaching Mather Corbin, sneaking up on our old enthroned founder from behind, I tried again to instill some cheer by pointing at my wife and saying, "Bow down before the idol, woman. Humble thyself before thy God."

But Edith was having none of it. "Stop it, Ruben."

"So you choose death for your whoredoms, woman?"

"It's not funny. I choose you cut it out."

"I'm sorry."

"I choose you let me be. I'm thinking."

I did, I let her be. Edith with her moods, with her winter coat and stockings. She adjusted her muff and picked at the dry skin around her nostrils. Under the gas-jetted lanterns, my wife was a winter coat and stockings and a weak chin that doubled when she focused on her feet, her spraddled gait like she was always wearing snowshoes.

Hastening off campus, the silence I'd been holding was dispersed by the winds, bringing the partying squalls and caws of bawdy Crows.

"I know it's already been decreed," I said, "that the adults will take downstairs and we'll fix the kids up in my study... but maybe we can put the kids down on the couch and let the adults have our room, so we can take my study together?"

"You're incorrigible, Ruben."

"It might be fun. Me and you and Judy's sleepingbag?"

We stood on a snowblasted corner, Edith looking behind us to the lanterned glow of the campus gates, where colleague-revenants were waving; taking leave of Dr. Hillard, who was heading back to his bachelor's cell.

"Remember when we were young, Ruben?"

"I do."

"When we were young, we took everything so seriously. Everything we read. Every exhibition and concert and book. All those poems. We were serious people and believed in things. In ideas. So sincere. And the way we talked: 'ethical aesthetics' and 'the moral passions of the culture'... The way we talked about politics: 'the freedom from fear,' 'the freedom from want,' and how it was honorable to serve your country, and how even being skeptical of your country could be a way of serving it... We were so earnest and principled but so intense, about democracy and love and death, as if we knew what those things were..."

"I remember. We were good little Jews."

"What's wrong with you? Who said anything about Jews? I'm sick and tired of hearing about Jews. I'm talking about the two of us."

"Sorry."

"What I'm trying to say, Ruben, is that meeting this horrible man and his horrible wife, it made me realize something. It made me realize I don't believe in anything anymore and not just that, but

I don't care. I have no beliefs and I'm OK with it; I'm more than OK, I'm glad ... I'm glad I'm getting older without convictions ..."

"What's Judy always saying, and her friends? 'It's copacetic'?"

"It's copacetic."

She retook my arm and we walked on, a pair of sweethearts in the snow. Our block was totally socked in. Hedgerows of snow. The pearly humps of cars.

We shuffled up the steps to our door, where the snow was soft and powdery and, even at the topmost step, under the overhang, calf-high.

I think of it as a blessing: may you never lock your door ... may you never have to lock your door ... I opened the door and—resisting the impulse to sweep her up like a bride—held it open for Edith. She stepped inside. She crunched onto the mat and bent down to untie her laces but stopped and turned and clung to me. I looked over her shoulder, through the lens fog, and saw our new television cabinet tipped over face-first, its screen shattered, and the youngest Netanyahu boy curled fetal atop a mound of gingerbread house scraps and glass.

He must've tugged the TV down atop himself like Samson with the columns. He must be dead, I thought, because Samsons don't get injured. But then he chewed some candied roof and shifted his position and the glass beneath him tinkled.

"He's asleep," Edith said.

I think she'd also forgotten his name.

She went to put on the lights and I, sensing some stirring upstairs, ascended, and halfway up noticed the middle boy, Benjamin, just past the stairhead, crouched like an Indian scout atop the carpet runner in the hall; his fat face lit in the lucent sliver coming through the slightly-ajar new door to Judy's room. As the downstairs lights flicked on, he turned and saw me and froze. He was a fat trapped baby deer frozen in the house-lights, looking down at me and then looking up at the cracked-open door and then looking down at me again and hollering—I think he hollered, "Yoni!" but like it had the meaning of "Geronimo!" and charged me; he knocked me into the landing wall and, pinballing against the banister, stumble-fell past me and off the landing and all the way downstairs. I recovered just in time to see the eldest boy, Jonathan, dashing stark raving naked out of my daughter's room, his headstrong rigid penis toggling with his stride between pointing rudely out to spear me and sticking straight up at the ceiling from within its dense coiled nest of jet-black hair. Too stunned to grab him—actually, unsure of exactly how, or where, to grab him—I flattened myself against the wall again, and as he bounded past me on the landing, the smell of heat and sex on him was unmistakable. Judy was at the door to her room, shrieking, hiding her nakedness behind the door. Edith was coming up the stairs now and pushing me aside and yelling at Judy, who in yelling back stepped out from behind her door and showed herself all breasts and bush and now Rockette legs afling, as she prepared to defend herself and her bumpless nose from her mother, who hurled herself atop her. I hurried up to pull Edith off, but got a wet boot-heel in the eye and slid down some stairs and struck my scalp and the name of the youngest boy came back to me, as Kiddo—Iddo was crying downstairs. I looked down but couldn't find him. I went down and looked around, threw open the closet, checked under the tray-table, checked by the piano and easel and shelves, and, spooked by a draft on my neck and a close-by cry, I spun around and saw him stepping charred from the hearth and sucking his thumb and tearing, his feet cut up and bloodied by screen shards, his toes coruscant with rainbow sprinkles. Behind him, a trail of glass, pulverized sweets, and bloody partial prints led out the open door and from there became troughs in the snow. I followed the trail outside, where it forked into zigzags and crisscrosses of my and Edith's making; into switchbacked paths like a wounded man had lurched onto the Dulleses' property, where I intercepted Dr. Morse and the Netanyahus. I looked past them down Evergreen; I looked across the street. I tried to avoid their eyes and had just managed to say, "You haven't seen your boys, have you?" when Edith came hurtling along the sidewalk like a sacking linebacker and slid directly into Tzila, tackling her into a snowbed, and the two of them rolled around rumpling the cold blanket of the Dulleses' lawn; Edith screaming—I don't think I'd ever heard her scream in public before, and I'm sure I'd never heard her curse—"Deviants! perverts! mad sex criminals! your sons belong in the fucking zoo for rapist animals!" I struggled to tug her off, tugging her by her ankles, as Dr. Morse and Netanyahu stood by stunned. "Go find your boys," I yelled, as I kept circling the thrashing tangle of women, trying to pry mine loose, "they ran away somewhere." Lights flicked on in the Dulleses' house and I said to Dr. Morse, "If you wouldn't mind, could you go up there and ask the Dulleses to call the police and say two boys are running around in this and one of them's naked?"

"He's naked?"

"Only one of them."

Dr. Morse hustled his bulk up to the Dulleses' door, and Edith was all-foursed atop Tzila with her hair hanging down like a veil, pinning her, panting, and the woman at bottom was laughing and hiccupping and babbling hysterically in Hebrew.

"What the fuck's so funny?" Edith gasped. "What the fuck's this loony bitch saying?"

Netanyahu, composed, dignified, said, "That loony bitch who is my wife is saying that you're a Puritan. And that it's she who should be angry with you because if anything sexual happened between any of our boys and your daughter, it's your daughter who's at fault, because she's older."

"Stop laughing. You're drunk."

"But she's not angry with you, not angry at all," Netanyahu went on translating his wife's babble, pausing to check a phrase and then scowling and continuing, "in fact she's happy that at least someone in this family is having sexual relations."

Tzila howled and Edith grabbed a fistful of snow and stuffed it down into her face and stood up and slipped and staggered up again homeward.

As Netanyahu helped his wife to her feet, I told myself: don't apologize; only a coward would apologize. "It's only the older two boys. They ran off. Iddo is still at the house."

Tzila spat snow. "And you're sure he's safe there with your daughter who seduces?"

Dr. Morse stepped out from the Dulleses', saying the police needed the boys' full names and ages and better descriptions than naked and known-associate-of naked.

I walked back to my property and into the garage for a shovel to dig out the car—I started digging out their car, because I wanted them mobile; I wanted them gone.

But they insisted I drive them, so I got behind the wheel of Rabbi Dr. Edelman's archaeological Ford and tooled up and down the hobbled streets.

It was hard to see with the single functioning headlight. The beam was weak and wavering and the snow was hissing down like static from a world signed-off, ash from the end of broadcast days.

"And in this weather you tell me they're naked?" Tzila yelled, from the backseat, where they sat together being chauffeured by me.

"Just Jonathan."

She cried, "Yoni!" but Netanyahu said, "What does it matter? If he would've said Bibi, you would've made the same noise too."

"And why you don't give them a chance to dress, I don't know—before you put them out? Yoni hates to be cold and what is Bibi wearing—his pajamas?" She thumped my seatback. "They'll die! Because of you, they'll die!" And then she tried to reach up and hit me with the shovel she'd brought with her into the car, but Netanyahu wrested it away from her and sat it back between them, like their substitute mute child.

I hunched down and squinted through the half-moons of visibility cleared by the car's one wiper, making out black stretches punctured only by the weakling twinkle of the few houses that still had Christmas tapers. Most of the houses were dark, with at most a lone bulb glowering up in bedroom territory. A tangle of tinsel was blown through the air and into a full black holly shrub where it glittered like my daughter's bush, and there, above the steering wheel, the Stop sign was a breast, scraped red and horripilated.

I stopped and oncoming headlights shone at me like a film projector, showing me Bibi, rolypoly in his footed pjs, grinding himself into the replacement carpet, as Yoni performed for him beyond the door-crack, grunting and thrusting and spurting ribbons...

The car shining into my windshield was blaring something Latin, something mambo, and honking in rhythm. I ducked down and nudged out into the intersection and braked, suddenly—so as to avoid running down the students who were crossing the street, and one of the varsity boys banged the hood with a bottle and another tossed a can at the side and some cheerleaders shook their pom-poms at me like radioactively overgrown snowflakes.

I wondered whether if I tailed them, we'd find the boys pledging at one of the tumbledown Greek houses, standing on their heads, guzzling from kegs.

Tzila hiccupped. Netanyahu held his silence.

A police cruiser pulled up and I lowered the window.

"You the folks out looking for the kids?" the officer yelled. "I was just on my way to this other mess but..." and he put up a hand and radioed in, "so I've got the foreign folks here in that beater Ford and I'll bring them down to check out the report from the Mews, but I'll be goddamned if Psi Upsi isn't throwing some kind of panty-raid rodeo with the Iota Alpha Phis..." and his radio garbled, and he radioed back, "got it, copy," and then said to me, "they'll take the naked frat boys, we'll take the naked kids... just stay on my icy ass, if that chicken coop can make it," and he cocked his head for me to follow and I fell in behind him and cranked and cranked but my window wouldn't be raised.

Snow flowed through and cooled my lap as we rounded the athletic fields and the cruiser's siren cast a seedy red over the whiteness. The goalposts looked like broken billboards. They looked like they'd once held screens. The tarp over the field was only visible by the flares marking its corners. The bleachers led up to the sky.

We came around toward the carceral Mews, the new prefabricated apartment-blocks where the school's support staff lived in a serried drab fortification overlooking the bus depot and derelict railroad tracks that protected the campus from the trailerparks and shanties of the poorest townies. The officer leading pulled in between blocks and continued through a miniature version of the inmost Bronx, transported here and only barely suburbanized: a narrow lane at the limits of the plowing, strewn with snowshrouded trash. We got out and walked, the officer leading, the Netanyahus and I trudging, as two more police cruisers came in behind us and from the windows above, black faces looked down in fright; the sirens—the soundless sirens, and more eerie for being soundless—sweeping by and blushing their fright, sweeping a blush across the blank flanks of their buildings. The two rear police cruisers were parked at angles, inclined toward each other and shining crossing cones of light down the lane at a battered dumpster dug into a gigantic glacier stuck with a forest of dismantled Christmas trees, and huddled up against the metal wall was a shivering fat boy in pjs and his shivering sticklimbed older brother cupping prayerful hands over the cold stump of his penis.

The last I saw of the Netanyahus, Tzila was wrapping her shearling around Jonathan's waist for an oversize loincloth and balking at her husband's attempts to wrap her in his, and the two of them bickering about it and arguing with the cops and Benjamin wandering over to admire the firetruck, which had just arrived.

I walked back through the Bronxian lane, got my shovel out of the Ford and, wielding it handle-down, used it as a staff to get me through the traffic-jam: an ambulance and a campus security van and a car from the office of the county sheriff.

The front passenger window was open and a dozing, thumbsucking Iddo was being passed through it, into the arms of an ambulance worker who held the kid far out in front and bore him forward to his parents like a soiled package.

I looked through the window and saw Dr. Morse, who gestured me in to ride in the back, like a beast in a moving cage, warm and rank. "What a night!" I said.

Dr. Morse grunted.

The Sheriff—whose face I never got a full sense of, besides a blonde moustache so long it was visible in wisps from behind—drove smoothly and commanded silence.

I tried to keep my shovel from bumping around.

The Sheriff slowed at College Drive and Dr. Morse got out. "Thank you for everything, Sheriff," and then to me, "Until tomorrow, Rube. It's been eventful."

Then he was gone and the Sheriff drove on.

"I can walk from Hamilton."

"I'm driving you home."

"That's not necessary."

"I know it's not necessary. But I wasn't asking you, I was telling you. I'm driving you home. I want everyone off the streets in this weather, even it means I have to be a taxi service for the evening."

"That's kind of you, officer."

"Sheriff."

"Sheriff... it's a turn up here..."

"I know where you live, Professor Blum."

I sat back, clutching my shovel atop the middle seat's hump, and looked through the backseat's bars: the snowpeople buried in their own element out in the yards, the lightless houses where my neighbors slumbered.

The Sheriff took the turn onto Evergreen and stopped in front of my house.

"Thank you."

"Thank yourself. Thank all the taxpayers."

I tried, but I couldn't get out. I just wanted to exchange this stuffy gaol for the one across the lawn, my home sure to be full of shrieking, my bruisenosed bareskinned daughter. But the cruiser's backdoors didn't even have handles.

"What a goddamned night," the Sheriff said. "Those fucking people. Excuse me, Professor Blum. But those fucking people."

Then he sighed and got himself out of the car and freed me and I clambered out to the sidewalk with my shepherd's crook shovel.

"Thank you, Sheriff, and I agree with you about those people. The parents of those boys. They're Turkish, you know," and I headed up the path.

But my front-door was locked and I didn't have the key, so I knocked, and as I waited for Edith to let me in, I kept waving the shovel back at the Sheriff and mumbling, "Turks...what did you expect?...just a bunch of crazy Turks..."

Credits & Extra Credit

FOUR YEARS AFTER the evening just recounted, the remains of Ze'ev Jabotinsky were disinterred from a cemetery on Long Island and flown to Israel, where they were reinterred adjacent to the grave of Theodor Herzl, atop Mount Herzl, in Jerusalem. The pomp and circumstance of the ceremony disguised with honor what was essentially a slight, a posthumous wounding—Ben-Gurion and the Israeli establishment having finally recognized that the only thing more damaging to Jabotinsky's dignity and legacy than the British having denied the man a burial in the land he yearned for was the modern state granting him a reburial in a tomb next to his rival's, atop his rival's hill.

In that same year, 1964, Jonathan (Yonatan) Netanyahu, age 18, returned to Israel and joined the Israel Defense Forces as a paratrooper. He fought with distinction in the Six-Day and Yom Kippur Wars, and earned a command position with the elite anti-terrorist commando unit known as the General Staff Reconnaissance Unit (in Hebrew, *Sayeret Matkal*), in which all three Netanyahu brothers would eventually serve. On June 27, 1976, Air France Flight 139 departed Tel Aviv for Paris with a stopover in Athens, where among the additional passengers it took on were two members of the Revolutionary Front for the Liberation of Palestine, and two members of the East German Revolutionary Cells. Soon after the flight left

Athens, these four terrorists hijacked the plane, rerouted it to Benghazi, Libya, for refueling, and then departed for Entebbe, Uganda, the country that, ironically enough, the British had first suggested for a Jewish national homeland, back when it was still called British East Africa. At Entebbe Airport, the plane's 241 hostages were crowded into the main passenger lounge of the old terminal. There, the Jews were separated from the non-Jews; the latter were allowed to return to France, while the former were held with the flight-crew for ransom. The terrorists offered to release them in exchange for five million US dollars and the release of 53 Palestinian and pro-Palestinian militants who were then being held in Israeli jails, and in the prisons of West Germany, Kenya, Switzerland, and France, a cohort that included affiliates of the Red Army Faction, AKA the Baader-Meinhof Group, and Kōzō Okamoto, the Japanese citizen who under the banner of the Palestine Liberation Organization killed 23 people at Israel's Lod Airport in 1972. If these demands weren't met, the terrorists warned, the hostages would be murdered. Meanwhile, as the Israeli government considered its response, the terrorists at Entebbe were reinforced by Ugandan army soldiers, on the orders of Ugandan president Idi Amin. On July 4, 1976, as America celebrated its bicentennial, Israeli special forces teams raided the Entebbe Airport, took the terrorists and Ugandans by surprise, and succeeded in freeing the hostages, sustaining a single casualty—Jonathan Netanyahu, "Yoni," a handsome curly-headed 30-year-old who, through numerous books and made-for-TV movies, became a national martyr-hero and an international symbol of Israeli military daring, crucial to the establishment of his brothers' careers and his family's political mythology.

After decades of shuttling between Israel and the States, for army service (*Sayeret Matkal*), school (MIT and Harvard), work in the private sector (Boston Consulting Group), and a stint as Israeli Ambassador to the United Nations (1984–1988), Benjamin (Binyamin) Netanyahu announced a more permanent return to the country of his birth and declared his aspirations to higher office, joining the Likud Party. At the time, his politics seemed solely predicated on opposing then Prime Minister Yitzhak Rabin for what he perceived as Rabin's desire to make territorial concessions to the Palestinians by evacuating Jewish settlers from the West Bank, under the framework of the Oslo Accords (1993–1995). He gave speeches accusing Rabin's government of being "remote from the Jewish tradition [...] and Jewish values" at rallies that featured effigies of Rabin dressed in Nazi uniform, and one that staged a mock funeral procession for Rabin replete with a coffin carried by kaddish-spouting pallbearers. Though he was alerted by Israeli security officials of credible threats to Rabin's life, Netanyahu refused to reprimand his supporters. On November 4, 1995, Rabin was assassinated by Yigal Amir, a religious Jew who'd attended Netanyahu's rallies and who cited rabbinical dispensation for the murder: he was, he claimed, taking one Jewish life only in order to save many Jewish lives, a murder that, to his mind, was not merely religiously sanctioned but required. In 1996, amid a spate of Palestinian terror attacks and mounting uncertainty surrounding the fate of the settlements under Rabin's successor, Shimon Peres, the Likud Party won a majority and Netanyahu became prime minister, the youngest ever to serve his country, and the first to have been born within its borders. After suffering setbacks through the Barak, Sharon, and Olmert governments, a decade-long stretch marked by the carnage of the Second Intifada, Netanyahu returned to the premiership in 2009, and was re-elected in 2013 and 2015, and in 2019—after his indictment for crimes including bribery and fraud, and in the midst of a series of inconclusive elections that failed to result in a parliamentary majority and left Netanyahu in power as acting prime-minister—he became the longest-serving head of state in Israel's history. *Bibi, Melech Yisroel*, his supporters call him, "Bibi, King of Israel." His reign, marked by the building of walls, the construction of settlements, and the normalization of occupation and state violence against the Palestinians, represents the ultimate triumph of the formerly disgraced Revisionist vision promulgated by his father.

Ben-Zion Netanyahu—who after a spate of adjunct positions at schools throughout the States became a professor of Medieval History at Cornell University—took a leave from Cornell after Jonathan's death and returned with Tzila to Jerusalem. He spent the next two decades laboring on his 1,384-page magnum opus, *The Origins of the Inquisition in Fifteenth Century Spain*, which he wrote in English, dedicated to the memory of his firstborn son, and published in the States in 1995. It remains an acclaimed, though controversial, text. Tzila died in 2000 at the age of 88, but Ben-Zion lived to enjoy the regime of his secondborn son, who through intensive propaganda efforts inflated his father's reputation to that of the father of American-Israeli relations—"the man who introduced the idea of the Jewish vote into the American political scene," according to one prominent historian of American Jewry, in an utterly baseless characterization that was repeated nearly verbatim by not a few obituaries and even by members of the US Congress following Ben-Zion's death in 2012 at the age of 102.

After completing his education and military service, Iddo Netanyahu—the runtling thirdborn, the Jew of the family—settled in Hornell, New York, a quaint former mill-and-railroad town at the western edge of Steuben County, where he established a radiology practice while writing numerous works of family history, or hagiography, which were invaluable resources to me while I was writing this text, works that were especially invaluable for what they omitted. Since his retirement from radiology in 2008, Iddo has split his time between Hornell and Jerusalem, and focused mostly on playwriting, producing scripts about the rise of Nazism, the theories of Viktor Frankl, and the fraught relationship between Albert Einstein and Immanuel Velikovsky. To this day, Iddo has rebuffed my every attempt at making contact—by email, by phone, by postal-letter—and when I stopped by his home in Hornell, he must've been in Jerusalem, and when I stopped by his home in Jerusalem, he must've been in Hornell. I met one of his children at a party—or an afterparty—or it might've been a rave—in Tel Aviv, but only realized that after I left. My cousin's cousin-through-marriage is a lawyer in Rochester who once sued Iddo for malpractice and, at a family bar-mitzvah, described him to me as "a sweet nice guy" and "basically harmless"—"try not to be a jerk to him, will you?"

I got to know the eminent American literary critic Harold Bloom only toward the end of his life and took to visiting him with some regularity at his house in New Haven, Connecticut. As someone who'd never been his student, and who'd surely never be his colleague, as a novelist whom he'd first met on the page and who was nearly fifty years his junior, I was something of an anomaly among his many well-wishers. I'd take a seat and examine the stacks of new books on his diningroom table as I waited for Harold to be wheeled over in his wheelchair and installed at the table's head, from which he'd commence his interrogations: he wanted to know what was going on in literature, in publishing; he wanted to know what I was writing and when he could read it, and what my opinions were on Kafka, Proust, D. H. Lawrence ("David Herbert Lawrence"), and Nathanael West ("Nathan Weinstein"); he wanted to know what books had just come out, and what books were about to come out, and which of them I'd read, and which of them were "palatable," and whatever rumors and gossip about the authors of those books that I could spare him. I did the best I could, trying to satisfy his curiosity quickly enough so that I could steer him—before he tired—to his own opinions, and, especially, to his stories, which, as we grew closer and he grew confiding, I came increasingly to cherish. If Harold was famous for his memory—his perfect recall of texts, a feat of which he was still capable, despite his advanced age and infirmity—he was most precious to me for his memories, plural, his occasionally perfect recall of the past, his stories of friends, enemies, cities, and quarrels. No one who has seriously read Harold can have any doubt as to why, among the many books he gave to the world, he never produced a book of memoir: for Harold, life and the texts he read were conterminous and, for a scholar of influence and its anxieties, to so directly address his own antecedents threatened to be an act of self-sabotaging literality. Still, he was certainly not without his vanity, and so with my prodding, the stories poured forth in that high-pitched nasal voice of his—a Bronx boy's dream of a donnish Brit's accent—along with spittle, slurps of water, bits of pills, and flecks of whitefish spread as amply onto rye bread as onto chocolate babka. He told me about his childhood on the Grand Concourse and first reading the poetry of Moyshe-Leib Halpern and Jacob Glatstein: the fish would come from the market wrapped in newspapers (the *Forverts*, the *Morgen Freiheit*), and he'd unwrap it and sometimes the ink would have run and lines of poems would be imprinted on the side of the fish and he'd try to read them; he'd try to read the fish and guess the author, from backwards Yiddish impressed onto wet iridescent scales. He told me about first reading the New Testament in Yiddish in a free copy brought to his door by intrepid missionaries ("I remember Jesus was Yeshua, but all the *shlikhim* [apostles] called him *rebbe* [rabbi]"); and about his earliest encounters with the Romantics ("The name, the epithet, continues to attract me"). There were stories about writers he'd known; about Bernard Malamud, who used to clean Harold out in poker; about Saul Bellow, who preferred Allan Bloom to Harold and had a kleptomaniacal streak when it came to bowties; and about Philip Roth, who created the protagonist of *Sabbath's Theater* by asking himself, "what if Harold, instead of making his parents proud and going to the Ivy League, had gone to seed in the Village in the '50s?"—this by Roth's own admission, apparently. Harold told me about fighting a bat infestation in a summer cottage he'd shared with John Hollander; a car crash he'd gotten into with Paul de Man; skinnydipping with Jacques Derrida ("he was quite fit"); croquet with Delmore Schwartz ("quite crazy and inviting of parody but never a self-parody"); and tippling with Dwight MacDonald ("a sincere Trotskyite—though one can't imagine an insincere Trotskyite—who was never sober"). There were anecdotes about T. S. Eliot ("it was unfortunate, his rejection of Milton"); Northrop Frye ("the rare colleague of mine who did not believe that Eliot was Christ's terrestrial vicar"); Susan Sontag; Camille Paglia; Toni Morrison; and Cynthia Ozick; and disquisitions on anti-Semitism at Cornell, where he was educated, and at Yale, where he was the first Jew ever tenured by the English Department. What else? Arguments with Anthony Burgess over limbo and purgatory ("as a lapsed Catholic, Burgess was going to hell, whereas I am still here and going nowhere"); chess with Nabokov ("it astonished no one that I did not emerge the winner"); and conversations with Don DeLillo ("I conversed, he didn't"), Cormac McCarthy ("he would call me on the telephone while soaking like a cowboy in the bath"), W. G. Sebald ("gentle, maybe too gentle"), and Gershom Scholem, "who when I'd visit him in Jerusalem at his apartment on Abravanel Street would invariably speak of himself in the third person ... so a typical English sentence would be, 'The judgment of so-and-so on this-and-that is such-and-such, but Scholem says'... a habit he shares with our current president, who likes to say, 'Nobody has done more for Israel than Donald Trump'... In literature, referring to yourself in the third person is called *illeism*." On my bachelorhood: "I urge you, dear Joshua, to reconsider"; on bachelorhood in general: "on the whole, dear Joshua, the literature on the subject does not recommend it"; on the homosexuality of Jewishness; on the Jewishness of homosexuality; on the intelligence of former students employed by *The New Yorker*, and on the incongruity of that intelligence with the mediocrity of *The New Yorker*; on John Ashbery: "I shall use my anger to build a bridge like that / Of Avignon"; on Hart Crane: "Migrations that must needs void memory, / Inventions that cobblestone the heart." What else? Feuds over identity politics (which he called "resentment politics," and of which he said,

"I find it curious that so many of our finest writers should regard 'resentment' as intrinsically negative"), relativism, deconstructionism, structuralism, post-structuralism, Gnosticism, Kabbalah, and the time he was asked to coordinate the campus visit of an obscure Israeli historian named Ben-Zion Netanyahu, who showed up for a job interview and lecture with his wife and three children in tow and proceeded to make a mess. Of all of Harold's tales, this was the one that stuck with me the most, perhaps because it was one of the last he ever told me, and following his death in 2019, I wrote it down, and in the process found myself having to invent a number of details he'd left out, and, due to circumstances I'm about to explain, having to fictionalize a few others. It should go without saying that "Ruben Blum," the prosaic professor of American Economic History, is not intended to be a portrayal of Harold Bloom, the furthest-thing-from-prosaic professor of English Literature, in the same way that "Edith" is not intended to be a portrayal of Jeanne, Harold's highly cultured, shrewd, and witty wife, who confirmed her husband's account of the Netanyahu visit and graciously blessed my use of it, on one condition: that I clear it first with "Judith." Though Harold and Jeanne never had a daughter, there was most definitely a "Judy," a younger female relative sent up to board with the Blooms to get her out of the Bronx—and that is just about all I'm going to say about her. I've never met her in-person—she didn't come to Harold's memorial—so I had to track her down online, and when I told her what I was writing, she asked me to leave her out of it. I replied that I'd do my best to make her unrecognizable, and in my attempts to do so, I found that the alterations I had to make to her character required me to make alterations to the Bloomian characters too, and soon the "Blums" took on a life of their own, even while the Netanyahus remained the Netanyahus. During this revision period, I noticed that, though "Judy" had never responded to my email agreeing to her request to render her unrecognizable, she had put me on her "Holistic & Homeopathic" email-list, so that at least twice a month and sometimes weekly I was receiving, I still receive, "blasts" from her about meditation retreats, magnetic healing, hallucinogen therapy, chelation experiments, Russian intelligence operations to undermine American elections, and, of course, the poisoning of the earth and the impending Anthropocene catastrophe. When I finished a full draft of the book, I foolishly responded to one of these emails by attaching the file and letting "Judy" know that I was keen to have her corrections and suggestions, if she were amenable to giving them, and this was how she wrote me back (original formatting preserved):

Dear Joshua Cohen,

I've just finished reading your 'book,' and I'm going to say it once and for all and that's it: Judaism is just another word for THE PATRIARCHY (and for PATRIARCHAL HEGEMONY). We're all one people, the Human People, with no differences between us. The planet is ruined, the machines are taking over, and none of this Jewish crap still matters. **WAKE UP!!!!!!** No one reads books anymore and the Jews are either on the wrong side of history or just irrelevant. IF YOU'RE HAVING AN IDENTITY CRISIS, I'm sorry, but your only choice is to expand your consciousness and join the Human People in our common struggle against pollution and technology or spend the rest of your life crying for a past that let's be honest couldn't have been that great if this is where it leads. Everything you believe in never existed, including your individual self, if you ever believed you could change that. Admit it, even literacy is dying—and when the last old Jew of you is finally as dead as (((God))) this proud nonbinary dyke **YES DYKE** IS GOING TO DANCE NAKED AS HELL ON HIS GRAVE.

J. C.
New York City
2020

JOSHUA COHEN was born in 1980 in Atlantic City. His books include the novels *Moving Kings*, *Book of Numbers*, *Witz*, *A Heaven of Others*, and *Cadenza for the Schneidermann Violin Concerto*; the short-fiction collection *Four New Messages*, and the nonfiction collection *Attention: Dispatches from a Land of Distraction*. Cohen was awarded Israel's 2013 Matanel Prize for Jewish Writers, and in 2017 was named one of *Granta*'s Best Young American Novelists. He lives in New York City.